Surviving The Evacuation
Book 2: Wasteland

Frank Tayell

Dedicated to my family

ISBN-13: 978-1495951985
ISBN-10: 1495951987

Other titles:
Work. Rest. Repeat.
A Post-Apocalyptic Detective Novel

Surviving The Evacuation
Book 0.5: Zombies vs The Living Dead
Book 1: London
Book 2: Wasteland
Book 3: Family
Book 4: Unsafe Haven
Book 5: Reunion
Book 6: Harvest
Undead Britain
(In the charity anthology, 'At Hell's Gates 1')

History's End
(In the charity anthology, 'At Hell's Gates 2')

For more information visit:
http://blog.franktayell.com
http://twitter.com/FrankTayell
www.facebook.com/TheEvacuation

The Story So Far

The outbreak began in New York on the 20th February. Within weeks, the virus had spread throughout the entire world. Nations fell, law and order gave way to chaos, and anarchy took grip almost everywhere.

Here in Britain, Sir Michael Quigley, our Foreign Secretary, took over after the Prime Minister's disappearance. An emergency coalition cabinet was formed that included Jennifer Masterton. Rationing, curfews, martial law, the piratical theft of overseas food-aid, the banning of almost all public gatherings, it wasn't enough.

Everyone in the inland cities of Britain were to be evacuated to enclaves established around the coast. To ensure that they left their homes, evacuees were promised a vaccine once they'd reached their evacuation muster point.

My name is Bill Wright. I grew up with Jennifer Masterton. We were friends. We were colleagues. The evacuation was my idea. It was my plan, but I didn't join those other refugees fleeing the city. My leg was broken on the day of the outbreak. Trapped in my flat, I watched as the evacuees left London. I watched those deserted streets, waiting for the rescue I was sure Jen would send. I watched as the roads filled up again, this time with the undead. The evacuation failed.

My supplies dwindling, my leg still not healed, I was forced out into the zombie-infested city. It took weeks, but eventually I managed to escape to the relative security of Brazely Abbey in Hampshire.

When out looking for supplies, I stumbled across a letter lying next to the body of a dead police sergeant. The letter said the evacuation was a lie. I went to a muster point, and I saw the truth for myself. The evacuees had all been murdered, poisoned by the vaccine they had been told would protect them.

I'd brought little with me from London, just my clothes, weapons, the little food I had left, and my laptop and a hard drive. On those were files sent to me by an American political fixer I only ever knew as Sholto. With little else to do, I finally found time to look at those files. I discovered that the virus originated at a demonstration in New York, witnessed by dignitaries from around the world. Most wore masks, but there was one that I recognised. It was our Foreign Secretary, Sir Michael Quigley.

Part 1:
Survivors

25th June - 2nd July

Day 105, Longshanks Manor

15:07, 25th June

After everything I've been through since the outbreak in February, I didn't think I'd have to worry about anyone firing a gun at me. Now, and in the space of only two hours, I have been shot at fifty times. I've been counting. The first bullet was a surprise. I didn't think Longshanks Manor was still occupied. Then came the second shot. That was when I realised what was happening.

I ran into the maze. I knew there was a wildlife park, and remembered the Manor was one of the more imposing stately homes in southern England, but I didn't know they'd put in a maze since I was last here.

Last year, when the maze must have rung with the sounds of happily lost children and frantic parents, the hedges reached over seven feet high. After half a year's sun and rain they've grown ragged, with fresh growth sprouting up so high that these new branches are bent over under their own weight. Ducking behind the large hedges was an instinctive response. Finding my way to the relative shelter of the gazebo at the centre of the maze was pure luck, but whether it was the good kind or bad, I'm not sure.

It's been one hundred and five days since the power went out in London and I started this journal. It's been a lifetime.

Fifty-one times. They're using a silencer so there's no sound of the shot, just a splintering crack as the bullet impacts against wood. Or perhaps it's a suppressor, I don't think I ever knew the difference.

As long as I keep my head down, I think I'm safe here, behind this gazebo. There's wooden panelling, about three feet high, running around the base to hide the concrete supports. Above that is a large open sided structure, about as big as a bandstand, made of ornate, hand-carved sections of seasoned pine. Every time a bullet strikes it, I can't help wishing they'd gone for something far uglier, but made of steel instead.

They can't see me and I'm giving them nothing to aim at, but whoever they are, that doesn't seem to matter. Sometimes the bullets come a few seconds apart, sometimes it's almost long enough for me to think they've forgotten I'm here. Almost long enough to make me want to stick my head up and check. Almost...

It's about three p.m. I found the watch, a wind-up one, in the house I took shelter in last night. It was hidden in a bedside cabinet, beneath a pile of old photographs and other similar keepsakes. Everything else of any worth, all the food and bottles, they were gone. Not consumed there, but taken away.

I had to guess at the time, and decided that dawn was as good a time for five a.m. as any other. So now it's about three in the afternoon, and I've been here for two hours.

I left Brazely Abbey three days ago. I didn't have to leave, everything there was fine and I had everything I needed to survive. Food, water, walls and solitude, what more can a survivor want? But surviving isn't the same as living, and it's not enough for me. Each day, first thing, I would go out and kill the few zombies who had wandered close during the night. Then I would tend to the vegetable patches and fruit bushes just outside the walls, repairing any damage caused by undead, trampling feet. Sometimes I would cycle off to loot one of the many houses nearby. The rest of the time I would climb up the scaffolding to the little platform where the stained glass windows once stood.

Looking out over the abandoned countryside my thoughts soon turned to the files sent to me by Sholto, and the one labelled 'Lenham Hill Trials'. It was on the laptop I'd brought with me from London, but without power I couldn't view it. Instead, I would look at a spot on the map, about thirty miles north of the Abbey, on the other side of the Thames, and marked down as an old aerodrome, where I know the facility is. The more I stared at the map, the more restless I became until, three days ago, I woke up and just started cycling north.

In the end I didn't reach Lenham Hill. As much as the ground allowed, I travelled across country, cutting through fields and along footpaths on which I was less likely to encounter the undead. Even so, by lunchtime I was growing anxious at how few zombies I had seen. I spotted an old barn at the top of a shallow hill. I climbed up the slight rise. Hidden by the building, and from a distance of about a thousand yards, I saw the M4 motorway.

On my way to Brazely from London, I crossed half a dozen reinforced roads. Those had fences barely seven feet high, often made of nothing sturdier than wire and wood. Every few hundred yards, there would be a gap where the fence had been broken. The M4 was different.

This was no flimsy barrier like on those other roads, nor even like the more desperately haphazard agglomeration of concrete and steel I'd seen along the bank of the Thames. This was a truly professional effort of interlocking concrete, with regularly spaced steel pillars supporting a double row of chain link topped with razor wire.

From that distance it was hard to tell its height, but abandoned in the middle of the road was a lorry, and the razor wire stood at least twelve feet higher than the vehicle's roof.

The walls hemming this roadway in, as impressive as they were, were not what first caught my eye. Inside this ribbon of steel and concrete, a grasping arms-reach apart, waited thousands upon thousands of undead evacuees, trapped by the walls they thought would protect them.

Approaching the motorway my spirits had been buoyed by the sparse number of undead I had come across. There were a few stuck in hedgerows or trapped by debris and obstacles on the road but otherwise, for a depth of about two miles this side of the M4, the countryside was nearly empty.

Looking at the motorway I saw why. In front of the fence, with nothing but a few weed filled fields between me and Them, were hundreds upon thousands of zombies. They weren't as densely packed as those caged inside the fence, but to me, standing there by that old barn, They were far more dangerous.

The nearest creature was less than five hundred yards away. If I were to shout or scream, or just cough loudly, then, within minutes, They would descend upon me. Hurriedly I turned around. I scanned the tree-line behind me, peered at the copse to my left then at the overgrown paddock to the right. All was still. There were no zombies, no animals, nothing. There was barely even any movement from the trees in the dry summer air. The reason for the nearly empty countryside was clear enough. The low atonal moan, the whispering of rotten cloth, the occasional scrape of flesh against concrete and chain link, magnified by the tens of thousands trapped in the motorway, taken together those sounds had summoned all the undead from the countryside around. Never have I felt both so exposed and so alone as when I stood there, surveying this final testament to my evacuation plan.

It was such a depressing sight that, at first, I didn't notice the bodies. Within the walled-in motorway and right next to the fence, there is at least one corpse every few hundred yards. Initially I thought that these were zombies killed by the evacuees during the panic. As I looked, though, I came to realise that, no, these are the bodies of the immune. Bitten, infected, they didn't turn, they tried to escape, but they couldn't. They were trapped, and they were torn apart.

I edged around the barn to the cottage next door, climbed up onto its roof and crawled along to the chimneystack. Hidden there, the extra height gave me a clearer view of that lorry. On its roof I could make out two bodies, more skeleton than flesh. Around them, half a dozen crows fought over the meagre scraps of sinew and tendon that remained on those sun-bleached bones.

In all these months I have never seen a bird, any bird, try and eat the remains of one of the undead. When I went to the muster point I saw, scattered amongst the bodies of the murdered evacuees, dozens of dead carrion birds. That same poison that the refugees had been told was a vaccine had killed those birds whose misguided opportunism had seen the thousands of corpses as a feast.

Those people on top of the lorry, they had not been infected, nor had they taken the vaccine. Immune or not, they must have climbed up, and taken refuge there, waiting for a rescue that was never going to come. Surrounded by death, they waited to die. Whether it was by dehydration or suicide, it must have been a dismal end.

I tried dividing the road up into sections, tried every trick I could remember, but there were literally too many zombies to count. Inside the motorway there are fifty thousand per mile, perhaps a hundred thousand, and it really doesn't matter which. Outside there are fewer, but there are still thousands of the undead. I don't know how long They will just stay there, or what might trigger Them to start roaming through the countryside. All I know is that it is just a matter of time and distance between me and Them. And if I want to get to Lenham Hill I've got to go over Them, and then through whatever awaits on the other side of the motorway.

One of the crows pecking at the bodies on the lorry's roof flapped its wings, flew up and then down towards the road. I watched as a dozen undead arms stretched up towards it in a macabre parody of a Mexican wave. I watched as other zombies raised their arms and the movement was copied for three hundred yards in both directions. I watched as the crow circled once, a few inches above their grasping hands, then returned to its perch on the lorry's roof.

I could have crossed the motorway then. Or I could have tried. There was an access bridge for farm traffic less than half a mile away. There were some zombies on it, but not so many I couldn't make out each individual one. I examined the road leading to the bridge carefully, judging distances, assessing which of the undead would be able to make it to the road and be able to attack me before I made it to the bridge. I stopped counting when I reached a hundred. "Zombies to the left of him, zombies to the right…"

Would I have made it? I don't know. I wanted answers and I wanted to get to Lenham Hill, but right then I didn't want to get there badly enough. Call it cowardice, call it prudence, call it whatever you want, that instinct that has kept me alive so far told me not to take the risk. But I couldn't just go back. Instead I climbed down from the roof and cycled west, following the motorway, to find out how far the fences still stood.

I travelled across country lanes, down bridleways and through fields, staying out of sight of the motorway but always within that two-mile empty corridor this side of it. It was slow going. Sometimes I came across a solitary zombie. Sometimes I stopped and dealt with it, other times I took a detour, so I ended up travelling a circuitous zigzagging route that got me one mile west for every three miles travelled.

Then I spotted a car. It was a saloon with a swept back roof designed to make a family run-about look like a sporty coupé. It had crashed into the soft earth of the verge, coming to a rest angled at ninety degrees to the road. The metal bodywork, exposed when the paintwork was scratched during the crash, was beginning to rust. A blanket of leaves and dirt covered the roof. Brambles snaked out from the hedgerow, trailing up the mud-covered windscreen. In short, there was nothing to distinguish it from the dozen or so similar vehicles I'd seen that day. Until the banging started.

She must have died whilst at the wheel. Then, the zombie she'd turned into was trapped inside the car. I think it was a she, though it's so hard to tell with those that have been dead more than a couple of months. Judging by the growth of vegetation on and around the vehicle, this one had been there since around the time of the evacuation itself.

The sad story of the end of her life was clear enough. She'd begged, borrowed and stolen enough petrol to get out of somewhere to the assumed safety of somewhere else. Sometime after the evacuation, when she thought the roads would be clear, she'd driven off. Then she had to stop, perhaps to help someone, perhaps just to stretch her legs. She got out of the car, was attacked, and infected.

She'd driven off at full speed, probably to find the vaccine in the hope it would be a cure, but then she died. The car crashed. She turned. Unable to open the door, the zombie was trapped. It became dormant, hibernating, waiting for someone, some prey, to come by. Then I did.

All of that flashed through my mind, but what really interested me was the petrol. With the weeks of rationing before the evacuation food is scarce, but fuel, well, that's rarer than life these days. With the petrol from the cars I'd found at the Grange Farm Estates, and the little I'd found in vehicles around Brazely, I had barely enough to get about twenty miles. Not enough to get from Brazely Abbey to Lenham Hill, let alone to get back afterwards.

Bang. Bang-bang. Bang. Its head and hands drummed out an arrhythmic staccato against the driver-side window. It wasn't loud, but in this silent world, it didn't have to be. Soon others would come, unless it was stopped. I dismounted and unslung my pike.

I've been modifying the weapon on an almost daily basis since I settled at the Abbey. It now has a two-foot long blade that previously belonged to a set of long-handled tree shears, bolted on at a right angle to the handle. At the tip is a foot long spike, and the base of the hollow pole is now filled with lead as a counterweight. It resembles a scythe more than anything else, but out of grim superstition I think of it as my pike.

I took a few practice swings. I'd hoped that with one blow I could break the glass, and with the next, impale the creature's brain. The position of the car was wrong. The spike kept getting tangled in the creepers trailing out from the hedge. I leaned the pike up against the bicycle, took out my hatchet and swung.

As soon as the glass broke the zombie's arm shot out. Its claw-like hand grasped towards me. It couldn't reach. The seat belt, which had stopped it from getting in the right position to break the glass, now prevented it from reaching me. I took another step forward, waited until it lunged again, and brought the hatchet down on the top of its skull. Bone cracked, and that reddish brown ooze They have instead of blood sprayed out, over the car, my sunglasses and the scarf covering my face.

I wiped the hatchet clean, then began a quick search of the vehicle. I'd been right in my guess at this woman's story, up to a point. There had been a veritable treasure chest of biscuits, cereals, pastas and what I think had been a circle of cheese. Time had done its work, though, and inside the steel sarcophagus was nothing but decay. I grabbed at the bag on the passenger seat and hauled it a dozen yards away upwind. There were photographs, keepsakes and once treasured possessions, all useless to me.

It was a disappointment, but not a great one. There was nothing I really needed, and there is little spare room in my bags to carry much. I just enjoy looting. It's one of the few pleasures in these dark times. I checked the fuel tank. It had been punctured during the crash and was empty, the fuel long evaporated.

I got back on the bike and continued heading west, keeping close to, but always out of sight of, the motorway. Every five or so miles I would dismount, creep closer and find a concealed spot from where I could survey the road, its fence, and the numbers of the undead within. Nowhere was the fence broken. Nowhere were the numbers less dense.

After a depressing day and a half, I'd covered close to ninety miles to get the thirty or so miles west as far as Swindon. There, within sight of that city, I stopped. I could see no point going any further.

15:45, 25th June

Fifty-two shots now, but I'm not worried. It's not bravado, it's the knowledge that it will be getting dark soon. For some reason these snipers don't want to come out here, so I just have to wait until nightfall and then I'll be able to slip away. They do seem happy enough to waste ammunition, though. That must mean they have a good supply of it, and I think that at least one of them knows how to use the gun. I think that he or she is teaching someone else how to shoot. That would explain the inaccuracy and odd length of time between shots.

Probably the only one who'd feel confident enough to come down here and take someone on hand-to-hand is the same one who knows how to shoot well enough to offer covering fire. It's conjecture, of course, but it's the only explanation I can think of right now. So long as I stay put, and literally keep my head down for the next six hours, I'll be fine.

It's funny. I mean really funny, I'm being shot at by snipers, and what I can't help thinking is that I have genuinely been in worse situations than this. Doesn't that say it all?

I reached Swindon, a day and a half ago. There is an atmosphere to towns and cities now, something intangible and forbidding. To me they have become nothing more than a testament to a world that was lost so recently yet already seems ancient and forgotten. These silent mausoleums of concrete and steel are a lifetime away from the cacophonous roar of civilisation whose memory has faded with each passing day, until now it seems less real than a fairy tale.

It's connected to the way that life seems to flourish all around me. The trees are overgrown, the fields are filled with weeds, and brambles encroach on roads slowly being reclaimed by grass and moss. All about me, the countryside is untidy, unkempt and not at all English, but it is alive. There are birds, there are insects, occasionally, and all too rarely for my tastes, there are even some small mammals. Not in the cities. They are dead.

Leading into Swindon is the motorway, the fence unbroken, the undead, undisturbed within. These were the evacuees heading to Bristol. Their fate should have been a life of drudgery on a farm or down some Welsh coal mine. It should not have been this.

I was at a loss as to what I should do. The motorway changed everything, but at the same time it changed nothing. That desire to know the truth of what happened still burnt strongly. As my mind danced with schemes to get around or over this barrier, I tried to come up with a plan that didn't involve returning to Brazely Abbey, however temporarily, with nothing to show for the trip.

Then I remembered the laptop. I had it, and the hard drive, in my pack. I carry them everywhere. It's totemic, I suppose, my last link with the past. Looking at Swindon, looking at the motorway, I made a decision. I needed to know what was on the computer, what was in the 'Lenham Hill Trials' file. I thought that, perhaps, I might discover that I didn't need to go to Lenham Hill, that I could just return to the Abbey and make my home there.

I have looked for laptops in the houses I've looted, though if I'm honest, I didn't look that hard. I had found tablets, desktops and phones galore, but the few laptops I found were all drained of power. I decided I would venture into some small town, or even into one of the cities, if I had to. I could begin a systematic house-to-house, office-to-office search. I took out my map, unfolded it and began to scan the place names. I searched my memory, thinking back on the places I'd visited, trying to remember the government statistics on internet usage that might give some clue as to where would be best to look. Then I saw it, Devizes, and I smiled with pleasure at the memory of a vicarious triumph.

During the last election, I'd been volunteered into doing some mid-campaign speech polishing. My job, after that incident in Burnley that the press described as 'a gaff too far', was to rewrite the stump speeches to make sure that the references tallied with the places the politicians were actually in, not those they'd just left.

It was a tedious job, and one I got by being one of the few outsiders the party trusted not to sell anything I heard or saw to the press. One of the stops on this mind-numbing round-Britain coach trip was Devizes. I remember it well, because it was the stop after the Chief Whip spilled mustard over my laptop. The computer froze, locking away that afternoon's speeches. Fortunately, there was a computer repair shop in the town, which managed to retrieve the documents just in time for the Whip to stand up in front of a crowd made up mostly of reporters and give them a few seconds of B-roll. He had the speech, but he'd forgotten his reading glasses, so he improvised. They didn't win that seat and the Chief Whip, after that clip was aired over and over, lost his. I felt really good about that.

The point is that I remembered there was a computer repair shop on the edge of Devizes. More than that, during that anxious half hour wait to find out if anything could be saved, I had noticed, and asked about, the stack of odd shaped boxes in the rear of the shop. They were portable power supplies, giant batteries that could be recharged from a car. What's more, the shop didn't sell them, they rented them out, mostly during the festival season to music-lovers who couldn't bear a night under canvas without the knowledge of a kettle full of boiling water the next morning.

I headed southwest, and had covered the fifteen miles or so before nightfall. The scene I found in Devizes was unlike any other I have seen since leaving London. Barricades had been thrown up across the roads, windows were boarded up, and about the streets, and inside the shops and houses, lay the dead and undead alike. A battle had taken place there, and it was clear the humans had not won.

The computer repair shop was still there, but only just. A fire had been started at the other end of the row, leaving half a dozen shops nothing but burnt-out remains. The door to the repair shop had been blocked from the inside. I had to break in through a window around the back, all the time listening out for the sounds of the undead.

I found only one power supply unit left. It was too heavy to carry on the bike, but it worked. That night, as I was waiting for the battery to charge up, I finally saw the files Sholto had sent to me.

16:05, 25th June

Fifty-three shots. It's such a waste. How much ammunition do they have? A lot clearly, but that's just a guess.

Around four a.m., yesterday, I realised there wasn't much point looking at the same video over and over again. I turned my attention to the map, once more trying to come up with a way of getting to the other side of the motorway that wasn't as suicidal as just cycling over some footbridge. I couldn't find one.

It was putting off the inevitable, just delaying the time before a return to the Abbey to face some hard choices. As I was leaving the town, unsure which direction to go, I saw a sign for Longshanks Wildlife Park, and thought, why not? If anywhere in the neighbourhood had become a refuge for survivors it would be here. It was only another fifteen miles out of my way. I thought it would only add an extra few hours to the journey.

I was wrong. It took all day to cover the distance. I had to keep backtracking to avoid roads blocked by trees, vehicles or the undead. After about the ninth diversion, and running low on water, I decided to stop for the day. I was only five miles away, but something about the houses I'd investigated was making me hesitate. The closer I got, the more I found that they'd already been looted, everything from food to herbs to bottles, even the jewellery, had been taken.

The last time I spent any real time at this rambling old estate on the western edge of Salisbury Plain, was about twenty years ago. Jen Masterton was packaged off here one summer and I, who usually spent my school holidays with her family, had to tag along. Back then, the wildlife park was little more than a home for animals rescued from crumbling zoos across the world. By the time the world ended last February, it had grown into one of the largest safari parks in Europe. I'd always meant to come back, but there was never the time. It was just one of many places I knew would be around forever, so what was the hurry?

With its lake and thick walls, and abundance of fresh and tantalizingly exotic meat courtesy of the wildlife park, it had everything going for it. At least, it did on paper. It was almost on the way, I thought, not really a diversion at all.

The bodies littering the ground should have been a warning sign. It's just that the only time I've seen zombies who have been shot was at that muster point. Even in Devizes, the undead had been killed with blade or blunt instrument. I suppose I didn't really know what I was seeing. Britain was not a country of guns. I just saw the bodies of the undead, the boarded up windows and lifeless house and came to exactly the wrong conclusion.

Fifty-four shots, now. There are at least two snipers. When the wind shifts I can hear the occasional snatch of conversation. I've tried working out the distance, tried to remember how cosines and tangents work, but if I ever knew how to do those kinds of sums, these are not the conditions to remember. All I've worked out is that they are either in one of the top floor bedrooms or in one of the towers that jut out above the roof, and that they are not worried about running out of bullets.

The hedges are a mixed blessing. They provide some cover, but with the elevation the snipers have, it's not much. More importantly, my only way out is going to be by pushing my way through those densely interlocked branches. Will they be able to see that at night? There's no cloud in the sky right now. It looks like it will be a clear night. Will they be able to see the rustling of branches above my head? I suppose I'll find out.

16:30, 25th June

I think this forced rest is actually good for me. I know that sounds odd, but I've spent so much of the last few weeks worrying over what I should do next, that I haven't really just stopped to think about where I am now.

Not that I plan to make a habit out of this kind of thing, but at the very least I'll make sure I carry more water in my pack. My water bottle was only half full when I first ducked into the maze, now there's barely two inches left. The rest of my supply is in the bag on the bike, and that's by a wall outside the grounds, about half a mile away. I thought it was better to approach on foot, leaving my hands free, less encumbered. You live and learn.

There's about another five hours to go until dark. That's not too bad, I'll be in the shade for most of that. It's hot, but not quite heat wave hot, though I can tell that's on the cards. Five hours, then I'll crawl through the hedges, sneak back to the bike and disappear into the night.

As a rule I don't do much travelling after dark. The undead don't seem to rely on sight as much as the living, but I won't need to go far. There's a ticket booth near the entrance to the safari park, just a few miles down the road, if I can get there, I can climb onto the roof and wait for dawn. Then it's back to the Abbey for supplies and then, with no more diversion, straight to Lenham Hill.

17:50, 25th June

"Look mate, we've got a night sight on this rifle. Make it easy on yourself and just stand up," a guttural voice called out about an hour ago.

That's the first human voice I've heard in… months, I suppose. Do I believe them? Yes. As to why they want to kill me, I don't know. I tried talking to them. They shot at me. I tried telling them I only wanted supplies. They shot at me. I tried saying I wasn't who they thought I was, whoever that might be. They shot at me.

Each time I tried to say something, they fired. Then I realised what they were doing. They didn't want me to talk. They wanted me to shout. They wanted the undead to come here and finish the job for them, but they were out of luck.

What's the longest you've gone without speaking? All I managed was a throaty rasp, barely intelligible as words even to my own ears. So now I'm silent again, and trying to come up with a new plan.

I could wait until nightfall and hope they were lying about the night sight, but if they were why waste so much ammo? Why do they want me dead? No, those kinds of questions can't be answered from here.

How long did the exchange go on for? I wish I'd checked my watch. Say it was fifteen minutes. Was that too long, did the undead hear us? The rifle might be silenced, but the impacts of the bullets aren't. How long before They come?

It seems I've a choice between heading towards the lake and being shot in the back, or staying put and hoping the undead don't find me. Neither is particularly appealing.

19:00, 25th June

Or I could head towards them. Or towards the house, at least. I'm almost positive they are in one of the bedrooms, which means they've got a pretty limited angle of fire. If I can make it to the house, and follow the wall around, I can make a run for the treeline from either the north side or the west. They won't know which side of the building I'm on until they've picked a bedroom and looked. So I've a fifty-fifty chance they'll pick the wrong one. Or, to put it another way, a fifty-fifty chance that I'll make it to the trees before they shoot me.

Are they good enough to be able to shoot a moving target? One of them probably is. Too many guesses and assumptions. What I do I know?

The only thing I know about night-sights is that they don't work in daytime. Obvious, right? But nor do they work in well-lit buildings or when a light is shining on them. Do you remember all those movies where the bank robbers would use a flash-bang to blind the SWAT teams? Well, I've no flash-bangs, and with no electricity except in a thunderstorm,

17

there's no prospect of the floodlights suddenly coming on, but I do have my torch.

It's about a hundred yards of lawn between the edge of the maze and the house. Probably about the same distance on the other side of the building. Perhaps more. Probably more, I don't know.

My right leg didn't heal properly from the break I sustained on the same day the outbreak started in New York. Now it's slightly twisted, an inch or so shorter than the left, and I have to wear the leg brace for support. I can walk, I can hop, I can skip out of the way of the grasping arms of the undead, but I can't really run. The limping lope I manage instead is still faster than any zombie can manage and up until now that is all that has mattered.

Day 106, Longshanks Manor

10:00, 26th June

Last night, I waited until about half past nine. It wasn't fully dark, but in the still night air I heard something approaching. The undead were coming. Fighting off one, or even two, whilst staying hidden from the snipers would be possible. Not easy, but possible. Except, when it comes to the undead, where there is one, soon after, there are more. If it's a choice between a bullet and being torn apart, well, what choice is that?

I took off my coat, wrapped it around the pike and raised it so it was just peeking above the corner at the other end of the gazebo. I moved it about for less than a second, then pulled it down just as a shot was fired. They weren't lying about the night-sight, but clearly it wasn't powerful enough to distinguish between a person and the oldest trick in the book.

Trying not to expose anything more than the tips of my fingers, I reached up and placed the torch on the gazebo's wooden handrail, pointing it towards the house. Then I tried the trick with the coat once more, this time raising it higher in a sudden jerking motion that I hoped would be interpreted as an attempt to clamber up over the railing. A bullet

18

flew through the jacket, hitting it dead centre. It folded over in what, even to me, looked like a fair imitation of a collapsing body. I let go of the pike, reached up and turned the torch on. Then I dived from cover towards the hedge.

In the near dark, with so much new growth, there was no point wasting time looking for a path through the maze. Three seconds after I'd left the shelter of the gazebo I heard a bullet striking wood. I dived at the hedge, shoving and pushing as the branches tore at my hands and face. Five long seconds later and I was through, just as another shot was fired. This time it must have hit the railing because the torch moved, rolling so its light now shone directly on the branches above my head.

I dropped to the ground and began to crawl, my hands outstretched, searching for a gap in the undergrowth. I found it as a third shot was fired, and the light went out.

As darkness suddenly returned, it seemed as if a deathly stillness settled on the grounds through which every last little sound seemed amplified. The water lapping against the shore of the lake, the trumpeting call of some far off animal, the wheeze of the approaching undead, even the click-clack of the next round being chambered in the rifle. I crawled on.

I was on my hands and knees, halfway out of a hedge when a sudden weight pushed me down. My chin smashed into the soft leaf litter, my teeth jarred upwards biting into my tongue. I could taste blood but I ignored this small pain, waiting for the agonising spasm when my brain realised I had been shot. It didn't come.

I breathed in, and it hurt to do so, but there was no bubbling rasp of a punctured lung, no numb collapse of a severed spine, no spreading cold of a mortal wound. I began to pull myself along, faster and faster. I was surprised to find that as my hands pulled at the branches and weeds dragging me closer to the next wall of the maze, my legs and feet started kicking out, pushing me along. I was sure I'd been shot but, somehow, I was still alive. Everything still worked, and though it ached to breathe, I knew I wasn't going to die. Not then, not yet.

At the next hedgerow I crawled along for a dozen feet before forcing a path through. This time, fighting my instincts, I didn't rush. I carefully brushed the branches out of my way, trying to make the hedge move as little as possible. When I heard a bullet whistling through the leaves I breathed a sigh of relief. It was nowhere near me, they didn't know where I was.

I kept crawling, my hands constantly searching out for gaps through which I could squeeze. Then I heard the sound of a body hitting gravel. The undead must have reached the grounds and the snipers must have seen Them. Perhaps they thought I was dead, perhaps they hoped the undead heading towards the maze would flush me out. Either way I knew I was no longer the focus of their attention. I waited until I heard another body thump to the ground, then I stood up and half dived, half fell through that hedge and the next and the next, until I fell flat on cool grass.

I picked myself up and hurried across the parched meadow that had once been a manicured lawn. I kept my eyes fixed on the house, holding my breath, gritting my teeth against the pain I knew must come when the bullet hit. But it didn't. I made it to the wall.

Standing with my back against it, I listened. I heard more gravel scatter, as another body fell. I gave a silent cheer. I was safe. Relatively speaking, of course. It sounded as if the undead were approaching from the same direction in which I had left my bike. That meant that I was leaving the Manor on foot. It dawned on me that with my pike broken, still wrapped in my jacket at the centre of the maze, I would also be leaving virtually unarmed.

I checked my belt. I had my hatchet and chisel and an empty water bottle. I was still wearing my pack, with a day's worth of food left, the laptop, the hard drive, the first volume of my journal, a rope and a few other essential supplies. All in all it wasn't much, but it was enough. I could find another bicycle, I could find more tools and make another weapon, I just had to get away.

I crept along the wall, listening carefully to the noises around me, expecting at any moment to hear the sound of the approaching undead.

When I heard a soft scratching sound, it took me a moment to realise it was coming from inside the Manor, from a room just a few windows away. I slowed as I got closer, and I saw that one set of windows was boarded up, not from the inside like the others, but from the outside.

Someone, or something, was trying to lever a window open. One of the undead, perhaps, trapped in the room for some macabre purpose. It had heard my approach and was now scrabbling at the glass, scraping at the paintwork, trying to get out. Except, what zombie would do that? Wouldn't it just hit at the glass until it broke? It made no sense. Then I heard a more familiar sound. The undead were coming. They were close.

I stopped a couple of yards away from the window. The sounds inside ceased but the sounds of the approaching zombies were getting closer. Whatever was inside, I didn't want to know. I was more than half way around the building, in a spot as good as any other. I braced myself and got ready to dash to the treeline. It was, I judged, less than two hundred yards away. If I could just…

"Hello?" a voice called from inside the room. A woman's voice. I paused. "Hi." The voice came again, slightly louder this time.

"Hi?" I replied and then closed my mouth, unsure what to say next, uncertain even how to say it.

"Can you help me?" the woman asked.

"You were shooting!" I replied, the words barrelling out in a rushed slur.

"You think if I had a gun I'd be trying to break out of here?" That was a fair point. I was having difficulty processing all of this, though. People, conversation, they're not what I'm used to.

"Would you mind?" There was an edge of impatience in her voice. "Let me expand on that. Would you mind levering off the board blocking this window?"

"Right. Sorry. Yes," I said, still off balance. I took out the chisel, raised it to the board covering the window frame and hesitated. I tried to work out whether or not she was a prisoner. If she was, should I let her out? The other windows were all boarded up from the inside, but if she was in league with the…

21

"Whenever you're ready." This time the impatience was coupled with sarcasm. That sealed it, I don't know why, but there's just something trustworthy about anyone who can be sarcastic in the face of adversity. I pushed the chisel into the gap between the wooden board and the window, hammering it into place with the hatchet.

"I meant quietly!" she hissed. "I assumed you'd understand."

"No time," I said. "Zombies." I heaved at the chisel, levering the board back. I repeated the action on the other corner. In the distance, another body thumped to the ground. Somewhere far closer, I heard the shuffling dragging step of feet on gravel.

I had both of the corners free, and began to pull and tug at the bottom of the board until there was a foot wide gap. I reached as high as I could and hammered the chisel in once more. There was another thump. I started counting.

The nails gave, and the board fell to the ground. Now all that was between us was the glass window.

"Stand back," I said. It was too dark to see, I just had to hope that she'd heard me. I swung the hatchet at the window. It broke. The tinkling of glass on the floor of the room seemed to echo all around the grounds.

"Well," I said. "Climb out."

"Can't. Chains. Wouldn't get far," she replied, stepping closer to the window. Under the reflected moonlight, I glimpsed an unkempt, haggard face. "Here, give me that." Her hand snaked out and snatched the hatchet.

I stood there, uncertain. Then there was a shot and the sound of a bullet hitting stone, but there was no corresponding thump of a body falling. I peered out into the night, wishing she'd hurry up. It was fifteen seconds before the next shot, and again it was a miss. The snipers had switched. I didn't know what that meant. I didn't like it, though.

"Hurry," I said, turning back to the room, but it was too dark, too filled with shadows to make out more than her outline.

"Stand by the window," she hissed back. "Get ready."

I couldn't see what she was doing, nor could I hear any sound of her breaking whatever chains were holding her. Unsure what I was getting ready for and because I had no better plan, I did what she said.

Close by, I heard the tread of a foot on dry grass. I turned to stare out into the night just as the door to the room opened. The light of a torch shone out onto the back of my head and out around the window frame, and into the night. Behind me, I heard a meaty thwock, and a man screamed, but I didn't turn to look. Before the light disappeared, as the torch was dropped, it had illuminated a zombie less than three feet away from me.

The torchlight had taken away my night vision. I was blind. I swung the chisel in a violent sweeping arc in front of me. Left to right. There was a second wet crunching sound from inside and the screaming stopped. Right to left, left to... It scored against something soft. I swiped again, slightly lower, and the chisel jarred against flesh. I pulled my hand back, ready to thrust it forward into where I thought the zombie's face was, but then it was on me.

Its mouth clamped down on my wrist. The chisel fell from my grasp. I pounded my free hand down on its skull. I pushed and I shoved and I pulled my wrist free. I grabbed at the creature, my hand closed around a handful of dank rotting hair. I twisted my grip, half turned and slammed its head into the brick wall of the house again and again and again, until it stopped moving.

I felt around on the ground for the chisel, found it, stood and listened for the next creature. Torchlight came through the window to illuminate the grounds. I turned.

"You al—" the woman began, and stopped as the torch in her hand shone down on my wrist. "Oh, hell," she murmured softly.

"What?" I looked down at my wrist. The bite wasn't that deep. "It's okay. I've had worse."

She looked at me with an expression of pitying disbelief. Then I realised why.

"No, really it's okay. I'm immune," I said into the silence, as I fumbled in my pockets for a bandage. I tied it off. It was a crude affair, but sufficient for the moment. Then I rolled up the sleeve of my other arm. "There, see," I said, and waited until the light was shining on the unmistakable, though no longer fresh, teeth marks. "So…" I waited a moment. "Look, this isn't the time to explain more. Help me in, or I'm clearing off." I tried to say it bluntly, but even to my ears it sounded petulant.

"I'm Kim. That's Cannock," she said, pointing the torch at the body when I was inside in the room. His right hand, still gripping a pistol, was almost severed at the wrist, a thin strip of flesh and gristle all that kept it attached. "Sanders is the one upstairs," she added, as she bent down over the body.

The scream must have come after that first blow nearly severed his wrist. The second blow had killed him. The hatchet was still embedded deep in the man's skull.

"Is there anyone else here?" I asked.

"No. Just them and me," she replied, as she fished in the dead man's pockets. She pulled out a set of keys. That was when I first looked at her. It was too dark to make out her features, but I could see that her clothes were ragged, torn and ripped into wretched shapelessness. Around each ankle was a pair of handcuffs, cuffed together in the middle.

"Who was he?" I asked.

"Cannock? Ex-military. Or claimed to be. He was a good shot, so who knows. Sanders… He's just…" she unlocked the cuffs. "He's…" she stalled again, unable to find words to describe the man upstairs.

I looked around the room. It was beyond spartan, it was bare. There was no furniture, not even a blanket. There was nothing to secure the window with and nothing to keep us here a moment longer.

"Come on," I said. "We should go." I walked over to the window. With the torchlight flickering around the room it was difficult to see far, but I could just make out the slow moving silhouettes making their way towards us. "Not this way," I muttered. "Sanders, he's in one of the bedrooms?"

"Top floor. Corner bedroom," she said, bending over the body once more. She gripped the hatchet and tugged at it. It came free with a sucking wet sound unlike anything I'd heard from the bodies of the undead.

24

I didn't like the feeling of being unarmed. I walked over to the corpse stepped on the hand until the fingers popped and the gun was released. I picked it up. It felt unfamiliar, flimsy compared to the hefty weight of the weapons I had grown used to.

"I think there's a back door," I said, "in the kitchens on the other side of the building. We should be able to get out there."

"I'm not leaving Sanders here," she said.

"You want him to..." I stopped. I was going to ask if she wanted him to come with us, but I could see in her eyes that was not what she meant.

I don't know why I stayed. Why I didn't just find a door and leave. It would have been easy. It would have been sensible. But I didn't. I moved the pistol into the torchlight, and checked where the safety-catch was.

"You know how to use that?" she asked. I hesitated and looked down at the gun. It was an automatic, the same kind I had found in the cottages at Grange Farm next to the former police sergeant who had died from the vaccine. I knew the theory well enough, but except for firing a shotgun at clay pigeons, theory was all I knew.

"Swap?" I suggested.

The hatchet was heavier than the gun, but it was a reassuring, almost comforting weight. We left the room, closing the door quietly behind us. Now that we were inside the Manor, silence descended. With it came a realisation of what it was I was about to do, what I had to do.

I have killed the undead, and these days I have few qualms about it, for I no longer see Them as human, but I have not killed another person. Until a few months ago, it would have been unthinkable, since then I have had neither the reason nor the opportunity. My mind replayed the perennial parliamentary debates about reasonable force, and the differences between self-defence and murder. I shook my head, trying to rid it of those unhelpful thoughts. I tried to focus on the journey, on moving stealthily, on each step, one at a time, and not on its terminal conclusion.

Halfway along the corridor Kim pointed at a section of wall. I looked back at her, puzzled. It seemed identical to all the others, until she pushed at an otherwise nondescript wooden panel. A door swung open revealing a hidden staircase. I was almost shocked. I'd always taken the stories about the secret passages to be no truer than those of the monster that lived in the lake.

Kim raised her finger to her lips, pointed at the stairs, then raised a hand with all fingers extended, then lowered it, then raised it again another eight times, then once with only three fingers showing. Forty-eight stairs. She turned off the torch.

I stepped in front of her, to go up the stairs first. Though it was almost impossible to see in the near darkness, I think she rolled her eyes when I took the lead. As we climbed, I began to hear more clearly the sounds from the sniper's nest. There was a click-clack each time the gun was reloaded. There was an odd muffled bump of wood against wood, an occasional flat tinkling as a spent cartridge fell to the floor, all against an incongruous, off-key humming.

I had to feel for the stairs with my hands. We reached a landing. The stairs twisted and climbed once more. Another landing, another twist, and with each step upwards the noise from the room grew. After the last twist, the stairway was illuminated by the thin ray of light flickering through the gap in the door, now only a few steps away.

Kim tapped on my ankle, once, twice. I don't know whether she was indicating that she was right behind me or telling me to hurry up. I ignored her.

I waited until I heard the soft thud of the rifle's recoil and a triumphant hiss. Then I pushed the door open and half fell, half ran into the room.

In such a silent world I'd misjudged how far those little sounds had carried. The bedroom was far longer than I'd thought. Sanders, half turning towards me, was still a good dozen feet away.

His expression, illuminated by a sputtering oil lantern on the floor, seemed determined as he swung the rifle towards me. I was ten feet away when he levelled the barrel of the gun at my chest. Eight as his lips curled in sneering triumph. Seven when he pulled the trigger. Six when he realised the gun wasn't loaded. Five when I twisted my arm behind me. Four when he let go of the rifle and reached for his belt. Three when my arm reached the top of its arc. Two when it bit deep into flesh.

His scream was terrible. The wound was fatal. In our old world it wouldn't have been, but here, now, where medical treatment is limited to bandages and antiseptic, he would die a long slow death. I remember thinking that, as I stared at him screaming and convulsing on the floor. The axe had dug into his shoulder, breaking the bone. From the way the blood was bubbling up around the blade, it must have nicked his lung.

There was a concussive explosion from behind me. Sanders slumped to the ground, dead, a bullet hole in his forehead. The headphones he'd been listening to fell out, and the room, now seemed to fill with the sound of tinny thrash metal.

"It's over," Kim said, before dropping the gun and collapsing to the floor.

13:00, 26th June

After Kim collapsed last night I didn't really know what to do. Unable to lift her, and unsure where I would carry her to even if I could, I covered her with a duvet. I threw a blanket over the corpse and picked up the mp3 player. As I turned it off, I saw that a corner of the room was littered with discarded smart phones, mp3 players, tablets and laptops. Going by the number of devices and variety of brands, they must have been taken from every house in the neighbourhood and beyond.

I was thirsty. I was hungry too, but I'm used to putting hunger to one side. I glanced around and saw a porcelain jug of clearish liquid by the table. I lifted it and took a sniff. It was water, but not fresh. It probably came from the lake. Would Sanders and Cannock have thought to have boiled it? I put the jug down and glanced around. There was a cooler by the bed. I rooted around in it and found a solitary bottle of iced-tea.

Unscrewing the cap, I walked over to the window and peered out. Perhaps it's the lack of light pollution, but the moon seems brighter these days. I could clearly make out the individual zombies heading down the drive towards the house. The sound of the two men's screams, the single, unmuffled shot, and the constant thumping of bodies hitting the ground, all put together it had been enough to summon the undead from miles around. There weren't enough to call it a pack, let alone a horde, but enough that I was beginning to feel that familiar sense of being under siege.

I lifted the rifle. Through the scope's green and white magnification the living dead resembled nothing more than a ghoulish parody of the horror They represented. My injured arm began to twitch with pain. I set the rifle down and picked up the torch, intending to go and ensure the house was secure. I walked over to Sanders' body, and hesitated over the gruesome task of retrieving the hatchet. Instead I picked the pistol up from the floor, telling myself that it was better, that if I needed to use it, the sound would wake Kim. I didn't believe the lie.

I went back downstairs, listening out with each step, but all I could hear was the creaking of wood and the sound of my own laboured breathing. I found the door to Kim's cell easily enough. It was still closed. Standing with my ear pressed against the wood, I thought I could hear the undead outside, pawing at the broken window frame. I looked around for something with which to barricade the door, just in case. There was an abundance of ornamental furniture dotted along the corridor. Ornately embroidered chairs that were never meant to be sat on, well-polished benches and delicately engraved cabinets containing now worthless antiques. I half carried and half dragged them all over to the doorway. The barrier was up to chest height before I realised how stupid I was being.

They can't climb, so there was no way that They were going to get through the broken window. If the zombies did, then the door wouldn't open unless They were able to turn the ceramic door knob. If They managed that, then since the door opened inwards, all They would need to do to get through the barricade is push. That is something the undead do well.

I collapsed into one of the chairs, throwing up a cloud of dust, and just sat for a while. I don't know for how long. Perhaps an hour, perhaps more.

When I came back to myself, I remembered the keys that Kim had used to remove the cuffs. The same keyring would surely have the door key on it. I was certain that it was still in the room, discarded next to the handcuffs. Wearily, I unstacked the pile of furniture and opened the door.

The moment I entered, the noise from the undead increased. The hissing groan of air, the snapping of teeth, the ripping of flesh and cloth on the jagged fragments of broken glass in the window frame, it seemed to fill the silent house.

Reaching through the window, a forest of arms grabbed at empty air as I frantically scanned the floor. I tried to keep the torch pointing downwards, but a shadowy sea of hands kept playing against the walls as undead arms grasped through the broken window. They shoved, They tore, They pushed, and the noise grew until... you remember that expression, 'loud enough to wake the dead'? Never was that more appropriate than when, with a splintering crack, the window frame broke.

I saw the keys, grabbed them, and ran from the room. I pulled the door closed, locked it, and slumped back onto the chair. Thirty minutes passed. This time I kept count. The noise didn't subside, but nor did it get any closer. I told myself They weren't getting in. I tried to believe it.

I stood up and walked a short way along the dark corridor towards where I thought the main doors were. I slowed, then I stopped. I physically couldn't go any further. I tried to force myself to take another step. I told myself it was stupid, foolish, childish even. That I was compelled by nothing more than a metaphorical desire to pull the blankets up to hide from the monster under the bed. Still, I couldn't take another step. I turned, went back down the corridor and piled the furniture back up outside the door.

I know it won't do any good, or the rational part of me knows that, but that's a very small part these days. Afterwards, looking at my barricade of once-priceless antiques, I felt better. Perhaps that is all that matters.

The main doors were more than secure, they were nailed shut. It would take at least a day's work to open them again. I found the old kitchen door, the one Sanders and Cannock must have used to get in and out of the house. The door was bolted, with a fridge dragged in front of it, but from the scuff marks on the floor I could tell that it had been frequently moved back and forth.

When you revisit places you knew as a child, they're meant to seem smaller. Not so with the Manor. In the dim torchlight it seemed to have grown. No matter which way I turned, which passageway I took, I never seemed to end up where I wanted. I tried to be systematic, tried to check each room in turn but really didn't do anything more than wander the halls with a disconsolate lethargy.

Tiring, and genuinely worried I might get lost and end up wandering the building all night, I retreated back upstairs. I moved a few benches to block off the top of the staircase, and moved some cabinets into the corridor on either side of the bedroom door. On top of this flimsy barricade I placed a pair of antique vases. My hope was that if the undead did get into the house, and upstairs, then I would be woken by the sound of breaking china. Only then did I go back into the bedroom.

Kim was still unconscious. Passed out or sleeping, I couldn't tell which. I stood watching her just long enough to reassure myself that she was still breathing. Then I closed the door and pulled a chest of drawers in front of it. I looked over at her again. The noise hadn't woken her.

I have found another survivor. More than that, I found three and whatever fantasies I had about this moment, they couldn't have been further away from the reality.

In the end, I didn't kill a man. I tried to, and I think that amounts to the same thing. I feel as though I should be examining my conscience, asking myself 'how I feel'. I don't feel anything, at least not about his death. I didn't know him, and from all I can infer, my world is a safer place without him in it. That isn't an answer, though, it's just finding an explanation for my lack of emotional response. Sanders and Cannock tried to kill me and now they are dead. That really is all that needs to be said.

It's this waking nightmare we are in, where none of the old rules apply. I feel I can't be certain about anything, that I can no longer even trust the evidence of my own eyes. It's not paranoia. It's just part of this never ending cycle of horror for which there will never be any therapy, never any happy endings, nor any prospect of it ever being over. With those, and a million other dispiriting thoughts running through my head, I collapsed into a chair.

I must have fallen asleep, because when I next opened my eyes dawn was just beginning to creep over the treeline. It was the sound of the rifle being reloaded that had woken me. A few feet away, the gun propped up on the table by the window, patiently taking aim at the undead below, was Kim.

"Morning," I muttered, standing up. The duvet I'd thrown over her, that she in turn must have placed over me when she woke, fell off and onto the floor. I looked around. Sanders' body was gone. She must have already moved it. So much for me waking up if the undead got into the house.

Kim had found some new clothes, or, rather some old, not-recently worn ones. A set of hard-wearing gear, more suited to a rain drenched autumn than the start of a hot summer.

I walked over to the window.

"How's your wrist?" she asked.

"What? Oh." I flexed it. It was sore, but I really had had a lot worse. "Fine. Thanks," I added, and feeling that was insufficient I went on. "How's... ah..." I stalled and decided to change tack "How many. Out there, I mean?"

"About a hundred," she said. "Give or take." Then she pulled the trigger.

"Are you familiar with guns?" I asked.

"Not really," she replied as she reloaded the gun with casual ease. I looked down at the grounds.

"I can only count about forty," I said.

"The rest are around the side of the house," she said.

"By the window to the... your..." I stalled again, unsure how to finish the sentence.

"About thirty. Another ten are stuck in the maze, a few others are scattered around the back. I checked first thing." She fired again. Now that I was looking in the right direction I saw her target collapse. Then I saw it try and move, its arms waving, its legs twitching.

"Chest," she said. "It's the suppressor, I think." She reloaded, shifted her aim and fired again. The bullet entered the zombie's head as it was trying to stand. "Less accurate, but less noise. Noise is definitely more important."

"I've never fired a gun before," I said, half to myself. "Well, I did fire a shotgun, once. At some clay pigeons. I fell over. The recoil."

"Right," she said, and fired again. I looked over to the table next to the rifle. One box of ammunition was opened, and already half empty. On the floor, other boxes were scattered about, all empty. Around her feet the carpet was littered with spent cartridges. Counting the shots fired at me yesterday, hundreds of rounds had been wasted on little more than target practice.

"It would be better to conserve ammunition," I suggested.

"Sure. Better. But you just said you don't know how to shoot, and I'm out of practice." She turned to look at me, and for the first time since we'd met, I saw her eyes properly. They were cold, hard, unforgiving, hidden beneath a haunted depth of recent experiences I can only hope I never understand. "And," she went on, "can you think of a better time to practice than this?"

Knowing that whatever she was doing, it wasn't target practice, I left her to it and went off to find some clean clothes for myself.

The more I loot, the better I'm getting at reading the signs left by the previous inhabitants. Washing still in the machine or dirty crockery in the dishwasher is a sure-fire indicator the occupants fled the night of the outbreak. A house that's immaculately tidy, with the beds made, the washing-up done, everything unplugged and the valuables inexpertly hidden under a floorboard, belonged to someone who went on the evacuation. A note on a kitchen counter or stuck to the fridge shows someone who left sometime in between. A note pinned or nailed to the front door shows someone who left soon after.

Then there are the places like this, which have been occupied since the collapse. The fireplaces, whether they worked or were just purely decorative, are full of ash and half burnt furniture. Usually, though not here, it'll be just the one fireplace, with chairs and stools pulled up close to it, giving a rough estimate of the number of survivors at that refuge's peak. The chairs aren't gathered there for heat, not entirely anyway, but primarily for light to read by, during the long sleepless nights.

The books, lying discarded by the chairs, provide an interesting insight into the specific crisis that the group faced and feared most. Encyclopedias, histories and historical fiction, biographies, maps, travelogues, cook books, DIY and how to guides, anything and everything that might provide even the most tenuous of clues to surviving another fear-filled day. The books closest to the chairs are the ones that seemed most helpful, or perhaps the most reassuring. Those whose charred remains lie in the grate, they are the ones found wanting. It is amongst those ashes that, if they had any in the house, you will find the zombie books. I did the same in the end, burning them out of desperate frustration when it became clear how far from this stark reality even the best fiction is.

Usually, in the room with the fire, there will be a table. On it will be every item that could possibly be conceived of as a weapon, but which was rejected when the survivors left. Cricket bats, hockey sticks, hammers, axes, knives, ornamental sabres, shovels, spades, the improbable and the implausible, all heaped next to open packets of nails and rolls of wire. The only thing missing will be the poker, usually left by the fire next to a sharpening stone, where someone has tried to add an edge to wrought iron.

These are the homes of the people who thought they could stay put and ride out the storm. They are the people who thought everything would work out. They waited for help that they were sure must come. At first they expected our government, then it was any government, that somehow, someone, somewhere in the world would come to save them. Then they were forced by hungry desperation to leave.

The Manor is like that, but on a bigger scale. It's hard to say exactly who was here after the outbreak, or, with the exception of two of them, who they were. When the evacuation day came, some left, some stayed on, perhaps for a week or two. Probably, judging by the bones in one of the kitchen bins, until the easily caught wildlife had been eaten.

The cupboards here are empty, but that's normal too. Long before the food ran out, packets of anything and everything with any calorific value, from herbs to toothpaste, would have been gathered together. There's always a notebook next to the treacherously inaccurate kitchen scales, where the survivors have laboriously poured over the nutritional contents of every morsel in the house. A menu of the inedible, for this time of the unthinkable, devised sometimes with loving inequality, sometimes with distrusting fairness.

Usually I find these grimly fascinating, here though, I recognised some of the names. Arch and Bell, Archibald Greene and Annabella Devine, the butler and housekeeper. When I knew them as a child, Mr Greene was always apparently furious with "these young'uns, messing up my house". Mrs Devine would always be ready with a kind word for a torn shirt or bruised eye after my almost weekly fights with Sebastian over my being orphaned and him being about to inherit one of the largest estates in the UK.

They can't have been more than forty back then, though that seems ancient enough to a child and they'd had a wedding anniversary that summer. I don't recall if it was celebrating ten years or fifteen or twenty or, perhaps, just one. The Duchess threw them a glorious party, for one night treating them and their guests as if they were royalty. Jen, Sebastian and I were decked out as footmen whilst the Duke even attempted to wait at table. It was my happiest of memories, now made eternally sad by seeing their names written down on that scrap of paper. I wished, then, that I'd never come to this house.

There is one aspect of the Manor that is very different from anywhere else I have been, the weapons. The gun cabinets were empty. Not that there were ever many here. The Duke had been invalided out of the service, returning home as a pacifist. He kept a few ornate shotguns, more antiques than firearms, but they had gone. The others, the older mementoes of ages gone and wars long forgotten, they adorn almost every room. If one wants a weapon, all one has to do is take it from the walls. I'm trying to remember what used to hang in the gaps. Morning-stars, maces, long-swords and lances, all already gone. There are plenty of weapons left, though.

I found six pikes hanging from the wall of one long overtly splendid room that was just as I remembered it. The twenty foot long, five inch thick, teak table, the ten foot tall portrait of the eighth Duke hanging over the fireplace, the Persian rug with its pile so deep you could lose a whole canteen of cutlery in it, and the candelabra to illuminate a room that had no electric lighting. It had been designed to awe and intimidate, a place to dine when unwanted guests arrived and needed to be dissuaded from staying the night. That was why, I had been told, every inch of wall space was taken up with ancient steel.

I don't think the pike I chose is a genuine antique. It looks and feels slightly different to the others. The blade is less pitted and discoloured, the handle doesn't have that worn-smooth-by-use feel and it feels lighter yet somehow more solid. Perhaps it is a genuine replica, an old replica certainly, but something made a few decades ago to replace an even older piece that rotted beyond service even as a decoration.

I found the sharpening stone exactly where I expected to. It was on the hearth next to the fireplace. A plain oak chair I once remembered as having sat by the window in the Butler's study, stood pulled close to the only spot in the house with warmth and illumination once the power went out.

Pike in hand, I returned upstairs. Kim was still in the same position, still firing.

"You should let your shoulder rest," I said. She looked up. "The recoil," I added.

35

She fired off one more round. I watched as one of the undead outside collapsed. It didn't get up.

"Head shot," she said, as she laid the rifle to one side, stood, and stretched. "Four in ten. My hit rate."

"Have you done much shooting, then?" I asked again. There was so much to ask, so many questions, but where is one meant to start? All those old conversational gambits about family and hobbies and jobs and schools, it all seems supremely irrelevant now.

"University," she replied, almost with an effort, as if she was reluctant to share anything personal, even something so pertinent to our immediate survival.

"What? A shooting club?" I asked.

"No. Year abroad. Oregon," she shrugged. "Host family were gun-toting, redneck, Republican stereotypes. Nice people. Really nice people," she added with emphasis. "Shooting range on Saturday, church on Sunday and hunting as soon as the season started." Her expression softened. "And there was me, a hippy liberal." She paused. "It was fantastic. I got very good at bowling, expert at charring meat on a grill, and moderately okay at shooting. Not good, not bad, but okay. It comes back to you. Like falling off a bike."

"Um," I stumbled trying to think of a response. The short utterance was enough to draw the veil back over her eyes. Desperate to say something, anything, I asked, "Do you want a cup of tea?"

She laughed. I didn't think it was that funny. Perhaps she was so highly strung, she was looking for, needed, any kind of release. The shooting was a manifestation of that, I think. The laugh was another, and I guess I also needed a release, because I started laughing too.

We found a bedroom that, going by the thick smell of mothballs and even thicker layer of dust, had lain empty since long before the outbreak. I opened the flu, letting out a shower of dirt and soot onto the ornate rug, doused the coal stacked decoratively in the grate with lighter fluid, and lit it. Despite the warmth of the day, we each pulled a chair close to the fire and sat.

"Cold toast," I muttered after a while.

"What?" Kim asked.

"Cold toast. I was looking around the room and imagining what it would have been like a century ago. Picturing the Dowager Countess lying in bed, spreading warm butter on cold toast whilst listening to a maid's downstairs gossip."

"Oh," she replied. "Why's the toast cold?"

"They toast it in the kitchen. By the time it gets up to the bedroom it's always cold. That's one of the things they used to say about the Lords and Ladies of those times. They didn't know toast came out hot."

"Huh." She poked the fire.

"The Duke, he told me that. Said it was why he had a toaster on the sideboard in the dining room. The Duchess hated it. Said it wasn't in keeping with an ambience of stately nobility. That didn't stop her using it, of course."

"The Duke of this place? You knew him?" she asked with genuine curiosity.

"Sort of. I spent a summer here with someone. Her family knew the Duke's family. I tagged along. It's... complicated."

"Right," she said.

Wanting to steer the conversation away from the past and the inevitable question of who that girl grew up to be, I changed the subject. "No water. I mean there's the water they were bringing up from the lake, but I didn't know how safe it would be to drink, even after boiling."

"So you're making tea with lemonade?" she asked as I cracked open a tin and poured it into a small saucepan I'd brought up from the kitchen.

"Yup. It works well. Think of it as tea with sugar and lemon," I added, pouring in a second can. The saucepan went onto the fire, and I sat back.

"It's old-fashioned," I said, as we waited for the saucepan to boil.

"Sorry?"

"The scene. Us. The fire, the saucepan, the setting, the whole thing. It's like the last two hundred years never happened. Thousands of years, even," I said. "I found some bones in the kitchen. One of them was at least three foot long. Giraffe, or Elephant, perhaps. I think they were eating the animals from the wildlife park."

"Wasn't us," she said. "Them. Those two, I mean. Whichever." She stared into the fire.

"You knew them, before?" I asked. There was a long pause before she answered.

"They thought we were the last," she said, and the words came out in a rush. "That of all the people in the whole world, only the three of us were left. They were certain of it, so convinced I think it drove them crazy."

"You knew Sanders?" I asked.

"Yes. Sort of. Not really." She grimaced. "That's exactly how to describe him. He was a friend of a friend of someone I used to work with. He was the kind of guy you'd just see around. I think Sanders was a nickname, but when you've been saying hello to someone for years you can't suddenly ask 'What's your real name?' Then he moved into a place on the next street, and I'd nod to him at the bus stop, or say 'Hi' when I saw him at the supermarket, you know? Nothing more than that. When the evacuation started, when they said everyone had to leave, we decided to head off together. Or he did. There wasn't anyone else close by, and he was familiar. He was safe, I guess that's what I thought. That's why I went along. And it was safe. Safer than if I'd been on my own." She stirred the fire with the poker until sparks danced up the chimney.

"We got trapped on the motorway. The M3. About five hours out of London. I don't know how far that was, there were so many people, all trying to go the same way, no one could get very far very fast. There was meant to be a lane free for buses and coaches to collect the stragglers, but the road was clogged. This great heaving, sobbing, swearing, shouting, mewling mob, all heading out to who knew where and who knew what.

"Then the screaming started. I think it was from in front at first, but a few minutes later it was coming from behind as well. Then everyone was screaming. Most of them, I don't think they knew why. They were screaming because everyone else was screaming. You know how people are. Were. Then it changed. Everyone started pushing. Everyone. Those behind, in front, to the sides, it seemed like every single refugee in that column, all wanted to be exactly where we were standing.

"Sanders saved my life. He dragged me through the crowd, over to the fence and practically threw me up it. I managed to claw my way to the top. It wasn't difficult, I mean, they'd not built this thing to stop people getting out. I got to the other side and didn't know what to do. I watched him as he helped other people climb up and over, and I was just standing there, unable to decide if I should wait for him or run or what. Then the screaming changed. Or maybe that was when it really started. Pain and terror, that's what it sounded like. Before it had been anger and fear, but now, now it was filled with desperation, and it seemed to be echoing up the entire length of the motorway.

"I worked it out, since. Thought about it a lot. Didn't have much else to do, but think. Those first screams, that's when the infected died. Someone standing next to one, when the body dropped, they screamed. Then the pushing, the shoving, that was when they realised what it meant. They wanted to get away, before the bodies turned. That last lot of screaming, that was from the people who hadn't managed to escape when those zombies started standing up.

"All those people who'd been infected, the ones who thought they were special. Who thought they were different, immune." She glanced at me. "If they'd just stayed at home, then maybe the evacuation would have worked. Of course if they'd done that, we'd have made it to the muster point and the vaccine. So, small mercies, right?

"Sanders managed to climb up and over, and then we ran. The last time I looked back I saw this huge section of fence just collapse outwards under the weight of about two-dozen people. Or zombies. Or both. I couldn't tell.

"We kept running, kept hiding up when we found food and water and moved on when we ran out. Then we met Cannock. That's when it went wrong. Some people are good, some people are bad, but most live their lives with their souls balanced on a knife's edge, just waiting for circumstance to push them one way or the other. Cannock was different. He wasn't just bad, he was truly evil. When he pushed, well, I guess

Sanders didn't really stand a chance.

"It was Cannock's idea to come here. When we arrived there was an old couple here. Not *old* old. Maybe in their sixties or seventies, but made a lot older by the rationing and the power cut and the fear of the undead, you know? Cannock killed the woman. Made Sanders kill the man. Said it was survival of the fittest. Said there was no room for passengers. Afterwards, he said it was the merciful thing to do. Sanders believed him, he wanted to. He needed to."

"The, uh, the man. Did he have a fussy little moustache? A Poirot sort of thing?" I asked, dreading the answer.

"Yes," she said quietly. "You knew him?"

"And the woman," I asked, ignoring the question, "was she short, rake thin, with a mole on her left cheek?"

"I think so. Who were they?"

"The butler and housekeeper," I sighed. "Good people. They didn't deserve to die."

"No one does," she said. "Not like that. I think that's when Sanders and Cannock both started to go mad, when the whole 'last men on Earth' thing started. It got worse, each day that no one came, each day they had nothing to look at but the empty skies. That's when I should have run, but where to? As days went by and we didn't see anyone, didn't hear anyone, I think I started to believe it too." She stabbed the poker into the fire.

"They'd go out sometimes for supplies, in that first week or so we were here. That's when Cannock brought back the rifle. I can't remember what it's called, but he knew the name and everything. He said it was the one the British Army sharpshooters had, said he'd used one of them in Iraq. I think he was lying, I don't think he was ever in the Army. He said he found it in the MOD Armoury on Salisbury Plain, and I think he was lying about that too. He was a good shot, though. He knew about the suppressor, knew it would make the rifle less accurate, but he also knew enough that silence was important. Everything had to be done quietly. Everything.

"The rifle made him happy, kept him… occupied, I suppose is the best way to describe it. Right up until they went out hunting. They made a big deal out of it, how they were the last people on the planet who'd ever bag themselves a rhino. I wasn't to go with them. I had to stay, prepare the fire, get everything ready for a feast that evening. Woman's work!" she spat, bitterly. "I should have run. They came back empty handed and soaked through. I said I should go out. That I'd been hunting, that I knew how to use a rifle. Cannock hit me. Then… well, you saw the cell, the handcuffs, you can work out the rest."

She stopped, lifted the saucepan off the fire and poured the boiling liquid into an antique china teapot we'd liberated from a glass display stand on the ground floor.

"Last men on Earth, Ha!" she went on. "That's one too many. They didn't go out after that, just stayed in the house, day after day. Cannock would have killed Sanders soon enough. Or maybe it would have been the other way around. Then I would've killed whoever was left." She poured the tea, and as she handed me a cup, our eyes met. There was no point putting it off any longer.

"I need to tell you something," I began. "About the evacuation—"

"That you came up with the idea? I know, Mr Bartholomew Wright, I read your journal." She shrugged. "Some of it anyway. Whilst you were sleeping." She sipped at her tea. "Too much angst for my taste." She took another sip. "It's how I knew about the vaccine. Cannock wasn't interested in it. I wondered what had happened to all the people, why no one had come. A house like this, I mean, fresh water, walls, I think I was expecting someone to come. Helicopters and Army or something. Maybe that's why I didn't run when I could." She shrugged. "I thought about killing you, I mean, that's what I'm meant to do, isn't it? I'm meant to blame you for everything. I'm meant to take it all out on you. At the very least I should be conflicted or something… something." She took another sip "I think," she said slowly, "that whatever happened, it was bigger than you. You were just another pawn, and me? I didn't even make it onto the board. I should say thank you, for rescuing me."

"I'm sorry," I said. "I am, for everything."

"Save it," she said, but not unkindly. She leaned back in her chair and closed her eyes. After a while, eyes still closed, she said "So. Bart."

"I prefer Bill."

"Hmm, yes, I can see why. Bill, then. What are your plans now?"

I hesitated. I didn't know whether I should tell her, but for some reason I trusted her, and besides that, she'd already read the journal.

"I'm going to Lenham Hill," I said. "I have to."

"Okay. Why?"

"It's hard to explain. There's a video on the laptop, it would be easier if I just showed you," I said, standing up.

"But didn't you realise?" she asked. "You were shot, or your bag was. Your laptop's broken."

I didn't reply, just hurried from the room. My pack lay where I had dropped it. She was right. That blow that had knocked me to the ground, when I thought I had been shot, I *had* been shot. It was just that the bullet had come in at an angle and had been deflected by the bag and its contents. The laptop was broken in two. Shards of plastic and circuitry were mixed up with the dirt and grime at the bottom of the pack. I knew at once it was broken beyond repair. The files on it were lost forever.

I emptied the bag out onto the bed. The external hard drive looked fine, I turned it this way and that, and couldn't see any damage, but without a computer to plug it into I had no way of knowing. I glanced over once more at the pile of mp3 players, net-books, tablets and laptops that lay discarded amongst the shell casings. I tried every device that had a USB port. The batteries were all dead.

"They kept their haul somewhere downstairs. I don't know where, but they brought back a lot of stuff," Kim said from the doorway.

It didn't take long to find the room she was talking about. It was filled with electronic gadgets, jewellery and even clothes. I remembered the house I'd spent the night in, how it had been stripped of anything that might once have been considered valuable. It must have ended up here, amongst this heap of worthless wealth.

I tore through the piles until, finally, I found an Apple laptop. I turned it on. Victory! It had power. I rushed back upstairs.

Click-clack. I heard the rifle being reloaded as I approached the bedroom.

I ignored Kim, as she fired off another shot, grabbed the hard drive and plugged it in. I waited, my fingers crossed until I heard the drive starting to whir. It was working. The green power light came on. A dialogue box came up on the screen.

"Disc unrecognised. Would you like to format disc? Yes. No."

I slumped despondently onto the bed. It wasn't a set back, not really. I hadn't looked at the files on the hard drive, but after what I'd seen on the laptop, that didn't really matter. I knew where I had to go, and why I had to go there. Everything else was just a distraction, a way of delaying the inevitable. I repeated those and another dozen similar sentiments and tried to believe them.

Click…

"Would you leave that rifle alone! Please," I added though it came out through gritted teeth.

She turned, and looked at me. "Alright," she said. "So tell me what was in those files. What's so important that you have to go trekking across the country?"

"There was a lot of stuff," I said, standing up. "There were accounts, supply lists, shift rotas and spreadsheets filled with millions of pieces of raw data, and those might be important, but I didn't have time to look at them."

"So what did you see that was important?"

"There was a video. It was a reply to some other message, a walk-and-talk presentation, explaining why the facility needed more funding. Obviously it was recorded before New York, but I don't know how long before."

"And?" she prompted.

"Out of context, without knowing to whom it was sent, what questions it was answering, it's hard to draw much from what they said. The scientist, the same one who was in that hospital in New York—"

"The one where the outbreak started?"

"Right. The same guy, he was giving a tour, I suppose is the best way of describing it. The camera was following him around Lenham Hill as he explained the facility's limitations. One thousand doses per day. That

43

was the maximum they could produce. He was stressing that wasn't enough. He was explaining, in a lot of depth, why they couldn't increase production beyond that. It was to do with air filtration systems, the need to focus on testing and refinements, on how the facility couldn't be run both for R&D and production at the same time."

"That doesn't explain why you think you need to go there," Kim said.

"I was getting to that. Like I said, it was hard to follow him without the context. I was trying, right up until he stopped outside of a room. It was one of those walk in vaults, containing rack upon rack of vials of this super vaccine, the virus that started it all." I stopped, and waited. When she didn't say anything, I continued. "Don't you see? What if it's still there? What if someone else finds it? It has to be destroyed. That's why I've got to go to Lenham Hill."

She continued looking at me for a long moment, then turned back to the window and picked up the rifle once more. Click-clack, pause, click-clack, pause. I stood there as she fired off three rounds and then I stormed from the room. I was furious. Couldn't she understand? Didn't she want to?

The fury quickly evaporated, turning to morose despondency as I turned down corridors I recognised as ones I'd run down as a child. I stopped by a portrait of the third Duke. Someone, I assume Cannock, or possibly Sanders, had slashed it. The canvas now hung limply from the frame. I stood there, looking at this wanton, purposeless destruction, until my resolve returned, and I marched back to the bedroom.

Click-clack. Pause. Click—

"We should go," I said decisively.

"We?" she replied, not turning to face me but pausing, one hand on the rifle bolt.

Of course, I had assumed she would want to leave with me. Not thought or considered or even asked, I had just assumed. "You want to stay here?"

"Alright, no," she said without much of a pause. "But I don't like the idea of some wild chase across the countryside to some research facility that may or may not still exist."

"But…" I began, and then stopped. "There's Brazely Abbey. I was going to head back there to get some supplies before heading north. It's a good spot. There's a well, fruit trees, and strong walls. You could stay there. If you want."

"Thank you, that's very kind," she said. I couldn't tell whether she was being gracious, sarcastic or a mixture of both. "But why the rush?"

"To get it over and done with, before someone else—"

"If it's still there now," she interrupted, "then another few days won't matter. Besides," she slid the bolt forward and removed the cartridge, "how much do you reckon one of these weighs?" She twisted slightly and threw the round to me. I fumbled the catch, dropping the cartridge on the bed.

"Well?" she asked again. I picked it up.

"I dunno. Half an ounce, maybe."

"So, in the real world we'd say between ten and twenty grams, right? How many do you think a thousand would weigh? Because that's how many are here. There were over two thousand, when they found the rifle. Now there's half that, but it's still too many to take out on foot and since there's no car here we *will* be on foot. Water, food, weapons and ammunition, it all adds up."

"Between ten and twenty kilos. I should get the scales, get an accurate weight for them."

"You're missing the point. Weight, size, call it what you want, but we're not going to be able to take all of them."

"We can leave them here then, come and collect them sometime in the future."

"Even if we were to come back, what is it you think you'll be doing with these bullets? One zombie is as good as any other. Kill Them all now, or kill Them all later, but they all have to be killed." She turned back to the window and slid another round into the chamber. "I'd like to stay a day or so. To recover. Then we can go to the Abbey, and you can head off on your quest. A day won't make any difference, will it?" She asked, and the edge to her voice had now gone.

45

"No," I admitted. "I suppose not."

She pulled the trigger.

19:00, 26ᵗʰ June

There's a line in Macbeth, "If it were done, when 'tis done, then 'twere well it were done quickly." That sums it up really. I want sanctuary, I want to get to Lenham Hill and destroy those vials, I want answers, an explanation for all of this nightmare, and I want it all now. I don't want to hang around, waiting, when there's a job in front of me. There's nothing wrong with that, that's who I am.

I didn't remember the quote, not exactly, and fine, I'll admit I'm mangling the meaning of the line to suit the circumstances, but so what? I'm hardly the first person to do that with Shakespeare. Why I feel I need to be honest to this journal, I don't know. It's something to do with Kim. I can't say exactly why, but somehow just knowing that there is someone else, another survivor, someone not that different from me, that changes things. It doesn't alter my resolve. I still need to go to Lenham. Someone needs to make sure that the place is destroyed, and if not me, then who?

I did remember the line was from Macbeth, so I went looking for a copy in the library and ended up spending the afternoon leafing through the plays.

I tried Julius Caesar first, but somehow the way the language has changed over the centuries makes the opening few scenes almost comical. Macbeth though, I can relate to that. It's strange that the distance of time, the almost alien nature of the language, makes it somehow more relatable than more recent works. Dickens and Solzhenitsyn, Steinbeck and Orwell, no matter how great and skilled the writing, the subject matter is now less relevant than the cheapest pulp science fiction. What does ideology matter when the species is virtually extinct?

Day 107, Longshanks Manor, Wiltshire

14:00, 27th June

I was woken by the sound of an elephant. I've always liked elephants, liked how they seem completely indifferent to the existence of us humans. Perhaps it was a hippo. Or a rhino. My knowledge of animals, and the noises they make, comes more from animated films than nature documentaries. It sounded big, though, and it's pleasing to know that at least some other animals have survived thus far.

It was refreshing, this morning, being able to wake up and do nothing. A reminder of those weekends, few and far between in recent years, when I had nothing to get up for. I spent an hour or so finding some new clothes, since there's no water to spare to wash my old ones.

There's enough tinned and dried food for about ten weeks for the two of us, and I'm not talking about crates of tinned peaches either. Breakfast this morning was kumquats in grape juice. If I had toast I could spread some 'By Royal Appointment' lychee and crab-apple marmalade on it. But I don't have toast. Spooning it out of the jar brought back some once happy memories, now bittersweet with all I've seen.

Then I wandered the halls, but the more time I spend here, the more the memories of happy times come back, and with them the realisation that everyone in those memories is probably now dead. Perhaps I do just want to get things over with, but by mid-morning I'd had enough.

"I think we should leave," I said. It had taken me an hour to find her, lying on the floor of one of the attic bedrooms, staring at the sky through the high, dirt encrusted window.

"Yes. I was thinking that too," Kim replied, sitting up. I'd been expecting a fight. I don't know why, perhaps I'm finding it hard to adjust to another person in my life. "Tomorrow morning," she said. "We'll need to pack first."

Bags were easy enough to find. There was a stack of them in the room with all the loot. I took another moment to look at that pile of jewellery, ornaments, trophies and the electronic gadgetry that would never work again. Other than the bags, there was little of any practical value, no first aid kits, no fire extinguishers, and no toilet paper. Sanders and Cannock had done nothing more than build up a dragon's horde of the shiny and worthless.

Next came weapons. I kept my hatchet and chisel at my belt, with the pistol in one of the many pockets of a thigh length jacket I'd found hanging in the Duke's bedroom. A set of carry-on luggage provided the strap for the pike. The contrast of nylon and plastic with the steel and wood was pleasingly incongruous.

Kim found an axe that she liked the heft of, hanging in the same room I'd found the pike. I don't know how a historian would describe it, but I would call it a killing axe. It has a three foot long shaft, with a single broad tapered blade and a flattened hammer head criss-crossed with grooves, surely designed for the crushing of armoured limbs and skulls. Too sharp to chop wood, too heavy to hammer nails, it is no workman's tool.

Added to the weight of food, the hard drive, can openers, rope, saucepan, matches and kindling, the last of the lemonade, and we were nearly overloaded. Kim thought my suggestion of taking a wok from the kitchen was proof I'd been on my own too long. Those were her actual words. I tried to explain how useful they were as portable fire pits. She just gave me a look. In the end, I had to concede that with everything else it was far too heavy.

Then we turned to the ammunition. Kim had been right. Weight wasn't so much of an issue as where to put it all. The bags were unpacked and sorted once more, with anything that could possibly be found elsewhere being discarded as we re-packed our gear for the first of many times.

18:00, 27th June

A light drizzle has begun to fall. It would be refreshing if we could walk outside. Water in the lake, water falling from the sky, water, water everywhere, but not a drop we can touch.

We've reached a compromise on the ammo and the food we can't carry. It's now hidden in a cupboard in the main kitchen. Hidden is probably an exaggeration. It's stacked neatly behind an ice cream maker, a waffle iron and what is either a deformed whisk or the world's largest milk frother. They're all still in their boxes and have the look of unwanted gifts from people seen too frequently for them to be thrown away. Any half decent looter would find our stash.

I want to leave a note, an apology and explanation in case anyone ever comes back here. I feel I owe them that, but Kim is adamantly against it. I think this is more to do with her experiences here than it is to do with effectively handing these supplies over to whoever may come here next.

Once we'd finished packing, we retreated to that small bedroom to eat tinned fruit by the unlit fire.

"Why?" Kim asked.

"Why what?"

"All of this. Everything. The zombies, the virus or vaccine or whatever it was…" she hesitated "I mean, you saw a video of the Foreign Secretary in New York. What's his name? Quigley?"

"Sir Michael Quigley. Former Defence Minister, Shadow Minister for Health before that. He's the one who took over after the Prime Minister disappeared during those first couple of weeks."

"Yeah, I wondered why he stopped appearing on the TV."

"I thought he'd had a breakdown, but now?" I shrugged. "I don't know. Quigley took over, he always wanted the top job. He was a career politician. I don't mean he went into politics straight out of university, I mean the other kind. The kind who mapped out their path to Number 10 whilst they were still at school. He did eight years in the Army before being invalided out, then spent just long enough in what was euphemistically called logistics to afford the sizeable donation needed to buy himself a safe seat and a cabinet job for life."

"Yeah, he was the one the press always described as dedicated, wasn't he?" Kim said. "Except they never say to who, or what, he'd dedicated himself to. I remember him. Wasn't he a friend of Masterton's?

"Lord Masterton, yes. They were old Cabinet colleagues."

"And he's the father of Jen. The one you worked for?"

"Worked with. I grew up with her. Sort of. During the holidays at least. Term time I spent at boarding school. I think it was Lord Masterton who paid for that, though I never asked, and could never work out why."

"Right. But you knew these people, you worked for them?"

"With them, but I don't think Lord Masterton had anything to do with this. He's been retired for years."

"Yeah, well you know what they say about retired politicians. So Quigley, then. And the PM and the rest of the Cabinet and whoever else that knew. The Americans, I suppose, since it was in New York. What were they doing? Was this an accident or a mistake or some kind of weapon gone wrong?"

"I really don't know."

"But you have an idea. You can make an educated guess. You've seen the footage, you know these people."

I thought for a moment but I didn't need to think for long because in truth I had been thinking about little else since I first saw that video. "It's a puzzle. I don't mean it's puzzling, I mean that there are all these little pieces that somehow are connected and whilst I've got some of them, I'm missing others. I'd thought if I put them together I might get a sense of the whole, but no matter how many different ways I arrange them I can't see beyond the outline." I shook my head and tried to gather my thoughts, whilst Kim just sat there, patiently waiting.

"Yes, it started in New York. That was the beginning," I said, carefully. "Those initial reports, the train stations, the freeways, that shopping mall, they all add up to it starting somewhere in the city. That video from the hospital ties it all together. I don't think those officials who were there to witness it knew what was going to happen. If they did, there's no way you'd get representatives of China, Britain, the US, and whoever the others were, within a thousand miles of that room."

"Why New York, then? Why not some out of the way lab in the middle of the desert or somewhere?"

"Easy. You can get pretty much any cabinet minister of any government in the world there on the pretext they're going to the UN. No one asks. No one questions it. It's how a lot of peace talks and back room deals get done. Got done. That's why it wasn't in the UK."

"But it was created here."

"Yes," I admitted. "The virus, the super-vaccine, they're connected, but whether creating and releasing it was deliberate? I don't know." She opened her mouth to speak, but I went on before she could say anything. "I could guess, sure, come up with a plausible hypothesis, but it'd still be just a guess."

"It was the planes," she said, after a while. "Diplomats on planes. That's how it spread so quickly."

"Probably. Almost certainly," I said. "After the whole bird flu thing, there were procedures in place to quarantine planes, and even entire airports. No one talked about them, but they were there. Didn't matter how important you were, didn't matter if it was a private jet and you were the principal donor to your country's ruling party, you'd get stuck in a plastic tent just like the guy travelling in coach. Except if you were a politician on a diplomatic flight. No one can ground that plane, not even in China if the passenger's on the Central Committee."

Silence settled between us once more.

"So what's your plan?" she asked, eventually.

"I told you," I said. "To go to the facility and make sure that everything there is destroyed."

"Yes, but how are you going to do that?"

"I don't know," I admitted

"And what'll you do if the place is still occupied?" she asked. "I mean, hasn't it occurred to you that of all the places in the world, that is the most likely one to be either a smoking hole in the ground or surrounded by soldiers?"

"Yes," I said, and it had. "That doesn't matter. I've got to at least try. There's just so much I don't know. Someone, and I don't really know who and I certainly don't understand why, but for some reason they dragged me into their grand scheme. I want to know why."

"So this is just about you then, not about those vials in that vault, or the future, or making the world a safer place." She stood up. "You just want to know why someone had to go and mess up Bartholomew Wright's little life."

"No. Of course not, it's more than that," I said, though the words didn't sound sincere.

"An evacuation could have worked," she said, seemingly changing the subject.

"What? Well, perhaps if—"

"No. It could. It was worth trying, and you must have thought so, otherwise you wouldn't have suggested it."

"I was different back then."

"Perhaps," she echoed mockingly. "But it could have worked. And it *was* worth trying. But it failed. It was sabotaged and that had nothing to do with you. It's over. Your part is done. You don't need to go chasing after pieces of the past because they don't matter. None of it does, not anymore."

"The past is all I have." I looked at her then, into those dark seemingly bottomless eyes. "It's all we have, you, me and whoever else might have survived. We're never going to build a new Camelot. There's never going to be that city upon a hill. All those people, those that became the undead, those who were murdered, and those who starved or froze or just gave up. Billions of people, an entire race, are dead. We need to know what happened, and then someone has to make sure it can't happen again. It's all there is now, at least for me. Ever since I saw the bodies at the muster point, I understood that there's no one else who can do it, no one, just me."

Kim walked over to the window.

"Except," she said, "you could have left yesterday. No, if you really believed that, you would never have come here. You would have crossed that motorway."

Day 108, Salisbury Plain

19:00, 28th June

This morning, I was woken again by that bizarre trumpeting bellow, more suited to the savannah than the English countryside. Though in many ways I wish I had never gone to Longshanks Manor, rescuing Kim notwithstanding, I will miss that sound.

In the end we did leave a note. It made no mention of Kim, or of the stash in the kitchen. Instead, we included a simple explanation of what Sanders and Cannock had done to the previous inhabitants and what we in turn had done to them. Perhaps someone will come along and find the food and my bike, and perhaps it will help them to survive. I hope so.

We gathered our gear and quadruple wrapped everything in plastic and cling film. I ran a dry test, so to speak, in a bucket filled with the undrunk lake water, just to make sure the hard drive would be fine. Then we checked and rechecked that we weren't leaving anything behind, nor taking anything extraneous with us. Then we escaped.

It was almost as simple as that. We'd taken two of the large oak doors off their hinges and carried them down to the kitchens. Then we placed them on top of two serving trolleys that had that old-fashioned sturdiness of an age when dinner was served with a dozen courses for two-dozen guests.

Kim had spent half an hour with the rifle thinning out the undead around the kitchen side of the house. The trick, we've learned, is not to shoot the zombies immediately in our path, as the sound of the body hitting the ground will attract the others. Instead, by taking out six to the left and right of the door, we created a zombie-free corridor down to the lake. All we had to do then, was open the doors and, pushing the trolleys in front of us, run straight down the path, onto the jetty and let momentum carry us out and into the water. That was easy. A lot easier than trying to clamber onto our improvised rafts once we were in the water.

They floated well enough, but every time I tried to pull myself up and onto it, the door would just sink and twist round. It was the weight of the brace, I think. In the end, I held on as best I could. Using the door like a float, I half swam, half drowned my way across the lake. Kim had it easier, and I swear she was grinning when she pulled me out of the muddy shallows. Then we just hurried away.

It took us all day to find two bikes. The first we found at lunchtime but didn't find the second until about an hour ago. We would have been quicker, but I wanted to check the cars. Brazely Abbey is about forty miles directly east, across Salisbury Plain. Without knowing where we'd shelter for the night, that's an impossible distance on foot. By bike, however, it's two days at most, perhaps one, and possibly far less than that. By car, with all the detours due to the blocked roads, it wouldn't be much quicker. That wasn't why I wanted a car. I'm starting to think that the only way across the motorway is at speed, preferably shielded on all sides by carbon-fibre and steel. No, that's not really it, either. That's an explanation, but since there was no way we could carry the extra weight of fuel, it doesn't explain why I felt compelled to check vehicles that were little more than scrap metal.

"Where will you go after?" Kim asked, when I was running some wire into the sixth fuel tank of the day. Of those we'd tried, only one had had any fuel. Not much, but even if it had, there was no way we'd be able to drive it anywhere. It had a flat battery an even flatter tyre, and scrapes and dents along the sides suggested it had been driven there with no consideration for anything but speed.

"After?"

"After you've been to the facility and done your saving the world bit. What then?"

"Back to the Abbey, I suppose," I said. "I think, with some work, it could hold up through the winter. It'll be hard with just the two of us, but perhaps we can find some other survivors. Or maybe we look for somewhere better, somewhere safer. I don't know."

"I think I've worked it out now," Kim said. "It's the future, that's why you're obsessed with the past."

"I'm sorry?" I asked.

"The future, it's uncertain, and you want to escape from the uncertainty. You think that if you keep running away, then one day you'll arrive somewhere. What you don't understand is that sometimes *away* is all that matters."

Kim doesn't talk much. Perhaps that doesn't come across in what I've written, but what I've written down includes pretty much everything we've said to one another. It's not that we don't have anything to talk about, rather it's that neither of us has anything that needs to be said. For the most part, I've enjoyed this quiet companionship, right up until she goes and says something like that. She didn't say another word as I went on to check the cars at the next three houses we searched.

This last one, where we found the second bicycle in the garden shed, and where we've decided to spend the night, has a little runabout in the garage. A four-door car with barely enough space for two. The battery wasn't flat, the fuel tank was half full, the tyres needed a bit of inflating, but otherwise it seemed sound. I thought about turning the engine over. But I stayed my hand. It would have been easy to take it, and really, how much noise would that engine have made? Surely we could have driven back to the Abbey with only a few zombies following. Two or three, or five or even ten wouldn't be a problem. We have the rifle, after all. Then, there would still be enough fuel left to get to Lenham, and back. Probably I would have taken the car, if it hadn't been for the note, sealed in a plastic folder, nailed to the front door.

"Dear Andie, we've gone to Maeve's. We'll be all right, you know us. But if you read this, come and look for us there. We left Gertie for you. We love you, Mum and Dad."

We found the car keys, along with six bottles of water, half a kilo of pasta, a jar of honey and two tubes of concentrated tomato purée, hidden in a box underneath a pile of ancient teddy bears. The one on the top, a hand stitched ragged thing, missing an eye and half an ear, had a ribbon around its neck that read, 'Love, Grandma Gertie'.

We took half the water, left the keys and I added a message of my own. I apologised for the theft and broken door and included a note about the Manor and the supplies there. I doubt, after all this time, anyone will ever come looking, but even so, I felt I couldn't do any less.

Day 109, Stonehenge

20:00, 29ᵗʰ June

I woke as the first light of dawn was playing through the avenue of trees by the edge of the road, causing eldritch shadows to dance along the walls of the bedroom. In that moment of half-sleep, staring at that immaculate white painted ceiling in that strangely quiet house, everything seemed, for one blissful second, to be normal once more. Then my leg began its morning round of twitching, forcing me to get up. Kim was already awake. I don't know if she slept. Perhaps she can't. I didn't ask.

We breakfasted on pasta with redcurrants, blackcurrants and some not quite ripe blueberries we'd harvested from the gardens of the neighbouring houses. Truly, the breakfast of champions! At least we had some coffee to go with it.

There was a narrow lane at the bottom of the garden that meandered vaguely in the direction we wanted. We followed it for a half mile or so, sometimes surrounded by trees, occasionally by fences, and sometimes by once cultivated hedges now grown ragged with a season's unchecked growth. We were quiet. We were cautious. We took our time. There was something in the air that made me reluctant to hurry up and leave it behind. I wanted to drink it all in, to saturate myself in this beautifully peaceful, so very English, summer day.

Eventually we did reach the end of the lane, and a small cottage whose garden backed onto Salisbury Plain. There were no signs of life, or the undead, about the house, but out in the rear garden, nestled between a mountain of flowerpots and a folded up cold-frame was a chicken coup. The wire was intact, no foxes or cats or anything bigger had come to prey on these animals. They had starved, or died from dehydration, when no one was left to care for them.

That brought us back to Earth, or at least it did me. Kim had maintained a stolid silence all morning. I stood looking at the dead birds for a moment, thinking about all that they represented. Then, as I turned to Kim, I spotted a gate half buried in the hedgerow. It was an old wooden affair, the supports tinged green with moss, which added an ominous shadow to the faces still visible in the once ornately carved pattern. It was ajar. Through it I could see fields and the wide expanse of the Plain beyond, but between us and the grassland squatted a solitary, stationary zombie.

It hadn't heard us and I don't think Kim had spotted it. I had. I wanted to test my new pike and here was the perfect opportunity. No, that's just an excuse and a weak one at that. I could say that it was some subconscious response to finally finding company and realising that everything, or nothing, had changed, but in truth I don't know what came over me. Perhaps it was just another one of those weird compulsions, something that doesn't have a reason, or if it does, where the reason doesn't matter. I motioned for Kim to stay where she was and cautiously stalked through the gate and into the field.

I was bent over, with the pike held parallel to the ground just a few inches above the grass. The zombie had its back to me, the tattered remnants of a red thigh length jacket blowing in the morning breeze. I kept my breathing shallow, as I took step after cautious step toward it.

I was twenty paces away when its back straightened. I stopped, counted slowly to five, then took another step. The creature didn't move. My eyes fixed upon its shoulders, I took another pace forward. Its head tilted suddenly to one side. I froze, my foot in the air. I couldn't hold the position for long, but I wanted to get closer. I could have attacked, right then, I could have moved quickly and swung the pike and finished it. But I didn't.

I breathed out and lowered my foot, but this time I hadn't checked my footing. As my weight shifted, a branch snapped with a crack that seemed to echo for miles, though probably it only carried a few hundred yards. The zombie heard it, though. It stood and turned in one quick motion. I shifted my stance and brought the pike up. As the blade reached the top of its arc, as sunlight glinted on the blade, as I changed my grip and altered my balance, the creature suddenly collapsed, a bullet through its skull.

"Don't do that again," Kim said, reloading the rifle.

Even on the bikes we couldn't travel quickly. Rabbit holes, mounds, and dips concealed by the tall grass continually brought us to a jarring halt. We got bogged down in the forests of weeds that made the corrugated earth of the fields beneath seem deceptively flat. Impenetrable hedges, and sturdy chain-link fences denoting the Ministry of Defence training grounds forced us to detour and double back. It was agonisingly slow progress, and as the sun rose in the sky and the dawn warmth turned to an early-morning simmer, I began to regret this tourist's detour.

Then we would come to some small ridge, clear enough of obstructions that we could pump away at the pedals, whilst all about us we could see nothing but a great open expanse of newly-wild splendour. We'd cover half a mile or so in little more time than it takes to write, but then the ridge would twist and we'd be forced to plunge, once more, into the morass of vegetation. Occasionally we'd stop, pause and look behind us at the flattened path we'd ploughed through the long green and yellow grass. As far as the eye could see, this furrow was the only sign of mankind in the encroaching wilderness.

It had been my decision to go to Stonehenge, at least I suggested it, and Kim didn't object. Actually, she didn't say anything at all, so we went.

It wasn't much of a detour, being only a few miles off our direct route to the Abbey. The stones may have stood for over five thousand years, and with the decline of our species they are likely to stand for five thousand more, but I felt this might well be the last chance I would ever have to see Stonehenge. The world has become much smaller now, stretching no further than the horizon, and often not nearly as far as that.

Who knows if I will ever pass this way again? That, and without any barriers or bylaws preventing me, I'd finally be able to get close enough to see the graffiti Christopher Wren carved into the ancient monument a few centuries ago.

There aren't many undead on the Plain. There are a few who have drifted onto the grassland, but until we got closer to Stonehenge we'd seen only a few dozen, and usually from miles away. At first, I was concerned that with all this open space, with no brick walls and shrubberies to hide behind, They would be able to see us from further away, that as soon as one did, we would become surrounded. Images of a last stand on some hill whilst They came staggering towards us in numbers too great to count played across my mind. It turns out we had little to fear. Over distances of more than a few hundred yards They are effectively blind.

Now I've seen it for myself, I should have realised this earlier. Their bodies become desiccated with time, drying up as the virus absorbs, or converts, or burns off, or whatever, the fluids within it. Without tears, grit and dirt would build up and scratch corneas, blinding Them.

In London, when I climbed to the roof of that office block, and saw the barricades along the riverbank and the sea of ghoulish faces turning to stare at me, I was wrong. They weren't staring. They hadn't seen me. They'd heard me.

I can't really stress how important a discovery this is to us. Knowing that, as long as we keep the bicycle oiled, our gear wrapped and a safe distance from Them, we can pass by unseen, unheard and undetected, is a great relief, but this discovery means so much more than that. It's another part of the reason I need to go to Lenham Hill. What else don't we know that could help us do more than just exist in this world, and where else can we find the answers?

We reached Stonehenge at around ten a.m. We missed the dawn, and this close to mid-summer it would be tempting to throw caution to the wind and camp out just to see the stones at sunrise. But even without the undead it would be too dangerous to stay here. The stones have a new guardian, one that has long been a danger to man, and judging by the evidence about us, one that is even more dangerous than the undead.

We knew something was wrong from a couple of miles away when we saw the first body. It was definitely that of a zombie, but it had been mauled. The face had been torn off, the skull crushed and most of a hand had been chewed away. Chewed, but not eaten. We found the discarded fingers a few yards from the body, where they had evidently been spat out. We stared at those remains. We looked around, wondering what new monster we faced, what horrific abomination the undead might have mutated into, and more importantly, in which direction it lay.

We couldn't tell, and since one direction was as good as any other, we headed on, faster now, until we crested a ridge and saw the animals, there amongst the ancient stones. There are lions at Stonehenge.

I always used to hate lions. Not just lions, I had a rule that anything that could, and often did, kill humans should be exterminated, not conserved. Polar bears, sharks, grizzlys, pretty much everything that lived in Australia. As for lions, to me they were nothing more than tigers with better press.

We watched them for a while, taking it in turns to use the rifle's scope. There's a male, a female, and at least one cub. They must have come from the safari park, but whether they escaped or whether they were purposefully released, I can't tell. It doesn't matter. That they are there, that is enough.

I watched the lioness disembowel one of the undead with its claws. I saw the male pounce from one of the stones, knocking a zombie down then crushing its skull between its jaws. I watched as the cub darted out between the two adults to nip at a zombie's ragged legs. I saw the female swat it back towards the ring of stones, before turning on the undead creature and ripping its throat out.

Again and again, the zombies came, in ones and twos, drifting in from the countryside. Again and again the lions dispatched the undead. They didn't rush, they took it in turns, they could have run at any time, but I think, no, I'm certain, they had decided that this was their territory, that they were in no danger, and that they were not going to flee. And that is why I am terrified of lions.

"The lions aren't infected," I said, handing the scope back to Kim. "They're not eating the zombies. They're biting Them, and they're not getting infected. So if lions have survived, why not goats and sheep and cattle and who knows what else."

Then we heard the lioness roar. That truly echoed for miles.

"We should go," Kim said.

"Sure," I said, making no move to leave.

"That noise travelled for miles," She said.

"Yep."

"We didn't hear it before. The lioness didn't roar until we arrived. We should go. Now."

After that we had to head further south than I would have liked, leaving the Plain and returning to the roads. We've stopped for the night a few miles from the city of Salisbury. Tomorrow we'll have to go even further south just to avoid going through the city itself, but then we'll be able to head back to the Abbey, and perhaps just a few days after that, I will be at Lenham Hill.

Day 110, Raysbury, Hampshire

09:00, 30th June

We're about twenty miles north of Southampton, and even from here I can tell the city is nothing but ruins. Smoke, drifting thinly into the sky, speaks of some great conflagration, perhaps one that engulfed the entire coast.

The main enclave for the south of England was meant to stretch from there all the way along to the nuclear power station at Dungeness in Kent. I've not thought much about the enclaves and the fate of those living there. After I saw the mass murder of the evacuees at the muster point a few weeks ago, I assumed that those in the enclaves must have faced a similar fate. Nowhere have I seen any signs that even the merest fragment of our old civilisation remains. I've seen no helicopters, no planes, no evidence of any gangs clearing roads or organised in state sponsored looting. If I needed it, then those few wisps of oily black smoke are all the proof I needed that if there is some bastion of humanity left on this planet, it is not in southern England. That isn't to say there is no life at all.

Raysbury Gardens is a building site that, up until a year or so ago, was the Raysbury Park House Hotel, and was in the midst of a conversion into the Raysbury Gardens Assisted Living Facility. It's a U-shaped building, with four storeys at the front, three on either side and a partly finished enclosed conservatory area connecting the two. Even if it wasn't for the brochure, or rather the seven unopened boxes of brochures, stacked in one of the downstairs rooms, it would have been easy to guess at the building's intended purpose. It's full of panic buttons, sit-down showers and stair-lifts. There was no food here, but we're four meals away from hungry and two litres of water away from being thirsty.

Outside the house is a stretch of would-be gardens. String squares, rectangles, and circles litter the ground, mapping where future flowerbeds and lawns now will never be. On the far side, ringing the grounds, is a twelve-foot high brick wall, covered in moss and ivy. It looks deceptively fragile, but in that way only bricks that have stood for a century, and will stand for a century more, can.

We came in through the main gates, to the southwest, on the other side of the wall, to the east, the road meanders along for about six hundred yards until it comes to a junction. The road continues east and south, until it eventually meets an A-road heading to the sea. But if you were to turn left at the junction, you would drive into Raysbury, with its award winning high street, and its pack of the undead.

We were cycling along the road when we saw the gates. We stopped. With a high wall on one side of the narrow road, and impenetrable scrub encroaching from the other, we were both getting a little nervous. Or at least I was. Kim's expression was as blank as ever. The gates were padlocked, but with the appearance of disuse that suggested it had been done before the outbreak. We broke in and re-secured the gates. The house looked empty, there were no odd footprints in the loose earth and none of the windows or doors had been broken.

We were about to go inside when the wind shifted, bringing with it the unmistakable susurrus of the undead, and with it something far more chilling.

They weren't close, but if we could hear Them, then the undead were far closer than I would have liked. We broke into the house and made our way to the top floor. We went from room to room, looking out the windows until we saw the zombies.

The high street is bracketed by a pub at each end. In between is a smattering of barber's, hairdresser's, bridal shops, florist's, tweed outfitters and a fish restaurant. Even from this distance I could tell it was a restaurant, not a fish and chip shop. It looks like the type that had pressed linen table clothes, squid ink risotto on the menu, and if they did do takeaways, they would very definitely not be served wrapped in paper. It's outside that restaurant that the zombies are most densely gathered. It's against that door that They are pawing and clawing, trying to get in.

"How many? A hundred?" I asked, handing Kim back the scope.

"Closer to a hundred and fifty. Factor in those we can't see, and I'd say two hundred. Probably more."

The wind shifted, and through the open window we again heard the unmistakable sound of a baby crying.

11:00, 30th June

"Two, maybe three survivors. No more," Kim said, still peering out the window. She'd barely moved from there. I'd walked the grounds, found a rusted gate on the village side of the wall, searched the house and taken the time to update my journal. She'd just stood and watched and, I assume, thought. What of, she didn't say.

"How do you know? Can you see them?" I asked, standing up and peering into the distance.

"Someone's comforting the child. That's why the crying is intermittent. That makes two. Any more than three and some of them would have tried to escape. Maybe they did. Either way, now there's two of them, maybe three, no more. And that's counting the baby." She emphasised the last word.

I followed her gaze to the high street. The pack wasn't moving much, some were clawing at the door to the restaurant, some at the walls and doors to either side. There was some heaving and shoving as those at the back tried to push through the others, but broadly speaking, They were static. No more seemed to be coming in from the countryside, and of course, none that were there had any intention of leaving.

"We have to do something," Kim said flatly, her eyes still fixed on the high street.

If it wasn't for the baby, if it had been an adult's cry of pain then I honestly can't say what I would do. But it was a child. Even if Kim wasn't here, with her clear determination to act, I would have done something, but standing there looking at the great mass of the undead, I just couldn't think what.

"There's nothing in the house. Nothing in the grounds," I said. "No car, no truck, no tractors." I had an idea that if we could find a heavy enough vehicle, a front-loading digger, perhaps, we could just drive through, crushing any zombies who got in our way. It was a disturbingly pleasing image, but there was no vehicle. "No. Nothing here," I repeated. "No chemicals for fire."

"Fire's too risky. Have you seen what happens when a zombie catches fire?"

I thought for a moment "No," I admitted.

"Neither have I," she said. "Probably They just stand and burn. You can't control fire. You can't stop it spreading to the restaurant."

"What about shooting Them?" I suggested. "There's enough ammo isn't there?"

"Maybe. If we had time. If I could see Them all. If I got Them with one shot each. Maybe. But probably not."

"You take out as many as you can, then I'll go in and kill the rest," I suggested.

"You'd be facing at least a hundred," she said. "So, no."

"Then," I said slowly, as an idea was beginning to form, "what if we could lure Them all away?"

Day 110, Heritage Motors
30 miles south of Brazely Abbey

21:00, 30th June

The rescue plan worked. Sort of. What we needed was a sound louder than an infant, and to hope that whoever was in that restaurant would realise what we were doing and quieten the child whilst we lured the undead away. An ice cream truck would have been ideal, but where do you find one of those in a world that came to an end in February. What we found worked just as well, at least as far as getting the zombies away from the village.

We left Raysbury Gardens, headed back out the main gate and in a long arcing loop across the empty fields to the north. We deposited the bicycles in the garden of an empty house on the road along which we planned to escape. Then we headed back towards the village, searching for a likely looking property. It took the best part of an hour. We ignored the places that looked like holiday homes, skirted those which looked as though they had been occupied since the evacuation and avoided the all too many which were now occupied by the undead.

In the end we picked a farm on the other side of the main road. The gates were closed and there were two zombies in the yard, but after a few minutes of observation we were both certain there were no more. They appeared battered, as if They had already been in a fight. The one furthest from the gate had an arm hanging at an odd angle suggesting the bone had been broken in at least two places.

With most of the ammunition left with the bikes and uncertain of what we may face later in the day, I motioned for Kim to put the rifle away. Leaving the relative safety of an old barn, I loped across the road and climbed the five-bar gate. Rain, sun, and inattention had caused one of the supporting posts to shift and break free of the cement anchoring it to the ground. The gate buckled and collapsed. I jumped forward, and as it fell to the ground with a resounding clatter of gravel, the two zombies stood up and began to move towards me.

As Kim had cut short my attempt near Stonehenge, this was the first opportunity I had to test the new pike. Its more professional construction made it far more manoeuvrable than my homemade one. Perhaps because of that, complacency had set in and I'd neglected to sufficiently sharpen the blade.

The first zombie staggered forward. Its clothes were mostly tatters except for a long, stained scarf, that kept tangling in the creature's arms as it swiped and grasped at the narrowing gap between us. I swung.

As the pike arced towards the creature, its head jerked towards me at the last second. Its teeth snapped out and bit empty air as, instead of slicing into its neck, the blade bounced off the top of the its skull, ripping off a chunk of its scalp.

The force of the blow spun the zombie sideways. It fell to its knees. Without the human reflex to put its hands out in front, it smashed chin first into the gravel driveway, an arc of brownish gore spraying out onto the sun-bleached stones.

I changed my grip and stabbed downwards with the spike. I missed. Some instinctive part of me had assumed the zombie would be stunned, that it would stay prone. But it didn't. It was already rising to its knees as the point dug into the dirt.

As it stumbled to its feet, its hand batted out at the wooden shaft, knocking the pike sideways. I was gripping it so tightly that I spun with it, and as I was staggering backwards, trying to regain my balance, the zombie was already standing up. The second creature was almost at its side. Kim tugged at my elbow, pulling me back a step, just as that first zombie snapped at me once more.

I levelled the pike and speared it forward just as the creature lunged, its own weight, adding to the force of my blow, drove the point through its skull. It collapsed, taking the pike with it.

The second zombie, the remains of a solitary ski boot on its left foot making its movement slow and awkward, tripped forward. I took another pace backwards, and another, as I tugged at the hatchet in my belt. My eyes still on the creature, I staggered sideways as Kim roughly pushed me out of the way.

She let the axe fall to her side as the zombie got closer. It was five paces away when its mouth opened and it began to snap. She gripped the axe, two-handed, and brought it round in a huge sweeping arc, down onto the creature's skull. It collapsed to its knees, its face split in two, the axe blade buried deep in its neck.

It was brutal. It was efficient. It was, in its way, stunning. Above all, it was terrifying. I had done something similar myself more times than I can count, but watching someone else do it is different. Truly, we have become the barbarians inside the gates.

"They move fast," Kim said, as she cleaned her axe.

"Not much faster than walking pace," I replied, retrieving the pike. "Maybe five miles an hour. Perhaps a little more. They haven't the co-ordination to run."

"Huh," she grunted.

"That was the first one you've killed. Hand to hand I mean?" I asked clumsily.

"Huh," she grunted again and headed towards the house.

The doors and windows were still closed and secure. The house was neither infested with the undead nor had it been looted, though rodents and insects had been there long before us. Anything edible and not impervious to small teeth had been devoured, right down to the labels on the tins in the cupboards.

"The glue," Kim said as she placed the last of three unidentifiable tins into her bag. "They eat it. The paper they shred for their nests."

We found the mp3 players upstairs in a pair of bedrooms that had once belonged to two teenagers. The portable speakers took longer, and we were about to give up and try a different house when I found two sets hidden, perhaps as a sanction during some inter-sibling war, in the back of one of the living-room cupboards.

We tested the players by me taking them into a cupboard in what we reckoned was the centre of the house, whilst Kim barricaded the outside with cushions, ready to hammer loudly the moment she judged the sound too much. I turned them on. They worked.

"If we had time," I said when I came out, "I'd prefer better equipment."

"Or a different selection of music?" she asked. "But we don't have time."

We left the house and parted ways. Kim went back towards the village to get in place to do the actual rescuing of the baby. I headed west, back the way we'd come, to create the diversion.

I needed somewhere close enough that the sound would carry to the village, but somewhere far enough away that the undead wouldn't be able to hear the baby if it cried whilst they were making their escape.

I found a low-slung shed, about a mile from the village, which had once been used either by pigs or cattle, or perhaps even turkeys for all I could tell from the scattering of small bones about the floor. I created a ramp out of some old planking and crates and climbed up to the roof.

Decades of rust had eaten away the bolts holding two of the sheets of corrugated steel together. I levered them apart, taped the mp3 player to the side of the speakers and jammed them into the gap. Then I climbed down and headed east towards the town.

It was pleasant being on my own again. Not nice, not good, way short of great, just pleasant. It was the solace of solitude. As I walked through the fields, I had that feeling of being alone in a vast world. I can see how it turned Cannock and Sanders mad, but not me. I felt alone, but not lonely, not the last man on Earth, because whilst it was pleasant to be out there on my own, it wasn't anything more than that. Company, stilted and awkward as it was with Kim, was far better than what I've known these last few months. No, I was relishing the brief pleasure of temporary isolation in the knowledge that companionship was only a short breadth of time away.

About five hundred metres to the north and west of the village is a field in which there is some kind of weather monitoring gear. I think the miniature windmill thing is for calculating wind speed, and the enlarged test tube possibly measures rainfall, or it might be humidity. I'm not sure.

During most school holidays, except the one I spent at Longshanks Manor, I stayed with Jen Masterton at her family pile up in Northumberland. We had the run of hundreds of acres, getting underfoot of dozens of tenant farmers desperately trying to provide for their families.

When, a few decades later, we were looking for a portfolio for her to specialise in, it seemed only natural to pick agriculture. It was when we were trying to put together a press release that we discovered that spending our childhood covered head to foot in dirt, was not the same as understanding anything about the crops grown in it. We stumped for nuclear power instead.

So that array could have been part of some RFID system to track the movement of a herd, or for monitoring the frequency of crop-circles, or counting the number of bees per field or any of a million other things. I'm going to assume it had something to do with the weather.

I stood up, careful to stand with the equipment between the village and myself. I thought I was far enough away that the undead wouldn't be able to see me, but I didn't want to take risks, nor be rushed. I strapped the mp3 player and speakers as high as I could reach, making sure they were secure. Then I hesitated.

This was the first music I was going to listen to since that dreary choral stuff they'd played on the emergency broadcast. I scanned the playlists, looking for some tune I recognised. I found nothing. I settled on the list with the most tracks and let the music play. A tinny base beat came from the mp3 player's built in speaker. I checked that it was set to shuffle and repeat, plugged in the speakers and turned them on.

As a guitar squealed, and the bass beat sped to a cacophonous crescendo, one by one the heads of the undead turned. I knew They weren't looking at me, not really, but it did seem like it. As the sound, surely the loudest heard since the death of our society, certainly the loudest in our silent world, seemed to bounce off the clouds themselves, the undead started moving towards the hill.

It wasn't an orderly march, as a director might have elicited from a cast of extras. Rather it was the shoving, pushing scrum of the mob. Some at the back, what had been the front of the crowd gathered around the baby and its refuge, now pushed through to the front. By dint of being less desiccated, or with fewer injuries or just by virtue of being younger when They turned, They were the ones with the greater strength. Some zombies were knocked down, and were trampled underfoot. Others staggered, and were shoved along as the pack shifted and started to flow away from the village.

I was standing, about thirty metres higher than, and two fields and a scraggly hedge away from, the road. I watched as the first zombie walked straight into the gate at the bottom of the hill. It was a small creature, possibly a child when it had turned. Its arms waved through the gate, not trying to push it open but trying to walk through it. The gate held. I hadn't considered that. I watched another walk into the hedge and become stuck in the brambles and thorns. I hadn't considered that either.

I panicked. I took two steps down the hill, as another zombie, a much larger one, walked into the gate. This time it moved with a jarring clang I could hear even over the music. Then another, and another and another, then the weight of a dozen bodies was pushing at the gate.

The track finished. I saw the gate start to shift and twist. The next song began, and as a saxophone began a soulful lament, the gate toppled into the field.

I turned and started to walk along the crest of the hill back towards the shed. I didn't hurry, though. I didn't feel any need. I thought I was safe, and I didn't want to tax my leg, not until I had to. Then I spotted another creature coming from the northeast, angling across the fields towards the music. That was just one more thing I hadn't considered, that I'd be calling the undead not just from the village, but from every direction around. That was when I began to hurry.

I was half way across the field, still half a mile from the shed by the time the first zombie from the village reached the weather station. It stopped. It wasn't intelligence. I know it looked like it at the time. That's something I keep looking out for, some sign that perhaps They are learning, even evolving, and when that zombie stopped I thought it had. I've thought about it since, and now realise that it had heard the sound, but when it was close enough to use its eyes, it could see no prey. I'm sure that's what it was. Others reached the top of the hill, some stopping closer to the music, some further away. More arrived, and a weird milling about began as They looked, or seemed to look, for the cause of the noise.

I hurried now, running in that skipping lope that my leg brace forces upon me. It took five minutes, maybe more, to reach the shed, long enough for another track to finish and the next one to start. After I'd climbed up onto the roof, I could see at least a hundred gathered around the meteorological gear. It wasn't nearly enough.

I set the speakers to full and turned the music on. I didn't bother to select a playlist, just continued playing from wherever its previous owner had left off. It was an upbeat piece about love in the summertime. Thoroughly depressing under the circumstances, and totally unsuited to my darkening mood, but it was loud enough to carry to the weather station. Heads turned. Then about a quarter of Them started heading towards me. This time They moved more slowly. I watched as a zombie stopped and turned back. It walked for a few paces towards the monitoring station before turning once more and began, with a more purposeful stride, heading to the shed.

I counted to twenty, watching as some of the slower undead only reached half way up the hill before changing direction. Then I climbed down, and headed to the road.

I don't know how far that music was carrying. Miles at least. The discordant battle between the two playlists would have, in the old world, been drowned out by traffic and tractors, people and planes and all the other symphonies of life. Now, it reverberated off the landscape in a discordant jumble of sound. It was beginning to give me a headache. Worse, it was calling in the undead from every direction. None that I could see were close. I think all the zombies nearby had drifted into the village over the last few months. The ones heading my way were from much further afield. They were still too distant to see me, or so I hoped, but if I stayed out in the open, one would spot and then pursue me. And where there's one…

I picked up my pace, and made for a tumbledown cottage that had been on the verge of collapse long before the outbreak. I didn't have time to check whether the house was occupied, I just dived into a gap between a woodpile and a broken-down shed. Then I waited.

Sometimes, during the occasional quiet sections of music I heard the shuffling sound of the undead walking along the road mere feet away. Occasionally I would hear rotten cloth tear or dead branches crack as They tried to walk through the impenetrable thickets of brambles and briers bordering the fields. Sometimes, during the brief gaps between songs, I thought I heard something else, a knocking sound close by. I sat. I listened. I waited.

It took a bit under two hours, for the batteries at the weather station to run out. Then there was a brief, glorious and wonderful time, when it was just the music from the old shed. Crouched there, hidden, my leg aching from cramp, my whole body tensed to spring up if I heard any sound closer than a few yards, I got to listen to seven songs.

I couldn't tell you their names. I couldn't even tell you if they were objectively any good. To me it was sublime. It was beautiful. It was transcendent. Music's always done strange things to me, and after so long with nothing but my thoughts playing inside my head, the effect seemed amplified tenfold. It was a watershed. It was the moment when I started to think that we could do this, we could do more than survive, we could actually live. It was as if these songs were shining a light onto the world that was and the parts of it that, one day, we could have again. Like I said, music does strange things to me.

And then, as the batteries died, the music stopped. I waited. Without any other sounds, except that of the undead, I could hear the knocking more clearly. It was coming from the cottage and now it was the loudest sound I could hear.

I was about two miles from where we'd stashed the bikes. The plan was that if I arrived first I'd backtrack into the village to find out what was delaying Kim. If she arrived first she'd wait as long as she thought prudent, depending on who it was she'd rescued and, if necessary, we'd meet up at Brazely. We'd mapped out a route, and the assumption was that since it was unlikely that whoever she rescued would happen to have a bike, or that there was likely to be one in the restaurant, they would use mine and I would have to find another one somewhere else. It wasn't much of a plan, but there hadn't been the time, and there were too many unknowns, to come up with a better one. The question for me then was had Kim managed to get out of the village?

The knocking got louder. I crawled out from my hiding spot and looked over at the cottage. The windows were smeared with something a lot worse than dirt, but behind it I could just make out the humanoid outline of at least two undead. That wasn't the worrying part. It was the way that the window was partially boarded up, with tape stuck to each pane of glass. I looked over at the door. It too showed signs of reinforcement. I wasn't getting in, They weren't getting out, so there was nothing I could do to stop the noise. I had to go, somewhere, anywhere, before more zombies came.

The rendezvous was two miles away, but that was two miles in a straight line. I could make out the sound of the undead, still moving through the countryside. A straight line wasn't going to be possible. The Abbey was closer to forty miles away than thirty. On foot, with the undead now roused from their torpor, that suddenly seemed a lot further than it had earlier in the day. I needed speed.

There was nothing but weeds in the cottage's driveway and I couldn't see any sign of a bike amongst the detritus strewn about the garden. Going by the state of the shed and the roof, if I did find one it would be more rust than metal. I had to look elsewhere.

I crawled away to a gap between two pine trees that marked the edge of the property. I vaguely remembered spotting a cluster of newer looking houses near a wider road on the other side of the hill. It was less than a mile. I glanced up and around. I could see movement in the hedges where the undead had become entangled. The idea of trying to head across the fields didn't appeal. If I stuck to the roads, then I would only have to face those zombies that had managed to push through the hedges. Of course those were the tougher, stronger ones, but what other choice was there?

I made sure the pistol was loaded, the safety was on, and that it was secure in my pocket. Easy enough to get out in need, but not likely to fall out. I checked my gear was tight, that there were no easy-to-grab straps, then I got up and I ran.

Running, or as close to it as I can get with my twisted leg, turns a mile into a marathon. It's a never ending cycle of one more step, one more step, one more step, just to push through the pain. I can't fight whilst I'm running. The pike has to be a staff, a third leg, it becomes all that's keeping me up. The further I get, the more the brace jars and rubs and abrades my skin, until blood mixes with the sweat seeping down my leg.

There weren't many of Them at first, just one every fifty yards or so. A hop-skip sideways was all I needed, then it was a straight bit of road until the next zombie. Then there were two, then three, then five, and then I stopped counting.

My vision narrowed. My world closed in. I danced left to right, right to left, forward and even backwards to avoid the grasping forest of hands and snapping sea of teeth. They seemed to be everywhere. In front. Behind. Coming through the hedges to the sides. I waved my free left arm, punching at their faces, pushing at their bodies, clawing back at Them. I screamed with the pain shooting up my leg. I yelled as I felt their hands tug at my clothing. I swore as nails clawed at my hands and face. I roared my anger and hatred at all They represented, all They had done to me, to my world, until my voice was hoarse and I needed all my effort just to keep going. One more step, then just one more, then one more after that.

Then there were no more zombies. I glanced around. They were all behind me. I looked ahead. The road seemed clear. I looked down and saw the surface of the road had changed, becoming darker, the lines less faded. I saw the turning into the small development. There were six five-bedroom houses, clustered in a crescent around a pair of converted barns. Not a large development, far smaller than I'd remembered it being. I ran down the cul-de-sac, stopping by the small roundabout, turning a full circle, looking about for a bike. I saw none. What was I expecting?

The garages, I thought. In February bikes weren't left outside, they'd be locked up in a garage. I turned around once more, looking with an indecision borne of desperation. I had so little time, barely enough to look in one garage, but which?

"Act," I told myself. "Just pick one."

I ran to the nearest and slammed my fist against the metal garage door. All I achieved was a resounding echoing gong and a bloody smear on the flaking paintwork. Of course it didn't move, didn't open. The keys would be somewhere inside the house. I glanced back towards the road. They were two hundred yards behind, and getting closer. I didn't have time to search for keys.

I could stay and fight, except I knew I would lose and I would die. I could keep running, except now that I had stopped I didn't know if I'd be able to start again. Desperate, terrified, angry at having come so far, having gained so much, determined not to lose it, not so soon, I stuck the tip of the pike in the gap between the bottom of the garage door and the ground. I heaved.

The door didn't move. What was it Archimedes said? Give me a lever long enough and somewhere firm to stand, and I'll move the world. I looked around. I made the mistake of looking back along the road. They were one hundred and fifty yards away. Almost too close. I spotted an old zinc-galvanised watering can by the drainpipe. Fulcrum, I thought. I grabbed it, threw it close to the door and tried again. Something snapped. For a moment I thought it was the pike, but no, it was something inside, some part of the mechanism. The door shifted, clunked forward a few inches. I grabbed the bottom, scraping my knuckles on the concrete drive, and heaved at the door. It swung up and inwards, sticking about halfway. There was a gap of about three feet. I looked behind, They were less than a hundred yards away. My hand went to my pocket, checking the now reassuring weight of the pistol was still in easy reach, as I ducked into the gloom of the garage.

There was a bicycle. The garage was packed with boxes and old time junk that would, in my universe count as a looter's paradise, but there was no time for it. No time for anything but the bike. I half dragged, half threw it outside. It wasn't even an adult's frame, it was one of those cheap BMX knock-offs, the kind you gave to placate a kid at Christmas when you know they'll have outgrown it before spring.

Seventy yards. I was tired. Dog tired, dead tired, whatever expression you want to use, I was beyond exhausted. I was drained, but I wasn't going to give up. I half carried, half wheeled the bike away from the road, through the back garden opposite, over the small fence and into the lane beyond. I kept on, until I got to the top of a slight rise, then I got on the bike and let gravity carry me down the hill and away.

I travelled east then south then west then north, a huge circling of the compass before I found a familiar looking road. I don't know how long it took, but surely it can't have been more than thirty or forty minutes. Perhaps it was, because when you add to it the time spent waiting for the music to stop, by the time I got to the rendezvous I wasn't surprised to find both the bicycles were missing.

A note, pinned to the door with a kitchen knife, read 'Bill. Gone to Abbey.' And that was it. I didn't stay any longer than it took to read that note. The undead were on my heels. We'd woken all the dormant zombies in the neighbourhood and now They seemed to be on every road, down every lane and I was barely keeping ahead of Them. I kept going, with no real plan except to head towards the Abbey, not thinking about the distance, not thinking about anything but the few yards of road in front of me.

The further I travelled, as yards turned to miles, as I outpaced the undead chasing me, I began to notice something different about the zombies on the road ahead of me. More and more were heading in the same direction I was. I realised that They must be following Kim. What else could explain it? I tried to pick up my pace, tried to catch up, tried to work out how far ahead she was. But the saddle was too close to the pedals. To push down I had to half stand. With my leg twisted, I could only manage that for a minute at most before I had to sit, rest, and freewheel until I caught my breath, gritted my teeth and tried again.

Once I had to dismount, at a spot where an old tractor had been abandoned in the middle of a country lane. Three of the undead were standing in the narrow gap between it and the hedgerow. I was too tired to use the pike. I took out the pistol.

The first shot hit the tractor. The second missed the leading zombie, hitting the outstretched hand of the one behind. The third shot hit the first zombie in the chest. With the fourth I killed it. It took nine rounds to kill those three and They were barely moving. Kim must have done more than just a little target shooting or casual weekend hunting to have become so proficient.

After that, twice, when the undead blocked the road, I dismounted and used the bike to push a way through the hedgerows, and took to the fields. It was slower, but safer.

I arrived here, at the garage, four hours after Kim. It's an odd little place, a mixture of high-end extravagance and fourth-hand wrecks. I'd seen the undead outside, six of Them, by the main gate. I was going to give it a wide berth, to head across the fields to shelter in a house I could make out in the distance when I heard the baby crying. I knew it was the one Kim had rescued, I don't think misfortune would extend to trapping two infants in this nightmare land.

June 30th – 10:15 p.m.

Instead of watching Bill exhaust himself even further, I've said that whilst he sleeps, I will write down the account of how I rescued Annette and Daisy.

Escorted, sorry, not rescued. Annette is reading this over my shoulder and she wants me to make that clear. This, then, is how I escorted Annette and Daisy out of the village. Where to begin? Daisy is the baby. I would say she is around nine months old. She's just working out how to crawl, and except when she's crying, finds everything absolutely fascinating. Annette is thirteen. She rescued Daisy from London, but that is another story.

After Bill and I split up, I headed back to the village. What didn't dawn on me until I was halfway there, was that I was also halfway between the zombies and the music that was going to start any second. We didn't think of that, either, did we Bill?

In the village, there is an annex to the old Post Office, which I think had been used for depositing parcels outside of opening times. In the building's new incarnation as a set of cramped flats, this partially enclosed hut was the home to a multi-coloured plethora of wheelie-bins. That was at the east end of the village, not on the high street itself, but off a side road. Through a knothole, across the road and along the alley between two cottages, I had a reasonable view of the edge of the pack of zombies.

I was concealed from the undead, that's true enough, but the bins, overflowing before the evacuation, were now filled with a sodden rotten mess. The ground was carpeted with a thick layer of moss and mud, which fractured under the merest pressure. Each shifting footfall, every tiny adjustment of weight, and the surface would crack, exposing the foul smelling slime underneath.

The music started. Through the knothole, I saw the undead slowly stream out of the village. That disorderly procession seemed to take forever.

The house opposite had a flat roof with a view of the high street. Once the stream had turned to a trickle, I left the annex, crept across the road, and climbed up. I shot the undead that I could see. It wasn't easy. Twenty-three bullets to kill thirteen zombies. It was wasteful, but it's not like target practice, it's not even like hunting. I'd learned on a rifle with a comically large calibre, a 'let's give it to the girl to teach her a lesson' gun. The hole one of its bullets would leave in a deer would kill the animal regardless of where it hit.

With the undead, though, it has to be a head shot every time. Not just that, but a good, centre shot. I hit one of them with a glancing blow. It was a lanky gangling thing, wearing the remains of a tattered kilt or tartan skirt, I couldn't even guess which. Its head kept bobbing back and forth, its neck twisting, craning round, whilst its feet seemed anchored to the same spot. I tracked its movement, tried to get a feel for the rhythm of it before I fired. It bobbed right when I was expecting it to go left. The zombie went flying, and I didn't realise, until it stood up a few minutes later, that the bullet had only grazed along its face, taking off its ear. No, it's not easy.

When I was sure I couldn't see any more, knowing that wasn't the same as killing them all, I climbed down and went into the village. I don't know how to describe those few minutes. How do I get across the feeling of isolation and impending dread as I walked down the narrow alleyway? How can anyone explain that gnawing expectation of pain and death as I stepped out into the street? How do I express the fearful doubt as the zombies turned towards me, the nausea, the almost overwhelming desire just to turn and run? I can't. If you've lived this long, if you've been through it, you know, and if you haven't, then be thankful.

There were three of the undead left in the high street. I unslung the axe. It was over in minutes. I went over to the restaurant, called out, and waited for a reply. That was when our plans hit another hitch. Annette had so thoroughly barricaded the door that there was no way in, not from the high street. We met up around the back. We had to leave the buggy behind. With the music still playing we couldn't risk taking the road, instead, with Annette carrying Daisy, and me carrying my axe, we headed off out through the village, and cut across the fields. Not all the undead had gone.

Practice doesn't make it any easier. I don't mean physically. This axe was designed for fighting knights in armour. The undead, they seem to burst under its weight. Each time, though, I can't help thinking that this is a person, someone like me who just picked the wrong straw. With the rifle, I can see their faces. I can take the time to apologise first, to wish them well on their journey. Walking through that waist-high grass, not knowing at what moment or from what direction a desiccated mouth would snap up at us, there was no time to do anything but swing the axe and hope.

Twice in that field we were attacked by the undead. They had been stationary for so long that the grass and weeds had grown up to ensnare them, trapping them in place. Even the sound of distant music hadn't been enticing enough to get them to struggle free of their organic chains. The sound of humans close by, of a girl crooning gently to a baby, that was different. One moment we were walking along, the next a snarling apparition, all teeth and hands, jumped up, appearing from nowhere. I swung. They died. I apologised afterwards.

By the time we got to the rendezvous I knew we couldn't wait for Bill. It wasn't safe there. It wasn't going to be safe anywhere that wasn't far away. We took the bikes, both of them. I felt bad about that, even though Bill and I had agreed it might be necessary. I rigged up a sling for Daisy, and carried her on Bill's bike. Annette took mine. There was no way of fighting, no possibility of doing anything but cycling as fast as we could. When we set off I'd actually been worried that Annette wouldn't be able to keep up. She outpaced me in seconds.

The sight, yesterday, of Bill checking for fuel had reminded me of being carted around car showrooms as a kid. I remembered how the cars were always ready for a test drive. How the sales reps even had the keys in their pockets, ready to throw a potential punter into a car where they'd be a captive audience for a long hour's drive of hard selling. I knew we weren't going to make it back to the Abbey on the bikes, not with so many of the undead on the roads. We needed a car and I could think of nowhere else to look.

No. That's not quite right. Bill was honest with what he's written, I suppose I owe it to him, or someone, or maybe to myself, to be honest in turn. I was scared.

It was suddenly being responsible for these two other lives. I can't explain exactly why, but everything then, and now, it isn't about me, it isn't about survival or escaping or anything else. It's about Daisy and Annette and their future. I'm not explaining this very well. I mean that it is ensuring that they get to have a future, and that there is a future for them to have.

This is the second car showroom we tried. Someone had already been to the first and taken all the petrol. They'd even left rubber tubing in half a dozen fuel tanks. That's a sign of planning, I suppose, and of a hurried exit. When that was and who they were, I didn't bother trying to find out.

When we arrived here, I closed the gate, checked we had a car that worked and enough fuel in the tank to get us to the Abbey. Then we decided to rest and wait until morning. Safer to drive then, when we could see the undead on the roads.

Then Bill turned up. We helped him climb over the fence, using the same improvised rope Annette had insisted on making in case we needed to make a sudden escape and couldn't use the front gate. And that's about it. We're safe, for now. We'll siphon off the fuel in the other cars, then drive back to the Abbey. What more needs to be said?

Day 111, Heritage Motors
30 miles south of Brazely Abbey

08:15, 1ˢᵗ July

I was woken at around five by the sound of Kim singing. We'd spent the night in the windowless break-room, and by the look of her I don't think she'd slept at all. She was holding the baby, crooning a quiet lullaby, Annette curled up on the seat next to her. I got up, and as quietly as I could, went into the relative privacy of the workshop to clean the leg and repair the brace.

There's a veritable foundry's worth of steel in there, more than enough to turn any car into a tank, if you know how to do it. I certainly don't. After I'd replaced the padding around the straps, I went from window to window, counting the undead outside the car showroom's fence, until I heard Annette wake.

"How many are out there?" Kim asked, when I returned to the small office.

"Not many. Perhaps a dozen around the gate," I replied. "About the same number scattered along the sides."

They're active as well, trying to get in," Kim said. "They won't, but it just doesn't feel safe when you can see their arms flailing through the gaps in the fence's metal supports. I've tried telling myself that there aren't that many, that, really, we are in no danger. It doesn't work. How far is it to the Abbey? Thirty miles?"

"About that."

"We'll have to drive back," she said. "What do you think?"

I took a moment before I answered, not to think about the question, but about the way she'd framed it. "It would be six hours by bike. At best," I said. "But we'd have to do it in one day. I can't think of anywhere between here and there that would be safe to stop for the night. On the other hand, a bicycle is quieter, and it would only be half an hour before we'd be far enough away from here that these undead wouldn't be a threat."

"Yes. Maybe," Annette said. "But then there's going to be more. There's always more. What happens when you find the road blocked and you have to take a detour, and then you're still a day away from the Abbey?"

I took a moment to work out what the question actually was. Kim stifled a laugh. It was a pleasant sound, at least from her and at least in that it made a change from her usual dour stoicism.

"If a road's blocked," I said, "it'll be blocked just the same, whether we're on bikes or by car. You're worried about Daisy—"

"No. That's not what I meant," Annette said testily. "I mean the unknown. You don't know what's out there, none of us do. However we get there, we don't know what's going to happen on the way, so why take the risk of an extra day or two when you can do the journey in a few hours? And it's not just Daisy. It's you as well. You wouldn't make thirty miles on a bike."

"It is dangerous—" I began.

"What isn't, these days?" Kim said. "Besides, you were looking for a car just a few days ago, so what's changed?"

Everything and nothing, I thought, as I looked over at Annette. She was studiously emptying individual sachets of coffee creamer into the saucepan. Of all the places one might expect to find food, a car showroom is not near the top of the list. All we had found to add to our meagre supplies was the coffee creamer and half a kilo of sugar, left open to the air so long it had turned into a syrupy glue.

"We should take all the fuel then, not just fill the tank, but every can and container we can find," I said, because I still mean to go on to Lenham, and there is still the question of what happens after that.

Four mouths to feed come winter. We'll need a lot more supplies, not just food, but clothes, crockery, books, and whatever it is that babies need. That's if I can make it back from the facility to the Abbey. The more I think about that motorway, the more certain I am that once I cross it, I won't be able to come back. Is it fair to leave Kim with the responsibility for these children? Don't I also have some kind of duty to Annette and

Daisy? Perhaps I can persuade Kim and Annette that we should all go to Lenham and after that, well, perhaps just going away will be enough.

Terrified activity followed by tedious boredom, that's what life has become, and right now I really want a few days rest and boredom. Yes, driving is a very good idea.

14:00, 1st July

That's five hours so far, spent siphoning the fuel from the cars. We've been taking it in turns. One of us on the roof of the office, keeping watch, the other with the rubber tube. Five hours and we've only managed a third of the vehicles. Probably less. I stopped counting an hour ago. I just didn't realise it would take this long. The only plus side to it all is that since my mouth tastes like petrol, I don't have any appetite. Are there any calories in petrol? If so I won't need to eat for a month.

18:00, 1st July

We're staying the night here. There's a good four hours of daylight left, but that might not be enough to get back to the Abbey. A couple more undead appeared during the day, but there are still few enough that it's safer here than being stuck out on the road. Yes, it's safe, even if it doesn't feel that way.

July 1st – 7 p.m.

Annette has asked me to write down her story:

"When they told us we'd have to leave home, Mum wanted to stay. She said it was safer. Daddy said no. He said the city wasn't safe. He said we should trust the government. They shouted. They were shouting all night. I must have fallen asleep because Daddy was shaking my arm, saying 'Wake up!' They had three bags packed. One for Mum, one for Daddy, one for me. The streets were full of people. I'd never seen so many before.

"Once, at Christmas, we went up to London to see the lights, and we went shopping to Selfridge's because Daddy wanted to buy Mum some chocolates. We'd had a family meeting and decided we weren't doing big presents that year. It was because Christmas had become too commercial, except I knew it was because Mum had lost her job and then Auntie Carla's boiler broke.

"She wasn't really an Aunt. She lived next door with her son, Maxy. He was two. Carla didn't have the money to pay for a babysitter so we'd look after him when she worked nights. Auntie Carla didn't have anyone else, just Maxy and us. It was sad. She was always sad." She paused for a moment.

"So that Christmas we went up to London. We were going to look at all the shop windows and see the lights and get some chocolates and it was going to be fun. It was going to be like Christmas without the cleaning up and the cooking and the mess and the spending money on things we really didn't need. It was meant to be fun, but it wasn't.

"There were so many people on the buses we had to wait an hour until one came by that we could fit into. Then, when we got to Oxford Street, we found they'd closed off the road, so it was just for pedestrians. Except there were so many people that you couldn't even get near the shops. Then there was the music, all these carollers all singing different songs, all competing so you couldn't hear any single one. Mum didn't like it, so we came home and got a takeaway instead and shared it with Auntie Carla. Which, actually, was fun." A smile briefly flitted across her face, before the memory was replaced with a more recent one.

"I think it was about a week after the zombies started, that Carla disappeared. One evening she came over to talk to Daddy. The next day I went round to see if I could help with Maxy. That was what I'd been doing all week, since the schools closed. The lights were off. That was normal though. Carla never had the lights on, even when she was in. Too expensive. I knocked. There was no answer. I went back and told Mum, and she didn't know where Auntie Carla was. When Daddy came back, he'd been out trying to find a friend he knew who would sell us some food, he said that Carla had told him she was going away. Then I was sent to my room and they had another row. One of the bad kind, the one where they didn't shout at all.

"When we opened the door, when we had to come out to join the evacuation, it was worse than London at Christmas. Everyone was carrying bags. Not shopping bags, but suitcases, piled onto buggies, prams and wooden carts. I saw at least two people who'd tied boxes and things onto skateboards and were just pulling them along. It wasn't right, not for London. Everyone kept looking around and bumping into people and shoving, but no one said anything. I mean, everyone was silent, even the people travelling together. No one said 'excuse me' or 'sorry' or helped someone if they fell over. It was like everyone was walking down the same empty street together.

"I don't know when I lost Mum and Daddy. We'd been walking for hours, but we were still in London. Probably it was hours. No more than four, though. We'd left at about seven and I wasn't hungry. I don't know where we were, either. It was the same shops on different streets. I was in front, you see. Mum and Daddy were behind, and Daddy had a hand on my shoulder. It wasn't like I needed to know where to go. We were just following everyone else. Step, step, step, step. I tried singing but Daddy shushed me. I don't know why. I think everyone would have been happier if they sang.

"Then I realised his hand wasn't on my shoulder. I turned around and he was gone. I looked for Mum but she was gone too. I tried to walk backwards, to find them. But I couldn't. There were too many people. Too many prams and buggies and bicycles. No one offered to help. I cried. I stood there and I cried and no one cared.

"So I stopped crying. What was the point? I pushed my way across to the side of the road and climbed up onto a bin. I couldn't see them so I shouted. I called out. They didn't answer. They were gone.

"I thought I might make it back to the house. Or I thought I should try. I knew we'd been walking for hours, but we can't have got far. I mean, how big can London be? It was all those people, all walking so slowly, that was the problem. I climbed down and tried to get back up the road. There were too many people. I knocked over this one man's suitcase. It was the kind with wheels, and on top he'd piled up a box with this blanket over it. When I knocked it over the blanket fell off and these tin cans rolled across the street. He started shouting at me. He tried to grab me with one hand and with the other he was trying to gather up his cans. I ran to the side of the road, and ducked under the barrier to a side street.

"I didn't know what to do. Daddy said if you get lost look for the police. Mum didn't trust the police. She said look for a firefighter or an ambulance. But I couldn't see one. It was just street after street filled with people leaving London. Too many people. I saw a pharmacy. Its door was broken. I went in. Bottles and boxes were everywhere. It was like someone had come in and swept everything off the shelves and dumped them to the floor. I went through to the back. The drawers and cabinets were open, and the medicines were all over the floor. It was such a waste. There was a storeroom behind there. It was filled floor to ceiling with nappies and shampoo. I hid. I waited.

"When I got hungry I'd go out into the shop for food. Rusks and baby food. Not nice, but better than what we had been eating. We'd not had a decent meal since the rationing started. We'd not really had a decent meal since Christmas.

"Once I heard people come into the shop. They were looking for something. When they saw all the medicines on the floor they swore and said someone had beaten them to it. Then they left. They didn't see me. Then it got dark and I slept.

"When I woke, I filled a plastic bag with some food. Mostly baby food, but food's food, right? I went outside. The streets were empty. Everything was quiet. It was wrong. London shouldn't have been like that. London should have been busy. But it wasn't. It was dead.

"I thought about heading home, but if I did, if Mum and Daddy were there, then we'd only have to walk this way again. If they weren't, then I couldn't wait there for them. There was no food in the house. If they waited and I didn't turn up then sooner or later they'd go out to join the evacuation. So I decided to follow everyone else. I'd go south and I would meet up with them in the enclave.

"It was easy to see where everyone had gone. The road was full of clothes and bags and all sorts of rubbish. Buggies and prams were pushed to the side of the road where people had left them. All of their contents were scattered over the pavement where other people had emptied them out looking for who knows what. Food, probably. Everyone was hungry before the evacuation.

"They said, on the TV, that there would be buses and lorries coming along to collect the people who'd not been able to keep up. No buses had been along that road. I could tell from the way that none of the rubbish had been crushed by the tyres. Sometimes I thought I saw a curtain twitch, but I can't be certain.

"Then I heard Daisy. It was from a window above a row of shops. The door to the flats was open. I went in. I went upstairs. I thought she was alone. She wasn't." Annette rolled up a trouser leg to show a small, perfectly formed set of bite marks.

"Daisy's brother. He must have been seven or eight. Daisy was on top of a wardrobe, out of reach." And that was all she said for a while.

"I don't know her real name. Daisy was what grandad called grandma. I always liked it. So that was what I decided she should be called. I found a buggy for her. There were lots to choose from in the street. Then I found another pharmacy. I had to bandage my leg. We stayed there for a couple of days, until I felt better. Then we left. I thought if we could get to the coast, to the enclave, it would be okay. We'd find my parents and there would be help for Daisy. I didn't think we'd have to walk the entire way. They said there was going to be coaches and buses, and I thought there would be helicopters out looking for people like us.

"It took ages. Weeks. Daisy would start crying and then we'd be chased and I'd have to pick her up and we'd have to hide somewhere until she quietened down. That would take a day or so, and then we'd have to go and find another buggy and more food. Pharmacies were the best place for that. All the medicines and bandages and stuff had gone, but never the nappies or baby food.

"It took about a month. Maybe less. I'm not sure. It was hard to keep track of days. Sometimes we'd manage to go for an entire day without being chased, and sometimes, if we found somewhere safe, we'd stay there for a few nights so I could rest. So maybe it was a bit more than a month, maybe it was less, but one day I was walking down a road, pushing the buggy, and I saw it. I'd been looking at it for hours, maybe even for a day, but I hadn't really seen it because I'd been watching out for zombies. It was a fire, a big fire. We got to the top of a hill and we saw that there was a city in flames. A whole city, and all along the horizon there was nothing but smoke and flames. I think that was Southampton. We turned around. I mean, what was the point of going on?

"I decided we needed to get away. I had an Aunt, a proper Aunt, my mother's sister, she lived in Wales. She didn't get on with Mum. I was about five when we went to see her. Just before the evacuation, Mum and Daddy were up late, talking. They didn't know I was listening. Daddy suggested we go there, that it would be safer, but Mum said it was too far away. I didn't know exactly where she lived, and Wales is big, but it's not as big as England, and where else was I going to go?

"Then Daisy got sick. She wouldn't stop crying, not even to sleep. We found a school, a really old, rambling one, built with red brick and with a tower at the top. We stayed there. It was empty and big enough inside that Daisy's crying didn't carry far outside. I was exhausted. I slept when she'd let me, which wasn't often, and sometimes I'd climb to the top of the tower to look out. Then one day, in the distance, I saw smoke. Not smoke like at the coast, but this thin wisp from a chimney. I went up to watch it each day. I liked being up that tower. It felt safe. Then, a few days later, I saw a flag, and it hadn't been there before. A flag and smoke from a chimney, I was sure that had to mean people.

"It wasn't far away. I was sure I could reach it, but not until Daisy stopped crying, except she wouldn't stop crying. We were running out of food. I had to leave her there. I had to go out to find food and hope she'd be safe. I placed her high up, on top of a bookshelf, way out of reach and went out. I..." she stopped and rubbed at her shoulder.

"I found food. It took a while," she went on, "but I mustn't have closed the door properly when I left. They had gotten into the school, dozens of Them. Daisy was safe. I grabbed her and again we had to run. I tried to make for the house with the flag. I tried to remember where it was, but it wasn't like I had a choice which way to go. When Daisy stopped crying, when I found somewhere to hide for the night, I'd become completely lost.

"I found a new buggy and we went off looking for the house. I'm sure we'd have found it eventually, but we kept running out of food. It was too heavy to take much with us and I didn't like leaving her. That's why we were in the restaurant. I had a new plan. This time I wanted the zombies to hear Daisy cry, I wanted Them to all gather outside the chip shop, then we were going to sneak out through the attics to the end of the street. We'd have been able to take enough food to last us weeks. Enough time to find that house." She paused and took a breath. "So, you see, we didn't need rescuing, but thank you anyway."

22:00, 1st July

Annette has gone to sleep now, so there's no danger of her reading this over my shoulder. She had less than a week's worth of baby food left for the two of them. That's more food than Kim and I were carrying, but still, it's not much. Whether she'd have been able to escape or not, I can't say. She had more of a plan than I did when I climbed through that window at the Manor, and she's survived well enough so far. It's not my place to criticise, certainly not to judge. I doubt I'd have done nearly as well in her position, nor acted half as calmly. Luck, I suppose that was it. The luck to be immune, but there's something else as well. What's that word they used in those old war movies? Grit, that's it. Luck and grit.

Before she turned in, we had a discussion about what we should do next, none of us quite sure whether it was "we" or not.

"I think we should find the house with the flag. That's what I'm going to do, anyway. Find other survivors. That's important," Annette said. She sounded determined. I didn't know that I could stop her, either. Not if I was intending on leaving her and Kim and going off to Lenham.

"But, after the Manor—" I began.

"I've got the rifle now," Kim said flatly. "From the sound of it, there's fresh water, and food at the Abbey. We'd just need more people and it could work. For all of us."

"There's food now," I said. "But in the winter, it's going to be cold and hungry just like anywhere else."

"Here," Kim said, pulling a small sachet out of her pocket. "Vinegar. To preserve the food through the winter."

"Right," I said, taking it sceptically. "Of course, we'd need more. A lot more. Perhaps we could cycle back there. Perhaps in a week or two the zombies would have dispersed."

"The point," Kim said, with exasperation, "I was making, is chip shops. There's one in every street of every town, or near enough. Salt and vinegar in every one, and who'd've looted it? Sugar too. Except Annette had eaten all that there was in that place."

"We should find her a toothbrush," I muttered, automatically, but I was thinking about that house, about how easy it would be to find. All we needed to do was go to a library and find a directory of private schools, then drive or cycle around until we found one with a tower. It wouldn't take long, just a couple of days. Then, as Kim said, with more people the Abbey could be turned into a fortress. The walls could be extended, more crops planted, the fruit preserved, furniture and fittings could be brought up from the houses in the village. It could be turned into so much more than just a pile of ruins. And all it would take was a just a little more time.

It seems the sensible thing to do, but it also seems like just another diversion, just a few more days of putting off what I have to do.

Part 2:
Escape

2nd July - 15th July

Day 112, Brazely Abbey, Hampshire

20:00, 2nd July

This morning, I know it sounds crazy and I wouldn't have said it out loud, I wouldn't even be writing it now if things hadn't changed, but as we drove off all that kept running through my head was; *Man, Woman, two children. We should have got one of those bumper stickers.*

Early, so early it was really still night, unable to sleep for Daisy's crying, I went outside and finished siphoning off the fuel from the cars. In the end we left with twenty ten-litre jerry cans, close to forty gallons, and a full tank of petrol. Take a map of Britain, stick a pin in anywhere and we had enough fuel to get there.

It was my choice to take the giant yellow four-by-four pickup truck. It was closest to the gates, the easiest to get out, and I liked how it seemed to loom over the other cars. According to the log book it's been sitting on the lot for two years. I can't imagine who thought something like that would sell in rural England. It seemed sturdy enough back in the garage, but after a day's driving I'm not so sure. It's got a high clearance, though, and I did find that useful.

Baby seats weren't a problem, either. Three of the smaller cars near the entrance, each emblazoned with an optimistic "Family Friendly" sticker, had them fitted in the back seat.

"You know where we're going. You drive. I'll open the gate," Kim said after we'd strapped Daisy in.

"You drive, and I'll do the gate," I said, trying to make it sound not like some chauvinistic chivalric response.

"I'll drive, you both open the gate," Annette said.

"You know how to drive?" I asked.

"No," Kim replied at the same time. "Get inside, Annette. You too, Bill. Yesterday you could barely stand." She turned and walked up the driveway toward the gate and its waving sea of hands. "Well?" she asked, her back to us.

93

We got into the truck. I turned the key. The engine roared. I hadn't expected that. I'd expected it to be loud. I'd half realised it would sound louder, since the only background noise was the low gnashing snap of the undead by the gates. It was far louder than that. It sounded louder than the music had been. We should have taken a different car, but overnight close to forty of the undead had gathered around the gates. I wanted to leave, and I liked the power the sound of the engine represented.

I watched as, with her axe in her right hand, Kim walked up the drive, and pulled up the bolts pinning the gate into the concrete of the road. Teeth snapped and hands clawed, as she unlocked the padlock. She hesitated, glanced back. I revved the engine. She pulled out the chain, and threw back the central bar holding the gate closed. Under the pushing weight of the undead it began to swing open.

She took a pace back, swung the axe into the widening gap, half severing the arm of the nearest zombie. I edged the car forwards, as she turned and started running down the slope towards the car. I eased forward, an inch at a time, waiting for her to get out of the way, waiting for her to move to the left or the right. She didn't. She kept running straight at the cab. One foot went onto the tow bar, the other up onto the bonnet and then there was a thud as she rolled over the cab and into the truck bed behind us.

"Drive!" she shouted, slapping her hand against the rear window.

I did. I put my foot down and the truck barrelled forward. There wasn't enough speed to do more than push the undead out of the way. As we crept up the incline toward the road, undead hands banged down on the glass, grotesque faces slammed into the window and Annette screamed. One of the side windows cracked and Daisy started to cry. Kim shouted "Drive, Drive, Drive!" as I glanced at the rear view mirror and saw her swinging the axe at encroaching hands and arms, and snapping mouths.

With a bump, we drove onto the road. The wheels were pointing slightly towards the right, so that was the way that we went. As the car straightened, I put the pedal to the floor. The speedometer edged upwards. Then the garage was behind us. We were through Them, and there was only one more zombie in front of us. It was coming out of an old bridle path at the edge of a field. I couldn't dodge it. The road was too narrow. I shifted gear, and accelerated again. The needle vibrated, edging up towards thirty as I gunned the engine and hit the creature square on. It went down and under the truck. The car rocked and nearly skidded off the road as we drove over it. Annette screamed again.

"It's okay. We're through," I said, as much to myself as to her. I looked behind. The undead couldn't keep up, but They were following. We came to a junction. I turned left and drove on for about a mile until we came to a slight rise. Then, after checking and double-checking the rear view mirror I stopped. Kim didn't get in immediately. She got down off the back of the truck, and took a moment to walk around the car.

"Much damage?" I asked, when she got inside.

"Not really. The cracked window's the worst of it. There are some dents, and we've lost a few lights."

"Right." I breathed out. Then I breathed out again, I felt like I was about to throw up. "Another hour, we'll be at the Abbey."

"Then let's get going," Kim said. We got in and I started the engine again.

"South, then east, then north and we'll loop around the Abbey and come at it from the west," I said, glancing over my shoulder and through the window. I saw a solitary zombie lurch out of a field and into the road three hundred yards behind us. "Where there's one…" I muttered, as we drove off.

Ten miles an hour. That's how fast it's safe to go. I had visions of putting my foot down, letting the engine sing, of hurtling down country roads, of putting the brakes on less than an hour later outside the gates to the Abbey. But the undead are everywhere. They hear the car coming, They head out into the middle of the road, and They come at us. At ten miles an hour, perhaps a little more, you can hit a zombie, knock it down and drive right over it. When I tried driving faster, a few times when the road ahead looked clear, we almost crashed.

It's a twofold problem. When a body falls out of the hedgerow towards the car, instinct takes over and I start to brake. I catch myself, but only after it's too late. We hit those zombies with the side of the car, pulling the creature under the rear tyres. As we drove over it, we'd lose traction, start to skid, and then Annette would scream, and Daisy would start to cry and Kim would sigh.

If we hit Them head on, there's a fifty-fifty chance of the zombie rolling up the bonnet to hit the windscreen. The zombie isn't dead, of course, and whilst its legs might be broken, its snapping teeth are just a few millimetres of glass away. Having that happen once was one time too many, so we stuck to ten miles an hour. That's a lot slower than cycling. Worse, at that speed we had no hope of outdistancing the zombies following us.

Annette bounced from seat to seat, peering out each window in turn, counting the zombies following us whilst looking out for that house with the flag. She kept up a constant litany of "No flag there… Twenty-eight… No flag there… Thirty-two… No flag… Thirty-five… No flag… Forty-six…" As long as it was distracting the girl more than she was distracting me, I didn't feel I could complain.

I knew where we were, but only in relation to the main roads and larger towns, not the smaller lanes where we might lose this comet's tail of death trailing behind us. After about thirty miles of circling, detouring, and back tracking we were barely any closer than when we'd started. I considered just forgetting about the Abbey and trying to cross the motorway instead. I almost did it, but it wasn't my place to make that decision for Kim and Annette.

"I'm turning towards the Abbey at the next junction," I said. "We can't lose Them. Either we head for safety or—"

"Fine," Kim said cutting me off.

I took a left, then a right a mile later. An hour after that we were twenty miles from, and heading straight towards, the Abbey. Then I saw it, running out of the field in front of us and heading towards the car.

My blood ran cold. I'd never seen one run before, nor seen one wave its arms so frantically. They didn't tire. They didn't need to sleep. Speed was one of the few advantages we had, but if They could run, then what chance did we have?

"Hold on," I said gritting my teeth and putting my foot down on the accelerator as I aimed the car straight at it.

"Stop! You'll hit her!" Annette screamed. Kim grabbed the steering wheel, shoving it hard left, then pulling it right again. We missed the woman by inches.

"Brake!" Kim yelled. I did, but mostly out of reflex. Only when we'd stopped, and I looked in the mirror and saw the woman jogging towards the car, did I realise that she wasn't a zombie.

I glanced around, looking for others. I spotted a figure falling through a hedge into the road two hundred yards further up. From the way its arms thrashed and spasmed, I was certain it was one of the undead.

"Drive, then!" the woman said, climbing into the back, next to Annette.

"There's no one else?" I asked.

"No. Just me. Drive," she snapped back. "You need to make a left half a mile ahead," she added, after looking around the cab. "The farm with the green-roofed barn. You see it? There's five of us. We've a car, but no fuel. No food either. Zombies got in, ruined our crop. Where were you heading?"

"An abbey with an orchard and fruit and vegetables," Annette said.

"Brazely," I added.

"Right," she said, firmly. "Strong walls?"

"Strong enough."

"You've spare fuel?"

"About forty gallons. In the back," I said.

"More than enough," she replied.

"What for?"

"I just told you. We've a car but no fuel," she said, as if that was explanation enough. Perhaps it was.

Even without the woman directing me, I would have known which farm was occupied. Rough timber boards had been crudely cemented along an old stone wall. Standing around ten feet high, topped with an occasional strand of barbed wire, it stood in stark contrast to the overgrown garden of the cottage opposite. It was the bodies, however, that were most striking. There weren't many, just eight or nine of Them, and They definitely were the bodies of the undead, scattered along the lane leading up to the farm house.

The woman opened the door before the car came to a stop, jumped out, and started pulling at the cords tying the fuel cans to their place in the truck bed.

"Stay here," I said to Annette, before getting out myself. I grabbed my pike and ran to stand in front of the truck, just by the road. In the distance I could see the undead coming.

A few were heading towards us across the neighbouring fields, but it was the larger mass, still in the distance, heading along the road that scared me most. They were minutes away, but if this inhuman mob, at least a hundred strong, reached us, we wouldn't stand a chance. I gripped the pike. My hand ached. I shifted my footing, trying to take the weight off my injured leg.

"We need to get out of here," I yelled. There was no response, except that now familiar click-clack of the rifle. I glanced behind, saw the woman grab a can of fuel from the truck, saw Kim standing in the truck bed, the rifle in her hands, tracking back and forth across the undead. As I watched she swung the rifle to the right.

"Over there," she yelled. I turned my attention back to the road.

They were in front of us. Seven zombies, coming along the road from the opposite direction, the one we would have to travel. Then there were eight, as a zombie pushed through what looked from that distance to be an impenetrable hedge.

The closest one doubled over. Click-clack. I glanced over at Kim who was reloading, then back down the road. The bullet had struck the zombie in the chest. It was already straightening up, a brownish stain almost invisible amongst the dirt and grime encrusted on its rotting clothing. It made only another three steps before it pinwheeled backwards, shot in the head.

"Hurry," I yelled, this time without turning my head.

Another zombie fell. The next shot was a miss. And the next. The next one hit, and then I realised that Kim wasn't shooting at those which were closest, rather, I realised, she was trying to thin Them out, ensuring I had time to recover between killing one and facing the next. I turned towards the truck, intending to shout a bitterly sarcastic word of thanks at Kim, when I saw Annette. She was standing by the truck's open door, a kitchen knife in her hand, looking nervous but determined.

"Back inside!" I yelled, and for the first time the girl obeyed me. I looked at the road, at the brick wall surrounding the drive. I tried to work out if we could just drive. If we could just go, leave these people, whoever they were. I glanced at the car to see what the delay was. The woman we'd rescued was still filling the car with petrol. At the back a man was loading some boxes into the boot. Another man stood just in front of the car, holding a shotgun. From there he would be able to protect the car, but not the truck, not us.

I don't really remember much of those odd few hours after we left the car showroom. I mean, I remember what we did and what happened, but I don't remember the emotions. They've become tied up in the rush of the moment, inextricably linked to each other and what happened before and what happened next, but I do clearly remember a shock of anger at this act of selfish self-preservation.

I turned my attention back to the road. I'd only looked away for a second at most, but one of the undead was now less than five feet away. I brought the pike up, holding it diagonally in front of me, then scythed it down. I missed the creature's head, but sliced into and through its neck. It collapsed, almost decapitated. I took a step to the left as Kim fired another shot.

"Hurry," I called out again, furious now that they were risking our lives to save whatever it was. Food, water, it didn't matter. Daisy, Annette, Kim, these were my people. I remember thinking that too.

I shifted my stance, one foot behind the other, holding the pike out as a spear in front of me. Trying, even as They got closer, to get a better feel for the weapon's weight and heft. I waited until the next zombie was two arm's lengths away, then thrust forward. The spear crunched straight through the cheekbone and into its brain. It collapsed as I pulled the weapon out.

"Ready?" the woman cried, then added, with what I swear was a touch of impatience "Hurry!"

"Kim?" I called out, not taking my eyes from the road.

"I've got you covered," she called back.

I didn't turn. I definitely didn't obey that command to hurry. I walked backward, my eyes on the undead. The nearest fell.

"C'mon, Bill," Kim said, calmly. Whatever fog of anger was clouding my judgement lifted. I ran back to the truck, threw the pike into the back, got in, and put my foot down. Kim was in the truck bed, Annette, Daisy and a man in the row behind me, that woman I'd almost run over was in the passenger seat next to me. The other three followed in the car close behind.

We didn't talk on that journey. I didn't even look at my new passengers. Adrenaline mixed with furious anger as I gripped the steering wheel, one eye on the speedometer, the other on the road, my foot aching with the pressure of not stamping down on the accelerator.

We drove straight back here to the Abbey. There seemed little point trying to evade the undead. The sound of two engines must have called all the zombies in four counties. As for how many followed us, I'd guess at hundreds, and think that that's being optimistic. It's getting too dark to count, but the woods are full of Them. I wanted company. Now I have it, and now I am trapped once more.

Day 113, Brazely Abbey, Hampshire

06:00, 3rd July

The woods are infested with the undead, but we are safe. For now. They can't climb the walls, but nor can we go out until They are dealt with. It's hard to get an exact count with the thick woodland around us, but there are certainly more than we have bullets for.

Kim spent the night in the truck, with Annette and Daisy. It's parked, next to the car, in the space in front of the gate. The girls slept, that I'm sure of. Kim spent the night rocking the baby, singing softly to her, lost in her own world. It was such a peaceful scene, I didn't disturb them.

I didn't sleep much. In my first few nights here I tried sleeping in the dormitory, but I was kept awake by the sound of the occasional zombie brushing against the exterior wall. Instead I created a sort of lean-to affair amongst the old stones in what was once the Abbey's nave. I liked the safety of being surrounded by thick stone, whilst being able to see the stars as I stared up through the long burnt-out roof. It was my Keep, my fortress. Thinking of it like that was childish I suppose, but I was able to sleep. Now, there's the snuffling snoring of the others inside, and the shuffling and pawing of the undead outside. I gave up on sleep at around four a.m., and climbed up here, to sit and watch and think. I didn't want to risk using the torch, but now it's starting to get light enough to write. So, who are these other survivors?

It's a good question and one I want answered since, last night, we didn't get much further than the most cursory of introductions. The woman I almost ran over is Sandra Barrett, though she just goes by her surname. Not Miss, or Ms, or Mrs, just Barrett. I don't know what to take from that. The only other people I've known who've gone by their surname alone, have either been militant mime-artists or reactionary aristocrats. She's around forty, lived somewhere near the coast and stumbled across the farm some time after the evacuation.

101

She'd gone off looking for petrol and food. This was her second such excursion, and I think that this one would have been as fruitless as the first evidently was, had she not heard the sound of the truck. I'm reserving judgement at the moment, I mean, I don't know any of these people, but that she wasn't on a bicycle, that is telling.

The driver of the other car is Daphne Mittley, married to Chris, the guy with the shotgun. They owned the farm this group was living on. The passenger in the back of the truck on the way back here is Stewart Walker. A quiet guy, who rescued Liz during an ill-fated supply run a few weeks back. Liz is an old university friend of Daphne's. She waited until after the evacuation before heading for the farm, as the most likely place she knew of that might have food.

Based on what I saw when we collected them, and from what little they've said since, they had planted crops, though I'm not sure of what variety, in most of the fields nearby, and had thrown up a wall around the farm house. Then the undead came, trampling their harvest. At some point, though whether it was before, after, or during this, the undead got into the yard. During the struggle they lost their water supply when one of the supports to their tank was knocked over. That was when they decided they should get away. I asked whether they couldn't repair the tank, but for some reason they don't trust the rainwater. I can't quite figure out why. And, for now, that's all I know of them.

Add in Kim, Annette, and Daisy, and this place is packed. It seemed so big before, now it's nothing more than a set of cramped old ruins. Change and a bad night's sleep, that's all this is. Time to see what the new day brings. At the very least, I'm sure it's going to bring some coffee.

22:00, 3rd July

I have retreated back up to the walls. I don't think the torchlight matters anymore. There are so many out there now, if the light was to attract another ten or twenty or even fifty I don't think I'd notice.

It hadn't registered this morning. There was just so much to think about, so much change in such a small space of time that the truly important things got ignored, right up until around mid-morning.

After we'd all had coffee, exhausted the small talk and finished taking stock of one another, we turned our collective eyes to the supplies.

The well is inside the wall. We have water, more, I think, than enough. That is the only good news. Inside the walls we have three fruit trees. One apple, one pear, one fig, none of which are yet fully ripe. Their branches are laden, though, and after it has been stewed, the fruit makes a welcome relief to a diet of miscellaneous unlabelled tins. Two-dozen apples, a dozen pears and six figs were eaten tonight. We may have been hungry, but that is still an over indulgence.

Then there are the boxes of military rations I found at the Grange Farm Estates. When I left there were fifty-six packs of the high calorie meals. I had already eaten a couple, one every other day or so, and taken four with me, three of which were, and I suppose still are, in the pannier of the bike back at Longshanks Manor. I was planning to keep the remaining forty as a reserve for the depths of winter. Six got eaten today.

The MREs were supplemented at lunch and dinner by lettuce from the two twenty-feet by three-feet salad beds. I feel slightly embarrassed by that. I thought it was rhubarb. Chris found that hilarious, typical townie behaviour, would starve in a hen house etc, etc. Not many calories in it, but it is food, and the leaves will grow back, if there's enough time.

The rest of the trees, the apples, the plums, apricots, peaches, greengages and others with fruit I've never seen in the supermarket, those were outside the walls. So were the beehives, and the vegetable plots. There had been more than I could eat, more than four of us, even more than the nine of us could eat. I had no plan for the beehives, no idea how to collect honey without being stung an absurd number of times, but I was secretly looking forward to trying.

That's all gone, trampled by the hundreds of zombies who came to beat at our walls. The chicken wire I rigged up to protect them from the handful of undead I used to get here each day has disappeared into the mud. Half a dozen fruit trees have already been knocked down, the others have been shaken about so much that most of the fruit has fallen. The car I had brought back here a few weeks ago, along with its meagre twenty miles of petrol, that's still parked at the edge of the village, two miles away. I thought it would have been a waste of fuel to bring it up here. It's of a far sturdier construction than the car the others drove back here in, but it might as well be in London for all the good it will do us now.

So that's that. We have two farmers here and no land on which to grow. Three fruit trees, the salad beds, thirty-four MREs, fifty-eight assorted cans and about ten kilos of rice, pasta and lentils. Tea, coffee, a little sugar, two cartons of UHT milk, a few jars of baby food and that's all there is to feed nine of us. You can call it eight and a half and a baby, and you can ration it however you want, but we'll be out of food in a few weeks.

We could try and kill the undead that are here. With the rifle and the shotgun and the pistol, we could certainly make a dent in their numbers, but there would still be hundreds to be destroyed hand-to-hand. It's not impossible, but then what? The fruit will be gone from the trees. Perhaps some of the root vegetables might be harvested, but probably not. We'd have to go further afield to find more food since I've already taken most of what was left from everywhere in a ten mile radius.

There was an old formula to do with the number of oxen you needed to cross a desert. I don't remember the details exactly, couldn't even tell you whether it had something to do with wagon trains crossing the American Plains, or from when Julius Caesar marched his Legions through Gaul. It comes to this, the further you travel the more supplies you need to carry just for the journey. If we eliminated the undead here, we wouldn't be able to use the cars. Not ever again, or we'd just risk the noise of the engine bringing more of Them back here. We'd have to use bikes, and we'd have to go out twenty miles or more, collecting whatever fruit and vegetables we could find now growing wild. After that, we'd end up scavenging from the sprawling suburbs of London. How much could we carry back, even on a successful trip? And how much could we carry on the trip after that, and the one after that, when each successive trip would take us further from the Abbey, to the point where it would no longer make any sense to come back.

The Abbey is no longer a sanctum. If we stay, we starve. So we must leave. Our only chance lies in the fuel, the car and the truck. I know where I'll go, but not whether anyone will be coming with me.

23:50, 3ʳᵈ July

Can't sleep. I went down to the car, to see if Kim wanted to swap. She said no. She's actually smiling, holding Daisy like that. She seems happy. So does the baby. Annette's snoring, which is definitely something I must remember to tease her about. The three of them, they seem right together, somehow, as if they fit. I'm the adjunct to that group, the guest, and that's okay. I think I understand why.

I had an odd conversation with Annette earlier.

"Have you kissed her?" she asked.

"Who, Kim? Why—" I began searching around for a way to answer.

"You shouldn't," she said, cutting me off.

"Why not?" I asked, unable to fathom in what direction her mind was spinning.

"You might be a carrier," she said flatly. "We did those in school. You think you're immune, but maybe you're not. You could be infected, just not turned. So you shouldn't kiss her."

I took my leave then.

I'd not thought of that. Up until Annette mentioned, it wasn't even something I'd even considered. Now, I can't stop thinking about it. Am I carrying this infection inside me? Is everyone who seems to be immune? It's just one more reason to go to Lenham Hill, but not the only reason I can't sleep.

It's the others and the casual way in which they can make me feel like an outsider, here in my own home. Fine, so I've only been living in the Abbey for a few weeks, but I have more of a claim to it than anyone else. I finished the work on making it a fortress, and those are my supplies that we're all eating. But is it really just that? No. It started with dinner. Breakfast was a slapdash thing, not really organised, more a tea and coffee thing that turned into lunch as we were all talking about the past and the future and everything and nothing. In the early evening it all came to a head. Barrett didn't want a meal. She wanted a dinner. That was fine with me, how else are we going to forge some kind of community here if we don't at least all sit down together.

No, it wasn't the idea of a sit down meal itself, it was the catalogue of complaints and corrections that she expressed before, during, and after. That Annette became one of her targets for criticism irked me, but since the others were similarly treated, I didn't feel I could do or say anything. And there is something odd about the others as well. They seem cowed, following Barrett's every lead and suggestion. Why, though? Is it fear?

I seemed to be the only one who escaped censure, but I could see Kim getting more agitated with each snide remark, so, looking to turn the conversation elsewhere I asked Chris why he didn't join the evacuation.

"We were a designated protected farm," he said, "or meant to be. I don't know who it was who did the designating or why they picked us. It was the 24th February, what was that? Four days after New York? About nine in the morning, this van drove up and a guy with a clipboard got out."

"Typical Londoner," Daphne added. "Wearing a suit and shoes more suited to the Tube than a working farm."

"And he was carrying a clipboard," Chris said, shaking his head. "I mean, when was the last time you saw one of those? He looked old-fashioned, that was the thing. He was one of those types who seemed to be in the wrong time, almost like someone from one of those old Pathé news films. Almost but not quite, 'cos out of the other side of the van, a soldier got out. Full camo, rifle, the works.

"The man with the clipboard, Cranley, he said his name was. He tells us that our place has been chosen as one of the Inland Farms. We're going to get a fence built around the place, and we're going to stay here and keep on going just as we would have done normally. The only real noticeable change, he says, is that instead of petrol we're going to use manpower, and instead of selling our crop we'd be giving it to the government for distribution. In exchange we'd get food until the first harvest, and all the other supplies we needed. Once the emergency's over, once it's all gone back to normal, we'd get to keep the improvements. Then he asked whether we were okay with that. Well, I wasn't too happy, but I can't say I was too unhappy, neither. It was my Dad's farm before he passed on."

"And my grandfather's before that," Daphne added. "Before the supermarkets bankrupted him."

"That was our land," Chris said. "Our birthright. Keeping it going almost killed Dad. I'd spent my life keeping the place going. Daph' too," he added hurriedly. "When she came back to see the old place, when we fell in love, it seemed like fate or destiny or something close. Then the world starts falling apart and there's rationing and people are dying and not staying dead. So if this man wants to tell us we'll get food, and keep the farm at the end of it all, well, we weren't going to say no, were we?"

"He wanted to look round," Daphne said. "See the farm, the equipment, see how we were set up."

"And he knew his stuff," Chris added. "I mean, he was dressed like the closest he'd come to nature was when he opened the salad drawer of his fridge, but he knew what he was talking about. I suppose he'd come from some meeting, hadn't had time to go home and change. Probably slept in his clothes too. Who knows? We went round the fields first, and that's when he started filling in the details. Our farm can't have been the first place he'd done this, because he didn't let it all out at once. If he had, maybe it would have been different. Then again, there was the soldier standing by the car, his rifle in his hands, so maybe not.

"We were going to have to turn the whole place over to potatoes. Nothing else. We'd be allowed a small garden plot by the house for veg, but that was going to be for everyone, all the workers, not just the two of us. This wasn't going to be some feudal dictatorship. He was clear enough on that, we weren't the lords of the manor. It was like this was going to be some kind of collective and if we didn't like it, we could leave and they'd bring someone else in to do the work. He told us there were plenty of farmers going to be evacuated."

"That was the first we'd heard of the evacuation," Daphne said. "I mean, the news had talked about some government plan, but they'd not said anything about an evacuation, not by then, anyway."

"Potatoes first," Chris went on, "then, depending upon productivity levels, yield, weather patterns and other factors, and he didn't need to say what they were, we may be moved into sugar beet. That's what the farm grew back in the War. We'd not get a say. I asked, you see, because we were mostly wheat, with the two fields down by Boxley rented out as grazing. He said no. It was all about the calorie yield. We'd be told what to plant, and for the moment that was potatoes.

"Well, that's when I started to think it wasn't as great as it sounded, but what was the alternative? So we'd have to work harder for a few years. So what? We'd seen the news, we'd seen how the world was falling apart. We'd talked about it, and couldn't think of anywhere that was better than where we were. By the sounds of it, everyone else was going to have it a lot tougher.

"He told us they were going to fence in the roads, run up this supply route all the way from the coast to be done by harvest. That was the plan, but until it was finished, all our supplies, and our workers, they were going to come in by helicopter. When the food was grown, it'd go out the same way.

"The first thing we had to do, he said, was to use the tractors to flatten out a section for the helicopter to land on. That seemed fair enough. He even gave us some diesel to do it, and that was a welcome gift, since you couldn't buy it anywhere, not even on the black market.

"Then it came to accommodation. That was the real shock. That's when he laid all his cards down. I didn't get it till then, the full extent of it all. He said we'd get a squad of five soldiers. Armed, of course, and led by Corporal Thompson, the guy who'd driven up with him. Their job, he said, was to protect us, and then to train us up to deal with the zombies ourselves. The Corporal was going to stay with us to begin that process there and then. Well, I knew what *that* meant. Insurance against good behaviour, they used to call that.

"He said that when the situation had settled down, when the farms were up and running, that there would be a mass call-up, a huge mobilisation of all these workers. Everyone was going to be conscripted so we could take back the country."

"I said," Daphne interrupted, "that five extra wasn't a problem. We could double up in the house, that some of them could squeeze into the office and the library. Even with a dozen or so extra people we'd all fit somehow."

"Right," Chris went on. "And that's when the man said no, that we'd need to keep the office and library for the doctor."

"Which struck me as strange," Daphne cut in, again. "I mean, why would we need a doctor if there were only ten or twenty of us?"

"So that's when he told us how many. Twenty in the first wave, probably in a week's time. Then another ten every week after that, until there were a hundred adults on the farm. Adults, mark you, that wasn't counting the children, and they'd be coming, too. Families weren't going to be broken up. He said to expect two hundred, perhaps more." He shook his head. "We had the barns of course, and you can squeeze people in there, and triple the kids up in the rooms in the house, but however you looked at it, it was going to be cramped, cold, and unsanitary, and that was looking on the bright side."

"That wasn't the end of it," Daphne said. "There was going to be more people coming, closer to harvest, after we'd expanded the walls."

"Yeah, he left that bit till last," Chris went on. "That was part of how Thompson and his lot were meant to train everyone. After the walls were up, we'd push them out, take in more fields, more land, and expand the farm. It would keep growing outwards until, eventually, it would meet up with the next farm along. This little man, who I was beginning to hate more and more each time he opened his mouth didn't say what would happen if we didn't expand the walls. He just kept mentioning that the weekly supply drops of food were only going to go to those who were supporting the National Endeavour. It was blackmail. Nah, it was worse. It was a gun to our heads, and we had no choice. We signed on the dotted line, and there was a dotted line, and another for Corporal Thompson to sign as a witness. Then he left."

"Thompson didn't seem like a bad guy," Daphne said. "We went inside, had a drink, and I cooked him some food. He hadn't eaten all day. Things were that bad. He explained about the evacuation, what he knew, anyway. The enclaves, the muster points, the fenced in roads, and how we were the lucky ones, and by the time we'd finished eating we believed him."

"We started right away," Chris said. "Him digging the latrines, Daphne on the tractor flattening out the landing field, and I started clearing out the barns, getting them ready for all the refugees. I went to bed exhausted that night. The next day, around lunchtime I went down to the village, to see if anyone was around, anyone who wanted to give us a hand."

"Thompson said that was alright," Daphne said. "He said if we got help from the village that would save them being shipped off to an enclave just to be packed off to the countryside again."

"A lot of people had already disappeared," Chris said. "I asked some of those who were left, but no one wanted to come and help us. Couldn't understand it."

"People didn't like us. Jealousy," Daphne said. "Petty spite. You know, small villages. Gossip."

"There was an old guy, Toby Hurley, him and his granddaughter, Annie, lived out by the woods, he used to do some work on the farm," Chris said.

"Only seasonally," Daphne added.

"Right. He'd owned his own place until a couple of bad harvests in a row forced him to sell up—"

"He got a fair price," Daphne interrupted again. "Anyway that's in the past."

"Yeah. He came up to the farm to help out. Him and Annie, practically moved in."

"Which there was no need for, he only lived a few miles away," Daphne said.

"Turned out we were grateful for the help," Chris said. "That evening, we got a delivery of building materials. Whoever was in charge of sending it must have loved paperwork, because it came with a twelve page docket, all to be signed and initialled and witnessed. We took delivery of load two of thirty-seven. What happened to the first load, and how they'd worked out we needed thirty-seven of them, well, I don't know. It wasn't much, a few I-beams and enough timber, wire and cement for a forty-foot section of wall about ten-feet high. I don't think thirty-seven would have been enough. Then, a day after that, we got a delivery of food, eighty kilos of rice, stamped 'UN Food Aid – White Rice'. A crate of tinned fruit, ten kilos of dried milk and a year's worth of vitamin tablets. That was our lot for the month, for us and the first lot of workers."

"And remember," Daphne said. "They didn't know Hurley and his granddaughter were with us."

"There was a note with that shipment," Chris said. "Saying it would have to be supplemented with whatever we had around the house or in the farm. That food was delivered in a security van, the kind with the bulletproof windows and the door that only opens from the inside. It came with a motorcycle escort. Four Coppers, all armed.

"We thought that in all the confusion some of the paperwork had got lost. We thought that at any moment a truck would turn up with the soldiers and the first lot of workers. We actually worried that the evacuees would turn up before the other thirty-six loads of materials for the wall and there'd be nothing for 'em to do. They never came.

"Three days after the evacuation was announced on the radio, Thompson went out to find out what had happened. He took his rifle, Daphne's car and, though we didn't find out until about an hour after he'd left, pretty much all the diesel we'd been left with. He didn't come back."

"When I turned up at the farm, they thought I was him," Liz added. "I'd watched all those people going by outside my window, heading off to the muster point, and I thought I'd wait until the crowds had gone, then I thought I'd wait a bit longer. I headed off the day I saw the first zombie walking down the street. I was at Uni with Daph'. We shared some classes, I'd stayed at the farm a few times, and it seemed like the obvious place to go. But it took forever to get here. I didn't have a bike, and back then I didn't like the idea of stealing one. I mean, theft was theft, right, and they had police on the streets. Except there weren't any police. I was pretty bedraggled by the time I did get to the farm."

"Bedraggled, ragged and cold," Chris said. "Took you for one of the undead at first. If Daphne hadn't recognised you, we'd probably've shot you."

"I figured that if you were a zombie and you'd come all this way then we had even bigger problems than we'd thought," Daphne said. "With Liz and Toby and Annie we stuck it out. We got some fences up on either side of the house, made ourselves a little compound, but we couldn't do much more than that. Not on our own."

"So I went into town," Liz said. "We needed some variety in our diet. That's when I met Stewart, or, when he rescued me, at least."

"It was nothing," Stewart said. "She'd been cornered in a shop. I just distracted the zombies, got Them heading towards me so she could escape. It wasn't anything really heroic." Though he said it with a tone that suggested that it was.

"We went out a few times, scavenging what we could, but there was little enough anywhere. There just weren't enough of us, not to farm and build walls and kill the undead," Chris said.

"That's how Hurley died," Stewart added.

"He was too old!" Daphne snapped. "Shouldn't have gone out there on his own."

"He woke early," Stewart said. "Earlier than any of the rest of us, old habits you know? If I got up at five, he'd already be dressed with the fire lit and a kettle on the stove. He was like that. The work was tiring, and maybe we were exhausted. Whatever. He got up before us, and we slept in, longer than was usual. It was a few days after we'd found a few dozen rolls of chicken wire. It wasn't much, but it was better than nothing. Every few seconds count, right? He must have decided to go and make a start on putting it up on his own. He was attacked and he got bitten. He killed the zombie, though, but by the time we got outside, there were three more in the yard, and he was lying there, blood pouring from his neck."

"He'd probably have died anyway," Daphne said.

"Probably. But we shot him. We had to. Just to be sure," Chris said, staring at Kim and I, as if daring us to judge.

"Then Annie—" Stewart began.

"She died too," Barrett said firmly, and then they exchanged a look, one that told me that wasn't even half the story.

"That was when we lost the water tank, and things just got worse after that," Chris continued. "This huge mass of Them came by, trampled everything outside. All that we'd planted. All gone. No food come autumn, and there was nothing left to drink. We'd been through most of the places within walking distance, but there hadn't been much there to start with, not after the rationing."

"That's when we decided to leave," Barrett said. "And for that we needed fuel."

"We looked everywhere. All the farms nearby, the village. Barely a thimble full," Liz said.

"Enough for a couple of dozen miles. At most," Chris added. "But where'd that get us?"

"That's when I went out," Barrett said. "It was all right, too. These zombies aren't that hard to avoid, not until some tank of a truck comes roaring by, waking up every creature in the county."

There was an awkward silence for a moment until Stewart made some comment about the Abbey and the Restoration, and after that the conversation drifted on in a desultory tour of historical Britain. From castles to monasteries, medieval university towns to Welsh mining villages, all were discussed as to where would be the best place to escape to. Their lack of enthusiasm suggested they'd been over the same ground many times. I chipped in occasionally, just for politeness's sake, but all I could think of was that I wouldn't want to travel very far with these people.

Barrett didn't share any more of her personal story, but then neither did Kim. I gave some details, skipping over the finer points, focusing more on being stuck in London. I told them what I'd seen and what I'd learned, at least as far as the places I'd been to, but no more than that. I think I would have told Kim the truth, even if she hadn't found the journal, but this lot? No. I don't know that I trust them. No, that's not it. It's not an issue of trust. I can't say why, exactly, but I just don't like them.

I told the others about the motorway. I repeated it, over and over, making sure they'd heard, but I don't think they understood. Kim was right. If we have to leave, if we have to escape I'd rather get it over and done with. I want to get to Lenham, and perhaps then I can then settle down. And if I'm honest, I want to do that with Kim and the children. As for the others, they can just fend for themselves.

Day 114, Brazely Abbey, Hampshire

17:00, 4th July

I'd been sitting at the top of the walls, watching the undead, trying to come up with a way of getting Them away from the gate. The best idea I could come up with was a sort of cage, like the kind they used to film sharks from in the old days. What I couldn't figure out was how we'd build it, or whether it would be possible to build some kind of crane or pulley system to lower it over the walls. I was heading down the scaffolding, on my way to see what the others thought of my idea, when I was stopped by Daphne.

"Come with me," she said, and led me into the prefab kitchen. She took a seat next to Chris, Liz and Stewart were sitting by the long oven, now useless without a gas cylinder. Barrett stood in front. Her expression was so grim, that at first I didn't notice Kim standing by the door, holding Daisy, with Annette by her side.

"Have a seat," Barrett said, pointing to a solitary chair opposite the other four.

"What's going on?" I asked, sitting down and stretching out my leg. "What's happened?"

"We read this," Barrett said, throwing my journal down at my feet with what, even then, I thought was overblown theatricality. "We know who you are."

"Right," I replied, bending forward and picking the book up. It was the first volume. The second, since I've been writing about these people, I've been smart enough to keep on me. To be honest, I'd forgotten that the first volume was still in my bag. Why and what they were thinking going through my possessions I don't know. What gave them the right? Well, whatever it was, having read it they clearly felt justified after the act.

"I thought I recognised you," Barrett said. "I wasn't sure from where. I'd seen you on TV, next to that Masterton woman. Always with the politicians weren't you, always standing behind them. One of those spin doctors, the consultants whom no one elected, but that didn't stop you from carrying on like you ran the country."

"I..." I'd been about to defend my former career choice, but I stopped myself. "No. The past doesn't matter. It's dead. It's over," I said.

"Over? After what you did," she spat.

"I moved to Bournemouth a few years ago," she said. "Four and a half if anyone's counting, and I certainly was. Four and a half years before the world fell apart. I had a job in London with a web design company. High end stuff, not your usual flash drivel. I started as a receptionist and worked my way up. The pay wasn't bad, I got a bonus and the chance to make more. Then my parents moved to Bournemouth. You know what they used to say about that place, how people went there to die, but often kept walking around long afterwards. City of the dead, and all that. It's not that funny now. They were happy, they had friends and the sea air was doing them good, right up until they got sick. Both of them, both within a few weeks of each other. Old age, that was what the doctors said. A 'combination of factors' was the more official term. They had some savings, too much to qualify them for state help, but not enough to pay for a nurse to do home-visits themselves. My salary wouldn't cover it and pay my rent as well, so I had to move. I had to give up my job, my life, to go and look after my dying parents. Where was your caring society then, eh?"

Kim took Annette's hand. "Come on," she said, loudly. "We've places to be." Barrett looked annoyed that this witness was being taken

115

away. For some reason I got the feeling that this speech I was being subjected to was for Annette's benefit, because it clearly wasn't for mine.

"You know how many jobs there are in Bournemouth for a web designer?" Barrett continued, after Kim had left. "I worked in a pub in the evenings and spent my days trying to carve out a life. It was too much for me, so we were going to sell their house, use the money to put them in a home. I'd even called up my boss and managed to get my old job back. It was all going to be okay. Not great, it couldn't be that when you've lost a year out of your life, but it was going to be okay. Then there was the housing crash. I mean, we all saw it coming, everyone did, right? Everyone except you lot." She paused. I don't know if she was expecting a response. I sat there, and said nothing.

"Their home wasn't worth half of what it needed to be. So no retirement housing for them. No return to London for me. Live in nurse by day, glorified barmaid by night. Everything you could possibly dream of when you're single and the wrong side of forty. They died last December. My mother went first. My father a week later. It was a combined funeral, and wasn't that a miserable affair. My old job in London was long gone by then. I was going to sell the house and go abroad. I didn't know where, didn't care either. I was going to take the money and just get out of this miserable country. I'd just put the house on the market when the outbreak hit. Four days later, I was in the restaurant when they came in."

"The undead?" I asked, surprised. I'd not meant to say anything, but surely I'd have heard if there was an outbreak in Bournemouth.

"No. Your lot. Government," she spat. "We weren't open, of course, but all of us staff used to go there and share what food and news we'd got. I know we weren't supposed to be meeting in groups, weren't meant to go out of the house except to collect the ration or go to the dentist. The dentist? That was you, wasn't it? One of your bright little ideas." She shook her head scornfully.

"When the rationing started, we'd just had a delivery, and there was enough to guarantee each of us a meal a day for the foreseeable. It was communal living, and didn't that infuriate the old Colonel who owned the

116

place. He was a true blue Tory, a dyed in the wool cold-warrior who loathed all things socialist. He was even suspicious of the NHS. But Paul was good to us, good to me. Now he's dead.

"They came into the restaurant. They were dressed like soldiers, led by a guy not exactly dressed like a civilian. He wasn't in uniform, except he had that look about him of the kind who was always wearing uniform even when he wore jeans. Suit, tie, overcoat, and if it didn't come from Saville Row, it was only because it came from some bespoke tailor in Baghdad. They were a little surprised to find us there. We had to explain who we were and at first they didn't believe us. They thought we were looters until we showed them the photo we had, one we'd taken at Christmas, all of us staff, standing by the bar. They said they were clearing out the town, evacuating everyone, final location dependent upon skill set, whatever that meant. Bournemouth wasn't worth saving. By their expressions you could tell they didn't think we were worth saving either. We were given two hours to be on the street out front, ready to walk down along the coast. Walk, mark you, from Bournemouth, a place where the average age has got to be at least eighty.

"Paul didn't want to go. He wanted to see the man's orders, demanded to speak to his superior, he even tried to pull rank. I don't know where he got the gun. Maybe it was a souvenir from some overseas posting, maybe it was an old service weapon, I don't know. One minute his hands were empty, the next he'd slammed the gun down on the table. He didn't wave it at the soldiers, didn't even point it at them, he just calmly told them to get out. The officer looked at the gun, then looked at Paul, then nodded to one of his men. The soldier shot him. Three bullets in the chest. The table, and all that wonderful, never to be seen again food was utterly ruined.

"After that we were marched outside at gunpoint. There were two lorries, both nearly empty, one an Army truck, the other a supermarket freezer van. We had to stand there in the rain as they emptied the restaurant. When they'd finished we had to follow the lorries as they went through every coffee shop, restaurant and fast food place in the area, loading everything into the back. Finally the officer felt he'd made his point, whatever it was, and we were escorted to the east side of the city where we joined up with the tail end of this much larger group that must have been made up of most of Bournemouth. Then they pointed along the coast and told us to walk that way."

There was a noise from outside. I don't think the others heard it, not over the shuffling and banging of the undead against the outside wall of the kitchen. Even if they did hear it, I doubt they would have recognised the click-clack of the rifle.

"It was a long walk," Barrett went on. "A brutal walk, all through the evening and into the night. I was glad I was wearing trainers. There were some buses running alongside to collect those who couldn't walk, but there weren't enough. It's not like we could even help each other. It was us or them. It wasn't our choice to leave them by the side of the road. That was you, you did that!" Her fists were clenching and unclenching with the memory. I straightened my back, expecting her to lash out and strike me, but she took a breath, and went on.

"By the time we got to the enclave, it was after dawn and I was exhausted. We were directed into a warehouse. There was a bathroom, or a toilet at least. One cubicle used by the night watchman now had to do service for about five hundred of us. There was no bedding. No blankets. Nothing. At one end, near the doors was a trestle table where they were giving out soup. They had bowls, but it was one per person, issued when you walked in with a stern warning not to lose it, since there wouldn't be any more. There were no spoons. Wasn't that absurd? I mean, they were collecting food from these restaurants, right, but no one had thought to gather any spare cutlery.

"One bowl of soup. That was all we got. Someone asked for more. A real Oliver Twist moment if ever there was one, and we were all hungry. No one was allowed seconds, but at least the people serving the food didn't make anything of it. They just apologised, said there really wasn't enough. But the worst bit was what they said next. They said we should make the most of it, because it was only going to get worse once they'd emptied the other cities. Some people found a cot and slept. Others collapsed on the floor where they were standing. That wasn't going to be me. I hung around by the doors, talked to the people serving the food until I found a guard. I… persuaded him to give me a chance, to get me a decent job, somewhere half comfortable.

"I found out a bit of what they were doing from him. They'd combined all of the south coast for about a hundred miles from the New Forest to Dungeness, and stretching ten miles or so inland, into this one giant zone, governed from the Isle of Wight. The Zone was then split into Districts. Each District was split into Control Areas, and each of those into Distribution Points. It was maddening. I mean, we had the old addresses, the councils, the parishes, and they could have just used those, but no. Someone thought this Byzantine classification would actually make things simpler. Our Distribution Point consisted of a dozen warehouses on an industrial estate by the railway line, a row of dilapidated terraces just outside the gates and a sports centre on the other side of the road.

"The sports centre was where I ended up. That was where the food was prepared. Nearly five thousand meals a day. No, that makes it sound like a restaurant or cafeteria or somewhere people would actually choose to eat. Five thousand people, needing a meal, once a day, and we were told we should expect ten times that come the evacuation proper.

"There was water and there was power, until… No, you'll hear the story in order," she said quietly, more to herself than to me. "They'd taken out the exercise machines, and thrown them into a heap in the car park. In their place were row after row of electric ovens, all the same model. They must have come from an outlet store, or even, maybe, a factory, if we still made things like that in England. They'd let us go up to the balcony if we wanted a bit of exercise, but very definitely nowhere near the armed guards standing watch over the food. That was in the indoor sports arena place. I don't know its proper name, the place with the tennis courts and five aside football pitches painted onto the rubber floor. The food came in, was sorted, and weighed, so only just enough was used each day. Only then did the food come to us, and that's where the system broke down. I mean there was no way of stopping us taking whatever we needed, and we were hungry too, right?" She looked over at the others, and after the briefest moment's hesitation, they all nodded.

"There were about a hundred of us," she continued, "split into three eight-hour shifts. A few of the people came from the warehouse, like me, but most of them seemed to come from prison. They'd emptied those, too difficult, too expensive to keep running, I guess. They'd been told this was a continuation of their sentence, and there was I, a volunteer. At the end of the shift, they were all taken back to the church they'd been billeted in. They didn't know how good they had it. It sounded like a far nicer place than the warehouse everyone else went back to. Everyone except me. When the shift was over I stayed, and just kept working. No one said anything. No one seemed to care.

"When I got too tired to go on, I found a small alcove near a storage room to sleep. All night long there were gunshots. Not many, just frequent enough to wake me each time I started to drift off to sleep. The next day, when the shift changed, when people who'd been in the warehouses came in, I listened to the rumours.

"Life in the warehouses was a life of queuing. You queued for breakfast, then you queued for the toilet, then you queued for lunch, then, for a bit of variety, you queued for a chance to climb up to one of the windows to look out at the sky, then you queued for dinner, then you slept. If you could sleep, with the people wandering around asking if anyone had seen their husband or wife or son or daughter. It sounded like almost everyone was looking for someone, and they kept on asking until they'd asked everyone. Then they would go outside to ask at the other warehouses. But there was a strict curfew. Anyone who went outside was shot.

"As more people came in, they started having to queue for a bed. But the numbers coming in didn't add up. It was a hundred here, a dozen there, not the millions rumour had us expecting. I worked, I ate, I slept. Compared to the warehouses it wasn't too bad, but only if you compared it to the warehouses.

"After a couple of days the fresh food was eaten. Then the porridge ran out. Then the delivery truck only brought carrots and onions, and we started bulking out the vegetable stew with flour and cooking oil. That must have been after…" she paused. "Only three days, maybe four. It seems like so much longer. The days blurred into one another. There was no end to the vegetables that needed to be scrubbed. I hated that. Looking back on it, after, when I had nothing to eat but dirt and air, I used to dream of those piles of carrots.

"Most of what I learned came from the guards. The cities were going to be evacuated. The Londoners were heading there, to us. There was a vaccine and they were going to get it first. That was the catalyst, the trigger, the tangible inequality which the refugees could grab on to and understand. The Londoners, who'd done nothing but bankrupt us, who took our money and ran our country into ruin, and did nothing for anywhere outside the M25, they were getting preferential treatment. It was too much. The refugees became angry. Then, one day, I heard shots in the afternoon. It was so loud, everyone stopped and just looked at one another. The guards on the door went out to check. They were visibly tense, expecting the worst. I'm not sure what they thought was happening, but they came back a few minutes later, looking relieved. They gave no explanation, but you could tell it wasn't the zombies that had been shot.

"That night when the shift changed I found out about the gunshots. I'd sort of shifted away from everyone else, into a corner. It wasn't exactly hiding, but just trying to be separate, making them think I was different, meant to be there. One of the guards came in with one of his mates, some soldier who'd been on a different duty that day. They'd come in to scrounge food and though they were talking quietly so they couldn't be overheard, they didn't notice me.

"The shots in the afternoon were a formal democratic protest. One of the warehouses had elected a representative. It was a show of hands thing, some former TV-gardener who everyone recognised. He'd taken a delegation of four of the more respectably eminent refugees, to meet with the person in charge.

"I don't know who that was. They got as far as a captain. A real captain of some real military unit, not someone thrown into a uniform at the last minute. The captain ordered them back to their warehouse. They refused. He shot them. He did it himself, I heard, a bullet in each head. It was the guard who'd told the people in the warehouse. He was a corporal in the Reserves, who lived in Yorkshire. The evening of New York he'd had a call and been driven down to the south. He was as outraged as anyone.

"He was the one who found out about the shipment of vaccine. There was a car park down near the port packed with lorry after lorry, loaded up with the stuff, all just sitting there. Why should it go to the Londoners first? How was that fair? That was what people were asking. When the morning shift came in, they were full of that same rumour about the vaccine and the same outrage that it should go to the Londoners over the locals. By the time the shift changed, half the lorries had driven away. The other half couldn't, because someone had got into the car park and released the air from the tyres.

"These weren't military grade lorries, just commercial vehicles that had been requisitioned, and now they each had four flat tyres apiece. People were pulled off work details left and right, even the elderly from the warehouses got dragooned into unloading the lorries so the tyres could be changed. Some of the vaccine was loaded into police cars, some into whatever other vehicles they had, but there weren't enough.

"The next morning there was no replacement for the night shift. One of the supervisors, a supercilious guy whose experience managing a fast food place had given him delusions of culinary grandeur, went out to check what was happening. He came back half an hour later. The warehouses, the churches, they were all in lock down. People had started dying during the night. Not turning, just dying. It was the same thing all over the enclave. People were just dying.

"There was no delivery of food that day, instead we got a message saying no meals were going to be served until further notice and we had to stay where we were. The whole enclave was in quarantine. We sat, and we waited, and we listened to the sound of gunfire.

122

"It took a while, maybe until afternoon, to find out what had happened, and by then it was too late. That corporal, the one in the Reserves, he came to tell us. The people who'd died had stolen the vaccine. Some had taken it then and there, some after they'd got back to the warehouse and shared it with others. That's how we found out. The Londoners, they weren't to be saved, they were to be euthanized. Put down like they were nothing more than animals. I almost felt sorry for them.

"Around midnight a lorry of food came in. Food was to be served at eight a.m., and that was it. We were back to work. At dawn a new lot of workers came in, and the others, those who'd been there with me all day, they went back to wherever. Not me though. I stayed, and I was glad I did. I didn't see any of them ever again. I could have asked someone what was going on, I suppose, but if you ask questions, then sooner or later you get asked them right back. Then and there I was safe, just as long as I kept my head down.

"After that, I got used to the shooting, an intermittent banging that went on day and night. Over that week I pieced it together. Scraps of overheard conversation and the things people didn't say. I suppose, if you had to call it something, you could say that that was our civil war. It was too big a thing, too tied up in moral certainties to be called a mutiny, too small and ultimately futile to be called a revolution. The soldiers, police and refugees who'd had friends or family or whatever in the cities, they'd had enough. There was no central command, it was just a bunch of individuals, all doing what they knew they had to. All fighting alone, together, and one by one, they died.

"It was about a week after the cities were evacuated that the guards came in and said everyone was being cleared out. They were emptying the warehouses, pulling back along the coast. They didn't say why. I'd had enough. I decided to stay and hide. Hours passed. I couldn't tell you how many. I wanted to see what was going on outside, and was half way to the office when it happened.

"Everything went white. The lights went out. All the little clocks on the ovens, they went off. Then there was a second light, just the same as before, this stabbing blinding glare shooting through the windows. It only lasted a second, but it was a second that lasted an eternity during which the world was nothing but light. Then it was gone. Then there was... I suppose it was the shock wave. The whole building shook. When it stopped, I picked myself up and went into the office. The glass in the windows was broken. I didn't notice that at first, because when I looked outside, I saw the mushroom clouds.

"One to the south, one to the east. I couldn't tell you how long I stood there, looking at them. Minutes, hours, seconds, I don't know. Then I went out to the lobby. The doors were locked. I peered through the glass, but I couldn't see any sentries. There was still gunfire in the distance, and that was all I could hear. I was safe inside. Safe until another bomb was dropped, safe until the food ran out, safe until the radiation reached me. I had to get out.

"I climbed out the window and dropped down to the car park. Then I ran. I just ran, heading nowhere but away from the sound of gunfire. I kept running until I reached the train line, then I kept running until I reached a tunnel. Then I stopped.

"I don't know what time it was, but it got dark soon after. Dark and cold. The shooting lessened during the night, but every so often there'd be a sudden flurry, a crescendo of sound that went on for twenty or thirty minutes. Then it would die off again, replaced by the occasional single isolated shot. I tried to stay awake, I mean, how can you sleep with all that going on nearby? But I fell asleep. When I woke the sun was high in the sky and the city was quiet. I got up, walked to the end of the tunnel and looked out. Pillars of smoke filled the sky. It was all on fire, in every direction I looked.

"I walked away, heading west, towards home. I saw my first zombie a half hour later. That wasn't the first body I saw, but those had been dead people. I hadn't thought to bring a weapon with me. Hadn't even considered it. It was standing in front of a bank, banging mechanically at the window. Its head turned. It saw me. It started moving towards me, getting closer. To me, then, it seemed as if it was about to burst into a run. I turned and sprinted away, ducking down alleys, not even daring to look back until I was thoroughly lost.

"I needed to get away. The road I was on ran north-south, so I ran inland away from the bombs. I saw some other people, other survivors, but I didn't stop, nor did they.

"They'd started building a wall around the enclave, but they'd not got very far. There were plenty of gaps, and it was easy enough to get out and into the countryside. I hid and scavenged, until I saw the smoke from the chimney and headed to the farm. I don't know which side it was who dropped those bombs. I don't even know how many sides there were. All I know is that it happened because of the evacuation. Because of your plan."

An expectant silence settled around the room, and I realised that she'd finished, and that they were waiting on my response. Of course, now, after a few hours to think it all through, I think I understand what it was all about. They had all heard the story before. No doubt they'd discussed it, and gone over every little detail, coming to their own conclusions, and their certainty in those conclusions had grown with each retelling until, now, they are certain that they are right.

And there was me, in that kitchen, an unelected representative of the old government, and the architect of the evacuation plan itself. I was being judged. This was my trial. They were my jury. I had no right to silence, yet nothing I could have said, nothing I can ever say will be sufficient. Not to them.

"Well?" Stewart asked.

I thought of saying nothing, of just walking out. I wanted to, but I didn't. I felt they deserved something. "The government was relocating to the Isle of Wight. That would have been one of the targets, the other was probably the nuclear power station at Dungeness," I said.

"What?" Barrett said. "That's it? That's all you have to say."

"I told you," Liz said.

"Alright," I went on. "Yes, I came up with a plan. As I saw it there were only two options. Stay put and starve, or evacuate and try and hold onto something. That was all I suggested. I wasn't in the government. I wasn't in the cabinet. I wasn't even in the meetings. I was in a flat in south London with a broken leg and not enough painkillers. I didn't know about the vaccine or the plan to kill off the population—"

"We read your journal," Chris interrupted. "You knew about the vaccine years ago. So you're lying to us now, you probably lied in that book. How can we trust anything you say?"

I stood up, moving my hands to my sides in an unsubtle gesture that ended with my right hand inches away from the pistol in my pocket. "In that case, like you said, you've read the journal. Believe it, or not. Trust me, or not. Just don't go through my stuff. Ever again." Then I walked out.

Day 115, Brazely Abbey, Hampshire

10:00, 5th July

An uncomfortable silence has settled over the Abbey, made worse by this morning's summer shower. The undead do not care. Ordinarily I would relish the cool rain, but not when there is a veritable storm brewing just below me. I have retreated, if that is the right word, to the top of the walls.

I've been up here since shortly after yesterdays 'trial'. Kim brought me dinner. She'd been teaching Annette how to shoot the rifle. It seems a waste to me. On the other hand, whose rifle is it? Whose ammunition? We aren't a community here, let alone a democracy. Besides, ten or twenty or fifty, they could shoot off every bullet, and we'd still be surrounded by the undead.

Dark thoughts breed depression, and that won't help. We are besieged. We need to escape, and that, regardless of the attitude of the others, is what I've turned my mind to. I think we could get the cars out of here. It won't be easy, but we could do it. If we created some kind of diversion on the other side of the Abbey, something loud enough to clear the undead off the track and away from the road, then perhaps we might be able to get away.

Two cars, nine souls, because regardless of their attitude, a life is a life, and that's now more precious than water. I mean that literally as well as metaphorically. The only real activity below me is the seemingly constant fetching of water from the well to flush the toilets in the shower block.

We've enough food for about two weeks. Rationing could stretch it out, but they won't listen to me. Nor to Kim. They seem to dislike her almost as much as they loathe me. Even if they did, what difference would a few extra weeks make? No, forget rationing, we're not going to be able to take much food with us. We'll take fuel and water since those are a lot harder to find, and that won't leave space for much else. We might as well eat it now as leave it here, so let's call it thirteen days to find a way out of here. And how we do that, I've no idea.

Do we leave together? Obviously I don't mean the others, I mean Kim, Annette, Daisy and I. Do they go where I go, because I know where that is. I haven't discussed it with them. There hasn't really been time since we left that car showroom, but I don't think they want to go to Lenham. Where else could we go? Where should we go after?

Allowing for a margin of error in my calculations, and the circuitous nature of any journey we undertake, then we've fuel enough for twelve hundred miles. Divide that by two for the two cars, and we could still reach pretty much anywhere in Wales or Scotland.

South is out, the bombs have seen to that. We have to assume the other enclaves met a similar fate, so that rules out southwest to Cornwall, or west to Bristol. There's east, of course, back towards London.

Of all the places in the country, of all the places in the world, London might just work out. If there was ever one national stereotype that wasn't built on ancestral hatred and local bias, then it has to be the English obsession with gardening. There were fruit trees and vegetable plots in almost every garden in the capital. Even the local councils got in on the act, planting fruit trees along the verges of almost every road. Then there's Kew. Every plant on the planet, or near enough, was grown there. Pineapples, coffee, chocolate, that would be our source of seeds. We'd find enough vinegar, salt and probably even sugar if we looked hard enough. We could find some place where the buildings were crowded together, and connect them with rooftop walkways. We could live without having to go down to the streets.

We could look for somewhere north of the river, in one of the old districts, and hey, if we're doing that then why think small? We could take one of the apartment blocks overlooking Buckingham Palace, or somewhere in Mayfair of Park Lane. Or why not the Palace itself?

Imagine that, the four of us living in the Palace. The idea of Daisy sitting on the throne is enough to raise an unfamiliar smile, but it would just be the four of us. Which would mean it is down to Kim and myself to ensure a place is secure. Could we do that with the Palace? Could we do it with a large Victorian block of flats? No.

I barely survived London once, completely unaware that radiation was a factor to be considered as well. How many bombs were dropped and where? We could find an apparently perfect redoubt, not knowing we were being poisoned by the air surrounding us until it was too late. No. If we had to, we could return to London, but it's a place to escape to, not a destination to journey towards.

North, then to Wales or Scotland, but where? I can think of a dozen places, I can think of a hundred, which would be ideal, if they had water, and if no one has reached there first, *and* if they are free of radiation.

What's left? One of the Scottish islands? Or would someone recognise me and turn me into a pariah there, like I have become here, an albatross around Kim's neck? The Americas? Now there's an idea. Somewhere in the north, somewhere so sparsely populated, so remote that the undead are few in number. We'd have to travel by boat of course…

Sailing off into the sunset, a new name, a new life, a new American dream, it's just another fantasy.

"Forget the where," Kim said. "You have a plan to go somewhere, but Annette's right. A road is blocked so you turn south instead of north. Plans change, where we go matters less than just going, so focus on the how."

As I was climbing down, Barrett, Liz, and Stewart pointedly went back inside the dormitory. A few minutes later, equally pointedly, Daphne came out and joined Chris by the fire. So I went to talk to Kim. She was showing Annette how to drive the truck. With the engine off it was very much a theoretical lesson, and of little practical value, but it keeps the girl happy and that's more than I've been doing.

"So," Kim went on, "how do we escape?" I hadn't realised it was an actual question.

"There's at least a hundred on the track between here and the road," I said, thinking out loud. "When the engines start, They'll hear and come running. Well, not running, but you know what I mean."

"And?" Kim prompted.

"And They'd block the road," Annette answered for me. "They'd gather outside the gate, and we'd never get the cars out. We need to distract them. So Bill," she added in a fair imitation of Kim's interrogative tone, "how do we do that?"

"Fire?" I suggested. "We could set a fire outside the walls. Throw out some Molotovs, or something. But we couldn't control the fire. The trees would catch, or the remains of their clothing would, and They'd set fire to the walls. Not to the Abbey, but the dormitory, the kitchen, the shower block, and all that timber I threw up in between. No, fire's out."

"Sound," Kim said with a shrug. "It's all we know that works."

"If we could get everyone to be quiet, or if we could get the zombies away from the gates, or at least some, then perhaps we could get up enough speed to drive out of here."

"Not everyone has to go," Kim said, quietly. "One car could escape. Leave the rest of the food behind. The people who stay can create a diversion."

I thought about that for a moment. "Then whoever stays would have to know and be ready to close the gates, otherwise it would just be murder," I said carefully, "and I'm not volunteering to stay. Are you?"

"Yeah, right," Annette said. Kim didn't bother to reply.

"I doubt any of the others would either," I said. "So it's all or none." The silence stretched for a moment. "So we need to get the zombies to move away from the gates to the walls on the far side."

"Right," Kim said. "Any ideas?"

"I was thinking about shark cages. You remember the TV shows where they'd send someone down into shark infested waters, and they'd film from inside a cage."

"Sure. No cages here, though."

"Right. But we could try some kind of platform we lower over the side of the walls. Something wide enough for someone to stand on. It wouldn't have to be big. One of the doors would probably do. Reinforced," I added. "Lower it, then lower someone down, kill the undead until there's a pile of Them, raise the person up, then raise up the platform, then lower it a bit further along."

"Use sound to attract Them," Kim mused. "With someone standing on a platform to get Them away from the gate. Then kill some to make space for more. Okay, maybe. You'll need spears, attached to a bungee cord. No, we haven't got any of that. Elastic? No, not strong enough. Spears attached by rope, then. Use one, pull it back up and use it again. It might work. How long before your arm gets tired?"

"An hour? Two? We could take it in shifts. But we're not trying to kill Them all, just make enough space for those around the gate..." I stopped to think for a moment. "How many could we kill before their bodies become a ramp others could climb up?"

"A prone body is, what, about twenty-centimetres high?" Kim said. "Bodies falling on top of one another don't stack neatly, but for every seven that fall in one spot say you create a ramp of about one metre. The platform is in front of the walls, so there'd be a gap behind this wall of the dead zombies, but gravity will fill that in." She thought for a moment. "How high's the wall?"

"About thirty feet," I replied.

"So, nine metres," she thought a moment more "I'd say, moving the platform along the wall… you could get between three hundred fifty and five hundred, depending on how They fell, but after that…" she didn't need to finish the sentence

"How many zombies are out there, do you think?" I asked, knowing the answer.

"A lot more than that," Annette replied. Kim nodded her agreement.

"It might work," I said. "I really can't think of anything else."

"You should see what the others say," Kim said. "There's a chance they might have a better idea. I doubt it, but maybe this is one of those times that if we're going to do it, then it's best to get it done quickly."

They didn't have a better idea. That isn't to say they didn't suggest anything.

"We could stay," Liz insisted again. "Why don't we just shoot as many as we can, and then you could go out and kill the rest with that pike of yours?"

"No," Kim said softly.

"But he says he's immune. So why not?" Liz demanded.

"No," Kim repeated.

"No," Annette echoed.

"Hey," Daphne said, "No, it's a fair point. I mean, why not?"

"Because I'm immune, not bite proof. They'd kill me. Probably very quickly," I said angrily before Kim had a chance to say anything. "Then I'd be dead and you'd still be stuck here, out of bullets and running out of food. And that's to say nothing of the radiation."

"Rocks. We just throw rocks down on Them," Barrett said.

"No rocks here," Kim said.

"Don't you know how to improvise?" Barrett snapped back. "We can use some of the stones from the Abbey!"

"That would actually make our walls lower," Kim said slowly, "and would help Them build their ramp."

131

"The advantage of using a platform," I said, "is that their bodies will fall away from the walls, not directly up against it. That nearly doubles the number we can theoretically kill before They can climb up and get inside. Look, we've no choice. We'll be out of food in two weeks. We have to escape, so unless anyone has a better idea?" I looked around, hopefully. "Then we need to create some noise to lure Them away from the track."

"And just how do we do that?" Liz asked. "You want us banging saucepans together on the battlements?"

"Music," Annette said. "Like you did in the village."

"No mp3 players. No speakers," I said. "I mean we don't do we? You guys didn't bring any with that stuff you brought here?"

"Use the cars," Annette said. "They have speakers, right? So that means they have music."

"That's true," Stewart said.

"We'd need to dismantle the speakers, rewire them, run them up to the walls, away from the gate," I replied.

"You know how to rewire car speakers?" Barrett asked.

"I reckon I know enough to take the wires out and splice them together," I said.

I didn't. However, with Stewart's initially reluctant help, we managed it. It took all day, with most of that time spent making sure we weren't pulling out anything important. I can't say we bonded, not exactly. That's too much of a Hollywood montage kind of word. By the end of it, though, we were talking about football, and cricket, and movies, and the usual stuff people talk about when they're trying to avoid talking about anything serious.

Whilst we were doing that, Chris and Daphne made the platforms. Most of the sturdier beams had already gone to reinforce the walls, but there was enough left over to reinforce a couple of doors. They seem strong enough.

Kim made the spears. Rough and ready, for the most part, knives stuck on poles with a weight added near the blade so we'll get gravity to assist with the force of the thrust. We pushed the cars up to the walls and checked that the speakers work. All in all, it was a productive day's work. It was only natural, therefore, that conversation this evening turned to where we would be escaping to.

"London should be our fall back. I've seen the cities. I know what they're like," Stewart said, adding in a grudging but conciliatory tone, "You do too, Bill."

"If it's still there," Liz said. "We don't know. We can't know. It's too much of a risk."

All afternoon she had made no secret that she still wanted me to go out and face the undead on my own, preferably dying after killing the last zombie trapping us here. It wasn't that she'd said it openly, at least not to my face, but all afternoon she kept finding opportunities to ask what we'd do if the plans didn't work.

"North, then. Across the M4," Chris said. "Then Wales, maybe?"

"But where in Wales?" Daphne said. "We're less than an hour's drive from the farm, a lot less, and we didn't even know that anyone was here."

"And the flag house," Annette said, continuing angrily when it was clear that the others weren't following. "The house I saw from the top of the school, the one with the flags. There's people there too."

"But we don't know where that is, dear," Barrett said, in syrupy tones that made her sound less like a concerned adult and more like a pantomime wicked witch.

"I know, my point," Annette replied, sounding more like Kim with each passing hour, "is that there are other people. Other survivors. Dozens. Hundreds. Probably more, and they're going to be everywhere, just holding on. We could find them."

"Not easily," Chris said, before Barrett could say anything. "And where would we start? We have to look after ourselves. We need somewhere concrete to go to after this. Somewhere we know we'll be safe."

"Scotland. One of the islands," Daphne said. "Far enough away from anywhere anyone would want to nuke."

"Why not New Zealand?" Kim muttered. Unfortunately she said it loudly enough the others heard. "Because," she went on, carefully, "it's the same difference. There are no ferries, no planes, so how would you get there?"

"The Thames," Stewart said. "If we had a boat, we could sail along the river, through London and out the other side, then we can follow the coast up to Scotland. That's got to be easiest."

"You know how to sail?" Kim asked.

"Don't need to," Stewart said smugly. "We've got petrol here, haven't we? We get ourselves a motorboat and chug our way along the coast."

"What about the zombies in the water?" Annette asked.

"The Thames is pretty deep, even this side of London," Stewart said. "We'll be going at speed, right over their heads."

"And if we let the tide pull us out, the fuel will go further. Much further than on land," Daphne added. I didn't think she was correct. The friction of the water would surely be greater than that of tyres on a road. How long would the fuel last? Not as far as it would powering a car, I'm sure of that.

"What if you run out of fuel and end up adrift at sea?" I asked.

"Is that any worse than being stuck here?" Barrett snapped back.

Personally, I thought it was, but I didn't want to argue. I was starting to get a feel of the direction this conference was taking.

"Alright," I said, leaving that point. "Where do you find a boat? I went up and down the Thames looking for one. They'd all gone."

"Ah," Daphne said, "Stewart knows a place."

So they'd been talking, planning it. Kim and I exchanged a glance.

"Well?" Kim asked.

"I knew this guy. He did boat hires in the summer. On the Thames, near Oxford. Day trips mostly, up and down the river. Usually, the tourists would get stuck somewhere, not be able to turn the boat, and have to call up for a lift back. That's how he made his profit—"

"But you don't actually know," Kim interrupted, "that there are any boats there now?"

"I can't be certain, of course, but he was out of the country in February. Off sailing around Australia, so he won't have taken any of them. As for someone else, well, he had two boathouses. One was for the hire boats. The other was for repairs. The hire boats probably are gone, but in his repair yard he kept his own boat. A nice one, always drained the engine of fuel, but otherwise it was ready to go."

"We'd have gone there weeks ago," Chris said. "But without the petrol and the—"

"Sounds perfect, doesn't it," Daphne cut in, loudly.

"Perfect? It's mad." I hadn't meant to say the words out loud, they just came out.

"Oh really? And what's your great idea," Barrett asked

"There are the bridges around central London, I doubt you'll get a boat through those ruins, but let's say you do, then what? You'll just drift down the river and out to sea with no chance of rescue. You'll die of dehydration drifting around the North Sea."

"That is," Barrett said softly, "a possibility. But we don't think it's a great one. We stick close to the coast, when we're down to our last few gallons of fuel we'll find a safe place to go ashore."

"That's easy to say," I shouted, "but you know, you must know, it won't be like that. It can't be, not anymore."

"Right," Barrett said, her voice still deathly soft. "So what's the alternative?"

"You're hoping that the engine works, hoping there's enough fuel, hoping there's enough water and food, hoping the boat doesn't sink, that somewhere along the coast there'll be somewhere safe. What if all the enclaves were nuked? What if this is it, this here, this small corner of England? What if it turns out this is all that's left of the entire world." I stopped. My voice had become nearly hysterical at the end as I expressed my secret fear, one that up until now I hadn't dared think, let alone express.

"So suggest an alternative," Barrett said, loudly this time, "or shut up."

135

"She does have a point," Kim said. "Of a sort. What is the alternative?"

To me there was really only one choice. "Lenham Hill. If it's abandoned there'll be supplies. If it's occupied, well, we'll see. But we need answers. We need to—"

"That's it, is it? Either join you on your mad quest no one else cares about, or go to an almost certain watery grave? What a choice!"

"Well, what do you want?" I asked, shocked at her sudden venom.

"What I want you can't give," she replied. "I want to know that there'll be a tomorrow."

What do you say to that? If I don't go there now, then I never will. We'll find a cottage in Wales or we'll end up on some boat trying to get out and away from this Island, and we'll never come back. Am I a carrier? How else can I find out? I should feel guilty that this now seems more important than making sure Lenham Hill is no threat to any future generations, but I don't.

Day 116, Brazely Abbey, Hampshire

07:45, 6ᵗʰ July

To get to the boathouse we'll have to cross the M4. I've drawn up a route from here to the motorway using the roads I remember being the most passable. After that, from there to the river, we're travelling through unknown territory. I thought of adding a little 'here be dragons' notation to the road atlas, but didn't think anyone but Annette would find it funny. Possibly she wouldn't either.

I slept little last night. The night before battle. I suppose I should have been standing watch over my armour, but since I don't wear any, I sat and watched the stars instead. It's odd, those little bits of history that you learn, but never really understand because you have no frame of reference. Knights and armour and castles and battles. It was all just words and movies. It was never real, not until I learned the smell and touch and taste and fear that goes with it all. Is this a new Dark Age? Will there, one day, be some myth told about our flight from this Abbey? No, this isn't the time for that type of introspection.

The gantries are ready. Chris and I are to go up onto them. Though no one said it, not out loud at least, they clearly wanted Kim to be the other person to go up, but I just don't trust the others. I swung the argument by saying we would need her to use the rifle to kill any zombies that still lingered on the track. Their quick acquiescence suggests, well, I'm not sure, not exactly. They're all acting oddly. Then again, we're all nervous.

It's going to be a tough few hours, but it's almost over. The truck and the car have been loaded. Fuel, water, and the rest of the space goes to the food. I'd liked to have packed differently, but that would have been too obvious a sign we're heading off on our own once we reach the river. And it is 'we'. I spoke briefly to Kim this morning.

"Annette and I have talked," she said.

"Yes?"

"The boat's a bad idea. So is Lenham Hill. But it's the best bad idea we've got."

"You don't have to come with me."

"Annette was right," she said, tilting her head to one side. "You really don't get it. We're not going with you. You're coming with us. Lenham Hill, then we'll keep going north. Out of the radiation zone, wherever that is."

And that was that, and since everything is in place, if 'twere done...

16:40, 6th July

My part of the operation went exactly as we'd hoped. More or less. The rest of it, well, we're still at the Abbey.

As soon as we lowered the platforms over the edge of the wall, the undead began pushing and shoving, their hands reaching up to claw at empty air as They tried to reach across the four feet or so between the gantry and their heads.

137

Half way down the rope, I paused to watch as a zombie lost its footing and fell. Somehow, it had managed to get this far still wearing a green baseball cap. When it stumbled and slipped, the hat flew off, disappearing into the crowd as the prone zombie was crushed underfoot by that great grasping mass of the undead. I saw the same thing happen again as I reached the platform, and again as I was testing my footing. I didn't think we would need to do any more than just stand and wait.

Then the music started. The track was one of those generic almost-hits that I sort of vaguely recognised from adverts and movies, but I couldn't tell you who it was by. I wasn't really listening to it. I was watching the woods.

They were pouring out, through the trees. Dozens, hundreds of Them. I turned to look to the right. They were coming along the side of the Abbey too, away from the track, away from the road beyond. It was clear enough, standing there, that the plan was going to work. The danger now was that it might work too well.

The spears were ready, tied to one of the ropes holding the platform in place. I gripped one, and took a step towards the edge. The platform rocked, tilting at a perilous angle. I grabbed at a rope with my left hand and shifted my right leg backwards, trying to stop the whole thing from swaying. That's when I wished we'd practised this inside the Abbey's walls. Standing as I was, one foot forward, one back, left knee bent, right held rigid by the leg brace, I couldn't see anything but the wood beneath my feet. If I couldn't see the undead, how was I to aim at Them?

"Tell me if I hit one," I called out.

Holding the spear as close to vertical as I could over the edge of the platform, I hurled it downward.

"Miss," Kim shouted back.

I grabbed at the rope and started to pull the spear back up. The undead batted at it, as it went by. I tried again.

"Hit," Annette called.

"Shoulder," Kim said. "I don't think this is going to work."

That was clear enough. I tugged at the rope, pulling the spear out of desiccated flesh. It didn't require much effort. The spear hadn't gone in deeply.

Clearly I needed to be able to see what I was doing. I tried standing on the edge, and by moving carefully, I managed to get a view of the undead beneath me without the platform tipping over. One hand on the support rope, the other gripping a spear, I picked one that was taller than the others, slightly fresher looking, its clothes less ragged.

I thrust the spear down. It entered through the zombie's skull. The creature fell. The rope attaching the spear to the gantry went taut. The platform rocked as the weight of the dead zombie pulled it down. I grabbed onto the ropes, trying to shift my weight to stop the swaying. When I dared loosen my grip and tried to tug at the rope to pull the spear back up, I found it was stuck tight. I had to cut the rope loose with the hatchet before I could try again.

I was one spear down, one zombie dead. Not a good ratio and I was starting to think we'd have to give up on this farce and just risk the road as it was. I tried again, this time picking a more wizened creature as my target. The spear went in, the zombie fell, and the spear came out. I tried again, and again, and again. Keeping balanced like that, judging the right force to use, only targeting the older, more time-ravaged, it wasn't easy, but it did get easier.

I lost the second spear with the fifth zombie, the third when my count got to twenty. By the twenty-fifth I was beginning to tire. I'd mistimed the spear thrust and it glanced off the creature's head. I'd lost all track of time. My world had narrowed into this one little spot containing the gantry and the undead beneath it. The scab on my wrist where I'd been bitten back at the Manor broke, and spots of blood began trickling up and down my arm as I raised and lowered it. The effort of keeping the platform steady was sending a pulse up and down my leg that I knew would soon turn to pain.

"Stop!" Kim called out at the twenty-ninth.

"What's wrong?" I croaked out. My mouth was parched. I'd not thought to bring down any water with me.

"Look down!" Annette shouted back.

"You'll need to move to the other side of the platform," Kim said. I looked down. There was a heap now, only a small one, but the zombies standing on it were noticeably higher there than elsewhere. I crossed to the platform's far side. In my head I started counting down as They fell. Twenty-nine. Twenty-eight. Twenty-seven. This time, I was a lot slower, but knowing that when I reached zero we'd have to leave or shift the platform, and that either way I'd get a break, made it easier.

I'd reached thirteen when I heard a scream. I glanced up at Kim, but she was looking away, towards the other wall and the other platform.

I had been lowered down first, ostensibly to work out any problems with the plan. I figured that my immunity did at least offer me a little protection. I may not like Chris and I may have no intention of travelling much further with him, but that doesn't mean I wish him or any of the others harm. Not then, not now.

It took an age to be hauled back up to the wall. Liz was meant to be helping Annette and Kim with the ropes, but she'd disappeared. By the time I'd reached the top of the wall, and then climbed down the scaffolding, I was the last to reach the small circle gathered around Chris.

He was sitting against the wheel of the truck, holding a bandage against his leg. He looked like a confused child, his face long, his eyes uncomprehending. The others were grouped, not exactly around him, but clustered together a few yards away. Daphne stood slightly in front, clearly unsure whether she should approach her husband or run from him.

"The rope. It caught on one of the stones," Daphne said. "I just didn't…" she trailed off.

"The rope broke," Barrett said, flatly. "The gantry slipped, toppled sideways. He slipped. Fell. The safety rope wasn't tight enough."

"You said to loosen it!" Daphne yelled at her husband. "You said you couldn't move! You told us to. You said you'd be safe!" The words trailed off into intelligible sobs.

Chris sat up, made as if to stand and go to comfort his wife. Daphne screamed. It wasn't a loud scream, but it was full of heartfelt terror. Chris slumped down again, and began to cry.

It should have been raining. There should have been thunder and lightning. It shouldn't have been a bright, cloudless day. A bird should not have taken that moment to chirrup a soft song from some distant perch.

"Do something," Kim said, before walking over to Annette, who was now holding Daisy. She took the baby in her arms and then took them both into the relative seclusion of the truck.

"You haven't turned," I said to Chris. "You might be immune." He looked up, his eyes brightening at the chance of a reprieve. "You might not be," I went on, "but there's a chance." I glanced around, considering our options. "We'll go into the kitchen. Just you and me, and we'll wait, and we'll see." I took a couple of steps closer then held out my hand. He stared at it for a moment before he took it. I half-pulled him to his feet. "Come on," I said, and gently pushed him towards the long prefab.

He sat on a chair, I sat on one opposite and we waited.

"How long's it been now?" he asked.

"Thirty minutes," I said, working it out and halving the result.

"And it was about half an hour after I got bitten before we came in here, right? So it's been an hour."

"A bit less. Fifty minutes I'd say," I replied. "Now just sit and wait."

"How long now? Three hours at least?"

"Time's funny like that. It's only been about an hour and a half," I lied.

"That's at least five hours," he said standing up.

"Sit down, Chris," I said, taking the pistol out of my pocket and holding it loosely in my hand.

"Surely it's five hours now. In your journal that's how long you said it would take. That was the maximum, wasn't it?"

"I'm not sure. It could be longer. We just have to wait."

"For how long? A day? Two? How long? How much longer?"

"Not long now," I said, standing up. "So calm down." In truth I had no idea. Some people turned quickly, some people took hours. I thought back then, and I've been thinking about it since, to the videos I saw. I remembered the footage shot at Grand Central Station, where the police chased an infected person down. I remembered how that person died, turned, was shot, but not until after others were infected. I remembered how some of those had turned almost immediately, how some bodies lay there for minutes before they reanimated. I remembered how others had fled the station only to turn outside. I remembered the terror in the recordings of the paramedics, radioing in for help, when others turned in the ambulances on the way to the hospital. I remembered all of that and a dozens of other videos I'd seen, and the simple answer was that I didn't know how long we would have to wait.

"There was a guy," I said, "at the mall. You remember the mall? The attack at that shopping centre in New York? The one that was broadcast everywhere?"

"Yeah," Chris said, though I'm not sure he was really listening.

"You read my journal. You know about Sholto, he tracked a guy from that mall, an everyday guy who was bitten and infected. He'd been in New York on a sales tour. Something to do with 3D printers. He was trying to flog some new refinement he'd come up with in his garage by driving his machine around from company to company. He'd driven there all the way from the Pacific coast. I can't remember where from, exactly. Somewhere near Portland I think. He'd stopped in that mall to pick up some souvenirs for his kids. Baseball stuff, you know? Jackets, hats, that kind of thing. An apology for being away so long. He's where I got the idea of five hours from. Where I think our government did too. That's how long it took him to turn. He drove from the mall, made it as far as Hagerstown, in Maryland, five hours later. He'd spent the entire time on the phone to his wife. The call was recorded. His death was recorded. Sholto got that recording, sent it to me. Sent it to others too, I think."

"Has it been five hours, then?" Chris asked, missing the point.

"I'm trying to say it might be longer. Why should it be five hours? Why not six, why not ten? We don't know, because none of us know how this virus works. We don't really know anything about it all."

"It wasn't easy, you know. Out there on the farm."

"No where's easy these days," I replied, only half listening to him.

"There are things you do. Things that you have to do, just to survive."

"We've all done them," I said. "Things we regretted even before the act itself. Those last desperate actions we take, when circumstance leaves us no other."

"But you shouldn't have made us," he said. "Shouldn't have said people should leave their homes. If everyone had stayed where they were, then none of it would ever have happened."

"No, everyone would have starved."

"Yeah, well that would've been better, I reckon. Better for—" Chris stopped in mid-sentence as the door opened.

"That's five hours," Kim said, walking into the dormitory. "I'll take over for a bit." She'd brought in a bowl of stew, one of the irreplaceable MREs. As she handed it to Chris I couldn't help thinking of it as a last meal. "Go on," she said, "you're needed outside."

"I'm not going without Chris," Daphne said, though she didn't sound like she meant it.

"I'm not going in a car with a zombie," Stewart said.

"How long do we have to wait?" Barrett asked

I'll admit it, I wanted him to turn. Not out of spite, nor as revenge for the petty bitterness he'd shown towards me, but so that I could kill him and we could leave. What else could we do though? We couldn't take the risk of being stuck in the car with him if he turned. Leaving him here alone, surrounded by the undead would be nothing but a death sentence preceded by the worst kind of torture. Nor could we kill him before he turned. That is murder, and there has been enough of that. What else was there to do but wait?

"It's been five hours, so the chances are that he's immune," I said, looking up at the sky. "As long as the walls hold, we're safe and I don't

143

think they're going to break any time soon. It's too late to go today, so we'll go tomorrow. That's how long we'll wait. Okay?" I looked over at Daphne. She didn't seem relieved. If anything, I would have said she looked disappointed. It was as if no amount of time would ever be long enough for her. I think she wanted me to say that we should just go then and there, and leave Chris to his fate. Perhaps that's judging them too harshly, it's been a long day for us all, but I do wonder what Chris was about to say just before Kim entered the room.

"There's another thing," I went on. "The undead outside the walls. Tomorrow, we'll need to attract Them away from the track again."

"There's no way I'm getting on one of those platforms," Stewart said quickly.

"Nor me," Liz added.

"I don't like the idea much either. But we may have to. I'll go and check," I added, forestalling another argument. I didn't go up there straight away. First I made a point of walking over to the fire and filling a bowl with stew. Then I went over to the truck, where Annette and Daisy were safely ensconced in the cab.

"You alright?" I asked.

"We shouldn't hang around. Daisy doesn't like it," she replied and for the first time I heard fear in her voice.

"Tomorrow. First thing." I looked at the gates. "But maybe before then. You stay in here." I thought for a moment. "You know how to drive?"

"Kim showed me. Doors locked, engine on, foot down."

"Good enough. Stay in the truck, then. I'm going to check the walls."

It's not as bad out there as I thought. Down there, in the compound, it sounds as if the zombies are tearing the place apart. They aren't. Not quickly, anyway. Their fingers are becoming, literally, worn to the bone against the stone walls. The timbers in the gaps between the prefabs seem to be holding, I suppose because most of those must be as old and weathered as the stone. No, if the undead break through, it'll be the prefabs that give first.

What to do then? They are gathered more thickly underneath the two platforms. Under the platform I was standing on, They are standing on the bodies of the dead, almost within outstretched grasp of the gantry. We could raise it a foot or two, and kill some more of Them. Is it worth the risk? It doesn't matter. I don't want to go back out there, and none of the others are going to, not after what happened to Chris, and I doubt he'll want to go back out either. We'll just have to risk it and hope.

Day 117, Brazely Abbey, Hampshire

03:00, 7th July

At about ten o'clock last night Kim came out of the kitchen.

"Chris is sleeping," she said. "I need to as well. Wake me in a couple of hours. We'll swap again." There wasn't even the suggestion between us that we would trust any of the others to take watch.

I sat on the steps leading up to the kitchen, my back to the door, remembering all the places I've ever been, trying to think of where we might go after Lenham. Where might be safe, which remote island, or peninsula might be defensible. Which country house or castle or cottage we could try to make our home. Nowhere I could think of was far enough away. Britain is just too small.

Around midnight I heard the sound of Chris getting up. I decided that it had been long enough, that I would tell him he was fine. I opened the door and went inside.

He was standing in the middle of the room, his back to me.

"Chris. Looks like you're—" I began. He turned around. It snarled. My hands went to my belt. It was empty. The gun was outside, so too was the pike. I'd taken everything out, left all the extra weight behind when I went onto the platform.

The zombie that had been Chris threw an arm out toward me. The hand grasped out across the ten feet between us, clutching at nothing as the creature took an unsteady step forwards. It snarled again and took another step, then another.

I looked around desperately, but there were no weapons nearby. I snatched up a chair and swung it with all my strength. The small room echoed with a crack as the bones in its forearm broke. It didn't slow down. Its left hand and bottom half of its forearm sagging downward slightly, it swiped clumsily at my head. I took a step back and swung the chair again. Its mouth snapped open and closed. I swung again as it took another staggering step towards me, the chair hit and cracked against the zombie's side. Its right hand snaked out. Its fingernails scraped against the skin of my neck. Pain seared through me, as it gouged out a line of flesh. I dropped the chair and slapped its hands away, punching it in the chest with little effect, then, as it raised its arm again, I ducked underneath and behind it.

"Chris has turned!" I shouted as it twisted round, but the words came out weakly from my wounded throat. It threw its arms towards me. I hop-skipped backwards banging my elbow into the counter that ran along the rear wall. The zombie was between me and the door, there was nowhere left to retreat to.

I could feel a thin trickle of blood running down my neck as my hands searched frantically along the worktop. My fingers curled around the handle of one of the large saucepans. I gripped it and hurled it at the creature's head. It hit it with a crunch of teeth. It staggered then came on once more.

The door opened.

"Chris!" Daphne cried out. Of all the people to come through the door first, it had to be the wife. The zombie turned.

"Chris!" she cried again, taking a half step towards her undead husband. The creature lurched towards her. Its arms stretched out as I ran forward and jumped onto its back. My weight knocked it to the ground as I tried to get an arm around its neck, my knee in its back, trying to hold it down.

"Move," I heard Kim say.

"No!" Daphne screamed.

"Move," Kim said again. I put my hands on its shoulders, pushing it down as I pushed myself up and away. I staggered back at the same time as Kim brought her axe down on the creature's skull.

04:00, 7th July

Dawn isn't far off. We'll be leaving then.

July 10th – 8p.m.
Riverside Links Golf Club, River Thames
Oxfordshire

One hundred and twenty days since the power went out in London. That was how Bill recorded it. I suppose that's how long it has been since the nuclear bombs were dropped on the south coast. That doesn't mean much to me. I'm not being callous, not intentionally, it's just that compared to the hideous fate so many billions suffered, an instantaneous death in a radioactive fireball seems merciful by comparison. I suppose I could count the days since the evacuation, or from when Bill rescued me, but why would I want to remember either date?

Today is July 10th, that's a more normal way of thinking about it. It's a nice, neutral, sterile way that conjures up images of summertime and school holidays, of sunbathing and beaches and last minute getaways. Not that I had any of those in the last few years. I couldn't afford them. I could barely afford the rent, not that any of that matters now. These days I could have my pick of the grandest mansions, the most resplendent jewels and the finest furs, but no caviar. It's a shame. I've never tried it, I never really wanted to, but now that I can't, now that I never will, I can not stop thinking about it. Caviar, lobster, Kobe beef, all gone forever. Luxury now is finding a sealed bottle of water, a few vitamin pills, and a pack of gum. That was all I had to show from my looting expedition when I got back this morning.

147

At least I think it was morning, it could well have been the afternoon. Bill's watch got waterlogged. It stopped at five minutes to twelve. That seems significant, but maybe, in times like these, you can find significance in anything. Right now, it feels like eight p.m., and that's as accurate as I need to be.

We're at a golf course on the north bank of the Thames, somewhere south of Oxford and west of London. According to the maps, this is Oxfordshire, but I found those maps hanging on the walls by the reception desk. They were printed at least two centuries ago, before the invention of trains, let alone cars. I could find a proper map in one of the nearby houses, but there is just so much else that needs to be done just to stay alive.

Bill would want a record. He'd want details. Well here goes. To the south of the golf club there is the River Thames, and that is how we got here. Along the north bank, runs a footpath dotted with little white painted metal rings for tying the boats to. Then there is a patch of grass, then an access road for boats being towed to the jetty a little way downstream. After the road there is a bowls green, a lawn, and a patio. Then there is this clubhouse. Downstairs there are double doors leading from the patio into the bar. I am upstairs, in the office with its door leading out onto a balcony. If I want, I can open the doors and look northward, over the remains of the golf course, a two-mile patchwork of wild overgrowth and barren dirt. Beyond that are trees which, I think, hide a railway line.

Next door is a boatyard specialising in 'Pre-Season Repairs;. There are no boats inside. I looked. The only thing there was a lifeless corpse. It wasn't one of the undead. How and why the man died, what story he was part of, I didn't bother to investigate. There were no boats, there was no fuel, and so the place had nothing to interest me.

On the other side of the clubhouse is the car park, beyond that is the main road, and a long, large storage building. I'm not sure what is inside there yet. The door is locked and withstood my brief attempt at breaking in. There's bound to be a key around here somewhere, I just haven't had time to properly look for it.

There is just so much to do, I haven't really had time to explore. When I do go out, I feel so lonely. It's an echo of that same feeling I had when I was locked in that room in the Manor, that an infinitely vast world is towering over me and at any minute it will come crashing down.

The clubhouse itself is still intact, but around us, including the greens in front and the gardens of the houses nearby, the grass has been churned to barren dust by the passage of millions of feet. It looks like a battlefield, like pictures of the Somme. Trees, hedges, lampposts, pylons, they've all been pushed down, trampled and crushed. About them lie scores of bodies, and some of those still move. Their legs are mangled, their backs are broken, and some are pinned under the wrecks of cars. These trapped undead twitch and grasp, and hiss and keen whenever I stray too close. I try and stay away.

Bill would probably have counted the footprints to get a more accurate figure of how many undead were in the horde that passed through here, but I'm not Bill. I could count the zombies out there easily enough, but to what end? I don't need to know how many are there, I don't *want* to know. They are everywhere, and everywhere I look is nothing but devastation and ruin.

I don't know what I was expecting the land here to be like. I didn't really give it much thought other than to hope that if Bill and I, and Annette and Daisy could just cross the river, everything would somehow work out, but when has the grass ever been greener?

We reached the river three days ago, on the afternoon of the 7th. Or was it morning. It must have been morning, because we left early and it can't have taken that long to drive from the Abbey to the Thames. It seems like a lifetime ago.

After Chris died, or after I killed the zombie he became, the atmosphere in the Abbey grew tense. No one shouted, no one threw around accusations or blame, not out loud. Daphne cried a little, but otherwise, at least on the surface, everything was calm. You'd have to be a total fool not to know that tensions were boiling underneath. Rigid politeness, that's what my father called it. Something had to give. I could sense it. I don't think Bill could. He was too focused on the details to see the wider picture. We didn't have a meeting, not exactly. We stood around, staring at the ground, the walls, the truck, at everything but each other.

"We should leave," Annette said, abruptly.

Those words broke whatever spell was being weaved. We filled the water bottles, loaded the car, and went through the plan. It seemed simple enough, not changed much since the day before. We would play the music one last time, and I would climb up to the section of the wall above the gate and shoot as many of the undead that I could. When I started firing, the music would be turned off, the speakers unplugged and the cars pushed into position. Bill would drive the truck with Annette and Daisy inside. Barrett would drive the car with Daphne and Liz inside. When they were ready, Bill was going to signal. I'd climb down, Stewart and I would open the gates, and then we'd jump into the back of the truck.

Bill had a route mapped out, one that he thought would be safest based on the roads he took to the M4 a few weeks ago. Honestly, the bit I was most worried about was whether Stewart might open the gates whilst I was still up on the wall.

It was simple, about as simple as it could be. All it required from pretty much everyone else was to get into a vehicle and sit in it. It fell apart whilst I was climbing up the scaffolding. By the time I'd climbed down again, Bill and Barrett were shouting at each other so loud that if they'd stood a bit further apart and a bit further away we wouldn't have needed to bother with the music.

Should I write down what they said? Bill would. He's scrupulous about that. I just can't remember, not exactly. I tried to listen, but all I could hear was a clock ticking down, all I could see was Annette shifting uneasily from one foot to another. All I felt was a growing impatient fury at what seemed like such a pointless delay. I was so wrong.

It was an argument over who should take the car and who should the take the truck. I think Daphne and Liz were in shock. They'd known Chris a long time. Even Stewart seemed distracted. Then there was Barrett. I couldn't work it out at the time but now I've had time to think, and now I have little but time to think, I see what it was. The words she spoke were full of concern, of pragmatism in protecting the young, in the need for leadership to overcome this next short struggle. Her tone, though, was judgemental, calculating, and dark.

It came down to this. Daphne wasn't any use. Nor was Annette, apparently, and didn't that make the girl kick up a storm. Daphne should go in the back of the cab with the kids. That was fine with me, fine with Bill too from what I could judge, since we weren't planning on ditching the others until after we got to the river. Since Stewart knew where we were going, he needed to be in the car in front. Since the truck would have to go first, so its bulk could push the undead out of the way, that meant Daphne, Annette, and Daisy in the back and Stewart in the front passenger seat. That meant it made more sense for Barrett to drive the truck, and for Bill and I to open the gates and follow in the car with Liz as our sole passenger.

Barrett went on about how we were more experienced, more capable in case the truck got into trouble and a dozen other unmeant platitudes besides, until that clock counting down in my head got so loud it drowned her out.

"Enough!" I said, and that was how it was decided.

Bill and I didn't get a chance to exchange anything more than looks after that, but personally I thought that since we had Liz as a hostage we'd get to the river and take it from there. I double-checked that Daisy's seat was safely strapped in to the back seat, made sure that the child-lock was off, and that Annette was ready to grab the baby and run. I gave them both a hug and then closed the door to the truck. I hated that moment, even though I didn't understand why at the time.

I climbed back up the scaffolding and got in place. I took a moment to survey the scene. I wish I hadn't. There were zombies everywhere. Those that were closest began beating furiously at the walls and gate a few seconds after I appeared. I signalled and the music was turned on. I waited. It took a few seconds for it to have any effect. Then, the few zombies along the track started moving towards the Abbey. I didn't look down, not then, but it seemed as if the entire Abbey was shaking as those closest to the wall redoubled their efforts to punch and claw their way inside. That was probably just the terrible fear that was beginning to take hold. I kept my eyes on the track, and the undead that we would need to drive through in order to escape.

At first the zombies headed straight for the Abbey. A sickening thumping began as they got closer and began crashing into the heaving pack only a few metres below me. Then, as the first song ended, I looked down. Slowly, almost as slow as a glacier, the mob was starting to flow away from the gate, sliding sideways around the walls, towards the sound of the music. I crouched down again, and as Bill and Annette, and the others down in the courtyard stared up at me, waiting, I closed my eyes and listened. The noise from the far side of the Abbey grew. The reverberation of fist on stone intensified, but I waited. For six songs, I waited, then I stood up. It had worked, not nearly as well as the day before. There was still a throng of the undead immediately in front of the gates, but behind them, the track itself was relatively clear.

I aimed, fired, reloaded. The music stopped. I fired again, and again, and again, until all the zombies around the gate were down, then I shifted my aim. I picked a target to the right of the track, a zombie with the tattered remains of a rucksack still strapped to its back. I fired. It went down. I aimed at a lanky creature, wearing a ski jacket that must have been too big for it when it had been alive. I fired. It went down. I aimed and fired, and aimed and fired, and sometimes I missed, but either side of the track the zombies were falling. Then, when I put my hand in my pocket, I found it was empty. I don't know how long I was up there, but I'd left a hundred rounds with Bill and that was now all we had left.

"Coming down!" I shouted, and half climbed, half fell down the scaffolding. Barrett had already started the truck's engine. I could just make out Annette, bouncing up and down in the back seat as I ran to the gate. I glanced at Bill.

"Ready?" he asked. I nodded. We pulled the gate open and the truck shot out. I got a brief glimpse of Annette and Daisy in the back seat before I had to dive out of the way. By the time I'd picked myself up, the truck was already half way down the track.

"Come on," Bill called, already waiting by the car. I ran over and climbed into the driver seat.

I had to drive. I don't know if Liz could drive, I never asked, but I wasn't going to trust my life to her. As for Bill, he could drive the truck, but not the car. With his foot twisted at that angle, and with the extra bulk of the leg brace, every time he tried to put his foot on the accelerator it came down on the brake as well. We followed the truck down the track. It started to speed up the moment it turned onto the road.

"You're too slow, you've got to match their speed." Liz barked. I put my foot down. Ten miles per hour, fifteen, twenty. The undead were everywhere, in the road, coming from the fields, their dried up snarling faces filling every window. Then, suddenly, we were through. The ghoulish faces were gone and I could see the road, the hedgerow, and the truck, getting smaller as it got further ahead of us.

"Faster," Liz said, louder this time. Twenty-five, thirty. I watched the needle bounce slowly up the dial, but the truck was still getting away. I saw it swerve, hitting one square on, its body came tumbling over the cab, bouncing over the truck bed and into the verge.

"They're going too fast," Bill muttered.

"You've got to catch up with them," Liz shouted, into my ear. I gritted my teeth and tried to ignore her.

A zombie staggered onto the road between us and the truck. I slowed, swerving at the last minute to avoid hitting it. The creature banged a fist on the side window. Liz screamed. I remember wishing she'd just shut up.

"Faster! You've got to go faster!" she whined.

"Relax," Bill said. "They'll slow down in a bit." I don't think he believed it any more than I did.

"Yeah. They'll slow down in a bit," Liz said, and began repeating it over and over.

I haven't driven much in the last five years. I didn't own a car, I couldn't afford one. I drove a bit last summer when I was on holiday, and I hired a van to move flats a few years ago, but I haven't really driven since

I got back from the US. That was an automatic on the back roads, backwoods and on a dirt bike round the back of the old wood plant. I had to concentrate. Clutch, change gear, accelerate, brake, steer, clutch… It was hard enough without the undead drifting onto the road. I kept glancing reflexively at the rear view mirror. Most of the time all I could see was Liz as she shifted and twisted in the back seat, but sometimes I caught a glimpse of the road behind us. They weren't close, but a horde of the undead were following us, and it was a horde. I've never seen anything like it and couldn't begin to describe it. At least we were driving away from them, that was what I kept telling myself.

The truck was half a mile ahead, and as it edged further away from us I realised just how loud its engine was. As we drove up a slight rise, I could see the undead getting caught up in hedges, bottlenecking at gates and low stone walls, an inexorable flood, pouring onto the road behind the truck. Which meant these zombies were now in front of our car.

Bill suddenly pointed at a fork up ahead "Take a left here," he said.

"You sure?" I asked.

"Can't you just go faster?" Liz pleaded.

"We can't catch up with the truck and we can't go on like this," Bill said. I took the turning. There were fewer zombies on this road, and those that I could see were, until they heard the putt-putting of our little car, heading toward the now distant roar of the truck.

"But," Liz complained, "how will you know where to go if we become separated?"

"We know where we're going. We have a map, we have the address," Bill said, calmly. "We've got half the fuel here, they're not going to leave us. This way will be faster. There's a fork ahead," he added, speaking to me. "Take a right. The road curves back towards the north after a half mile or so."

"Hey! You've got to stick to the plan. We've got a plan. Stick to the plan…" Liz started muttering that over and over as she rocked on her seat. Shock. I suppose that's what it was, though at the time I just thought it was pathetic. Maybe she realised what I hadn't, that we'd been betrayed. I don't know. All I could think was that she was distracting me. I gave Bill a meaningful look.

He turned in his seat. "We're heading to the river. There's another bridge over the motorway about a mile from where we were going to cross. It was closed down, scheduled for demolition in April. That's our best bet."

"But if it was going to be knocked down, how do you know it's still there?" Liz asked and I swear she sounded petulant.

"Because it's a bridge. Bridges don't disappear. They don't just fall down, and no one leaves them to collapse, not in the UK. It's got another ten or twenty years' worth of life. Who's going to have bothered blowing it up since the evacuation?"

"They did in London."

"Then if they did that here, we head due east, there's a rail bridge about five miles down. And," he added loudly to forestall the next whine, "if that doesn't work we keep going until we get to Windsor and we'll look for a boat there. We've got half the fuel, remember? We'll catch them on the river." He turned back to face forwards once more. "The road branches again in about a mile, you take the left, then there's a hard right after a hundred yards. Your seat belt's on?" he added half a question, half a statement. "And if we can't find a boat at Windsor, then we head out of town to a level crossing and get onto the tracks and follow the train line. Now," he said turning once more, "put your seatbelt on."

I took the turn, slowed, and took the hard right. We were now running roughly parallel to the planned route.

Was Bill lying? Not about the heading to Windsor bit, with what happened after, I know that was all for Liz's benefit. I mean did he honestly intend to find a way to catch up with the others and the children? Maybe he was planning on just crossing the river and getting to his precious Lenham Hill, but I don't think so. I don't think he would have abandoned the girls.

Driving a car along the train tracks sounds like a good idea. Maybe it just sounds fun, right here, right now, as the night draws in. The nights are the worst. During daylight I can look outside, I can see whether the

155

undead are out there. At night, all I can do is check the doors are locked and hope that morning comes.

July 11th – 3p.m.

It's too hot to be outside now. What I wouldn't give for air conditioning. What I wouldn't give for ice and a fan and something cold to drink.

I went out first thing. Not for food, there's more than enough of that here, but there's so little else, and so much I need when my worldly possessions amount to nothing more than what I can carry on my back. Clothes, bandages, matches, thread, a map, a torch, books, water, toilet paper, medicines, every time I sit down I find there's something I'm missing.

There's a storeroom downstairs, behind the bar. Whatever was in there had been looted long ago, but at the back was another door. I didn't notice it at first, not with the stack of posters, banners and sandwich boards stacked in front. The door led to a pantry. That's where I found the food. Half a dozen catering sized tubs of instant soup, some beef, some tomato, some mushroom, and there was instant coffee, tea, and enough ketchup and mustard to sauce a thousand hot dogs. There'd been biscuits too, but those had gone mouldy.

It's interesting that the rats and mice didn't get in there. I wondered why until I remembered the footprints of an uncountable number of feet, the huge swarm of millions of the undead that had trampled the countryside. Either the rodents fled before it, were crushed under foot, or, for all I know, have barricaded themselves in their holes, hiding like the rest of us.

After I found the powdered soup, half of the immediate problems were solved. The other half, that's the lack of water. It's been nearly a week since it last rained, and that wasn't anything more than a light shower. Now it seems like a heat wave is setting in. Finding water is a daily task. Toilet cisterns, hot water boilers, long forgotten bottles of water left in glove boxes. It's out there, but each day, I have to go further to find it. Then it's back here, to boil it up. It takes all morning. Getting it from the river is very definitely not an option. Not when it might contain typhoid, cholera, and who knows what other diseases.

I don't want to stay here, but there is nowhere nearby that is any better. Besides, I won't be here long. I've enough water for today at least, so until tomorrow, and whilst there's still daylight I might as well make use of it.

We were in the car, heading north. Once I'd worked out the rhythm of the road, driving became easier. It was a case of drive on the left, then swerve to the right, then straight on for twenty metres, then swerve to the left, then straight on and swerve and so on. I managed to avoid head-on collisions, but still I kept hitting the undead with the side of the car, and it was taking a real beating.

After ten minutes we lost the right wing mirror. After fifteen we'd lost the left. After twenty-five minutes I was starting to worry that the sides were going to be so dented we'd never open the doors if we needed to escape. For all Bill's talk of plan B, and plan C, and plan X, Y and Z, I didn't think we'd make it more than a few more miles, let alone to the M4. I was just concentrating on the road, hoping we could get close enough to the river that we could run the rest of the way.

"I'll take the wheel for a moment," Bill said suddenly. "You wrap up your face. It's okay. It's a straight bit."

"Why?" I asked, but I was already pulling my scarf around my face leaving only my sunglasses uncovered.

"You too, Liz. I don't know that these windows will take much more."

In the rear view mirror I watched her wrap her head in one of the blankets covering the spare fuel cans.

"What's coming up, Bill?" I asked, as I retook the wheel.

"Nothing," he said, looking at me, and I knew he was lying and he knew I knew. "We're coming up to the bridge in about three miles. Try not to stop, but if you have to, throw the car into reverse and just go backwards as fast as you can." He pulled out the pistol and half turned in the seat. "Liz, you've got the back. If the windows break, just push them away. Don't waste your time trying to kill them, okay? Right. You've got a weapon?"

In the rear view mirror I saw her hold up a cleaver, the blade and handle covered in neon-pink plastic. It wasn't ideal under the circumstances, not a proper butcher's tool, but the kind for the home kitchen where every utensil had to 'match'. The hairs on the back of my neck stood up just at the thought of her waving it around in such close quarters.

"This isn't going to be pleasant," Bill said, "but it is going to be quick. We'll get through to the other side then it's just a short drive to the river. The zombies around the motorway will have heard the truck, they'll be heading that way."

The way Bill said "through to the other side" struck me as strange, then I understood what we were about to do. My mouth went dry.

"How far?" I asked.

"About two miles," he said.

I stretched in the seat, hunching forward slightly, flexing my shoulders, gripping and ungripping the wheel, trying to get in a better position. The number of undead in front of us thinned out. We'd entered the dead zone that lay before the motorway.

The road bent, and then I saw it, the M4. Inside and in front were the undead. They were too far away to make out any details, but it looked nothing like I'd imagined. Where he'd described a quiet, waiting mass, now it heaved and shoved and pushed as it headed towards where the truck must have crossed. As we got closer, the sound of our little engine was drowned out by the pummelling, moaning, bone-cracking crescendo of thousands upon thousands of zombies. I tried to focus on the road ahead and nothing else.

Then I saw the bridge, but it was the motorway that went over it. Our road went through a tunnel underneath. I didn't say anything. Bill knew, and what Liz didn't know, she couldn't scream about.

"Good luck," Bill muttered quietly.

"Same to you," I replied.

We were five hundred metres away, when the movement of the horde started to change. Slowly at first, in ones, then fives, then tens, the undead in front of the motorway began to stalk our way.

I glanced at the fields to either side. Thousands of feet had turned them into a crater-pocked landscape. I looked behind. The road was packed. There was no going back, around or to the left or right. There was nothing but going forward through the tunnel. I tried to evade them, twisting the car left and right and left again, keeping around twenty miles an hour, wanting to go faster, but afraid we'd crash if I did.

Then we hit a zombie. It was a glancing blow on the side of the car that made the whole vehicle shake. Gritting my teeth I pulled my foot up and off the accelerator. Fifteen miles an hour. We hit another. The lights on the left hand side of the car smashed with the impact, the body rolled up over the bonnet and thumped into the window before sliding off and down.

Now we were less than two hundred metres from the tunnel. We hit a third, it was dragged under the wheels, and the car thumped and skidded as we drove over the living corpse. Then a fourth, then a fifth, then their hands were swatting and scraping at the paintwork as we drove over and into them. The windows cracked. The roof buckled as one rolled up the bonnet and over the car. The exhaust rattled and coughed as it thumped against the still grasping hands of a zombie, knocked down by the scrum as the mass of the undead tried to reach their prey.

A hundred metres before we reached the tunnel, we hit a zombie square on. The front bumper hit its legs, smashing bone, and flipping the creature up, momentum carrying it head first through the windscreen.

"Close your mouth and eyes," Bill shouted as he levelled the gun and fired. The sound was immense. I felt the splatter of gore and bone over my covered face.

Liz was screaming, I remember that. I think she'd been screaming for a while, but I just hadn't noticed. I opened my eyes. With the dead creature obscuring my view all I could see was the fence around the motorway. It was starting to bow and flutter like a sail, as the zombies inside pushed and tore and were crushed against the concrete and chain link by the pressure of those behind.

I put my foot down as Bill pushed the dead zombie out of the way. Speed would kill us, or it would save us, but right then and there I knew that dying in a crash was infinitely preferable to being forced to stop. There was no going back, no evasion, no retreat, nothing but death unless we kept going on.

Liz screamed again as one of the side windows smashed. I kept my eyes ahead, swerving the car to the left, then to the right, accelerating into them whenever there was a slight gap. In my peripheral vision I saw Bill turn with the gun pointed into the back, but Liz must have dealt with that threat because he didn't fire.

Then we were under the motorway. Automatically I flipped the lights on. Nothing happened. They were all broken. About us was near darkness. I sped up once more, my eyes now fixed on the thin light at the end of the tunnel.

There was a deafening cannon of gunfire as Bill fired again, this time without warning, and this time Liz didn't scream. All I heard was a meaty thump of dead flesh. I was half deafened and three quarters blinded by the explosion of gunpowder. I couldn't tell where Bill had been aiming, whether he had hit anything or what was going on in the back. I tried to grip the steering wheel tighter, I tried to accelerate, but we kept hitting the undead. The collisions rocked the car. Liz swore and I was actually relieved to know she was alive. I tried to focus on the light ahead, I remember thinking, one way or another, it would be all over soon.

The car lurched to the right as one of the tyres blew. I over corrected, and we started to skid, the rectangle of daylight shifting to the right. I took my foot off the pedal, turned the wheel, but I over-corrected. I turned the wheel again, this time the rectangle of light was back in front, and much larger, but we'd slowed to little more than a walking pace. I put my foot down again. The gun fired. Liz screamed. The light got brighter. The driver side window broke. An arm came in. The gun fired. The arm disappeared. The engine coughed. Bill fired. I hit another zombie. Its body rolled up the bonnet, lodging against the window. I couldn't see the sky. I couldn't see the road. In the sudden darkness I couldn't see anything except a thin thread of brownish ooze trickling down onto the steering wheel. Bill shoved at the body, pushing until it fell away. I could see again, and I saw that we were out of the tunnel and the road ahead of us was almost empty of the undead.

Carefully, conscious of the flat tyre, I eased my foot down and we picked up a little speed. Bill was twisting this way and that in his seat, checking the sides, checking behind.

"We're clear," he said, what seemed like an hour later, but couldn't have been more than a few seconds.

"We're clear," I repeated. "Tyres gone," I added, and now that the blood had stopped pounding in my ears, I could hear the metallic scrapping of the exhaust dragging along behind us. I raised a hand to the mirror, to where the mirror had been. At some point it had fallen off. I turned in my seat, looked behind and saw the motorway. I saw the fence. I saw it give way. I watched as thousands of the undead fell, pouring down one after the other onto the road behind us. Thousands and thousands. Hundreds of thousands. Every time I close my eyes that image is all that I see. There's a line from some song or poem or something that I learned at school, and that's the only way I can think to describe it: 'I turned and I saw, the gates of Hell had opened and darkness poured through.'

I glanced at the dashboard. The plastic was fractured, the speedometer was stuck on ninety, and the needle on the fuel gauge was stuck on empty.

"Which way to the river," I asked.

"We want to take a right in about five miles," Bill said, as he reloaded the pistol. "Then it's about three miles to the boathouse. You think the car can make it?"

"Your guess is as good as mine," I replied. "I can run eight miles. Can you?"

"You run, don't worry about me, I'll be following. What about you, Liz," Bill said twisting in his seat, "you ever done any marath— oh, hell."

I turned and saw Liz was holding up her hand. She'd thrown a hasty bandage around it, but there was no mistaking the blood, nor what it meant.

We made it to within a mile of the boathouse before the exhaust finally fell off, another half a mile or so and the engine started to splutter and die. Bill had spent the drive with the gun in his hand staring at Liz. For her part, she'd said nothing. She wasn't catatonic, but had the silence of the condemned about her.

"Out," Bill said, unnecessarily, as the car chugged to a halt. I grabbed the axe, rifle, the ammo, and my pack. Bill grabbed his pike and his bag. Liz stumbled out of the car, clutching nothing but her injured hand. I took a moment to load the rifle, then slung it on my back. I looked at the fuel cans, but there was no way of taking them with us. Then we ran. We didn't bother to stop to kill the undead. Bill on the left, me on the right, Liz in the middle, we didn't look back. What would have been the point? We were about ten miles from the motorway, two hours ahead of that horde. Time was against us.

We saw the truck first. That beautiful yellow beast. Between it and a low building on the water's edge were the undead, eight or nine of them, but they hadn't seen us. Then I heard the voices, coming, I was sure, from inside the building. I couldn't make out the words, but I recognised Annette's strident protest. Then an engine started. They'd found a boat.

"Keep quiet!" I hissed to Bill and Liz. The temptation to tell them we were coming was immense, but we had to keep silent as long as possible to avoid alerting the creatures ahead of us. Then Liz yelled. It wasn't loud. She was out of breath, and suffering from blood loss. I doubt if any of the others heard it, but the zombies did. Their heads swivelled our way, then they started their ponderously grim march towards us.

I shifted my grip on the axe, and looked ahead, the doors to the boathouse would be locked or barricaded by the others. We weren't going to get in, but we could make it down to the jetty, and get on the boat there.

"Head straight to the riverbank," Bill said, thinking the same as me. He'd fallen behind slightly, either by design or because of his leg, but now he pushed ahead, his pike shifting in his hands as he ran straight at the undead and the truck that blocked our way to the riverbank.

I would have laughed. Even under those circumstances, I almost did. He was moving with this hopping-sideways skip that seriously did him no favours. I almost laughed, until I heard Daisy cry. Then I picked up my pace. I left Liz to fend for herself. It wasn't exactly everyone for themselves, but I wasn't sure that hers was a life I could save, whereas up ahead were Annette and Daisy.

Bill reached the zombies first. They were clustered together, a horrific clump with three in front, almost abreast of each other. He swung the pike up behind him, his left foot leaving the ground as he pirouetted in a three hundred degree twist. The blade scythed down in a huge arc, hitting the front three between shoulder and ear. The first two went down, not dead but knocked over from the force of the blow, a thin brownish line scarred diagonally across their dirt-streaked faces. The pike had stuck in the third, buried deep in its neck.

I stopped watching him then, as I was now only a couple of metres away from one of the undead. Half its scalp was missing, on the other half, lank strands of red hair whipped across its face as its hands lashed out towards me. I swung my axe up in front. It was a two-handed blow that slammed the blade into the creature's chin with a sickeningly damp crunch of bone. The momentum knocked it from its feet. I didn't wait to see if it was dead. I changed my grip and swung the blade at another. It sliced through outstretched fingers and bit deep into its neck. I pushed back as it crumpled towards me, and pulled the axe free.

In another couple of paces I was at the truck. I clambered onto the roof, unslung the rifle, and began to fire. I didn't have time to think. I barely had time to aim. There were now a dozen there on the jetty, another twenty or so coming up on us from the road and I don't know how many pouring around the buildings to our south.

Bill was moving around too much. I remember pointing the rifle at the group near him, trying to find a target, but he kept getting in the way. I turned my attention to Liz. She'd been bitten again, but she was still alive, half crawling towards the truck. A creature was about to fall onto her. I fired. Its head exploded. I picked another target, and I fired again, and again. Liz reached the truck and I started firing at any target I could see.

Seconds or minutes later, I'm not sure how long it was, the engine noise from the shed changed. I glanced over my shoulder and saw the boat edging out of the boathouse into the river. Liz started waving and shouting.

"Bill! The boat's coming!" I yelled. I took a step backwards, fired, and then glanced down at the distance I'd have to jump from the truck. I fired again, and as I reloaded I looked down at the fuel cans still in the back of the truck. With the ones we'd left in the back of the car, they couldn't have taken more than nine with them onto the boat. Not enough, I was sure of that. Nowhere near enough if Bill and I were going to take some to drive the girls somewhere safe. There was no way I was going to be able to swim carrying one, but I thought, that maybe, when the boat got close to shore, I could throw a can on board. Fuel equals speed equals time equals life, that was what I thought as I stood there, on the roof of the truck.

I fired again, glancing towards the river between shots. The boat was out of the boathouse now, its turn almost complete. I couldn't judge how close it was going to get. I could only afford to spare the briefest of glimpses, and they weren't nearly long enough to gauge how far into the water the concrete jetty extended. I knew we'd have to wade, and I was starting to think we may have to swim.

I looked over at Bill. He was still surrounded by the undead. He seemed to be holding them off, but he'd already been forced to retreat a half dozen paces. I fired again. Another one fell, but the undead seemed to be coming from everywhere. I knew it couldn't go on. One misstep, one slip, and he would fall under their numbers. I fired again, then glanced towards the river, to see if the boat was close enough yet.

Liz was at the water's edge, half walking, half crawling down the slipway into the river. She was screaming at the boat, shouting at them. I couldn't hear what she said, or maybe I just can't remember. I glanced back to Bill, looked at the pack surrounding him, fired, and made a decision.

"Fancy a swim, Bill?" I called out, as I reloaded the rifle. It took him a moment to answer.

"Right," was all he grunted back in reply.

"Or float," I added, turning around to look at the boat, once more. Something was wrong. I could make out Barrett behind the wheel. She was staring resolutely ahead, not looking at us, but that wasn't what was causing my anxiety. The boat was in the middle of the river, but it wasn't turning towards the shore. Then the boat's engine was turned off, and I thought I heard Daisy's faint cry. I breathed a sigh of relief.

Liz was in the water now, swimming. Her arms thrashing frantically, but she would make it to the boat, that was clear enough. But could we?

She'd been bitten at least twice. Probably more. I don't know how the virus works, but surely each time you get bitten increases the chance you'd turn immediately, unless you are immune. I'm sure that was it, looking back on it, I'm certain that she was immune. Even if she wasn't, if she was infected, right then, there would have been no way for anyone to have known.

"Bill. We've got to go. Count of five," I said, firing once again. I missed. The shot grazed the zombie and ploughed into the chest of the creature behind. "Four. Three." I reloaded. Bill swung his pike, nearly decapitating the zombie my bullet had missed. I wanted one more shot before we left. I looked down again at the fuel. "Two." There was no way of taking it. "One." A gun fired, but it wasn't mine.

The shot echoed across the landscape, bouncing off buildings, and reverberating around our little world. I turned to look over my shoulder. Stewart stood in the boat, shotgun in hand. Where Liz had been, now there was nothing but a growing red stain in the water.

Stewart stared at me. I stared back. He began to raise the shotgun. From that distance I doubt it would have done any damage. I could have shot him, though, and easily enough. I don't know why I didn't. The engine started again, and the blood stained water churned as the boat picked up speed.

As the boat pulled away down the river, I thought I saw Annette, Daisy in her arms, trying to get up onto the deck. Then she was pushed back down into the cabin. I knew there was no way we could swim out to the boat, no way we could reach the girls.

"Kim!" Bill called up at me, and he must have been calling to me all that time. I looked back the way we'd come. The undead were still flowing towards us, their numbers growing as they drifted in from the countryside, down the road, and around the houses and offices along the riverbank. From every direction they came, and I knew that behind them, not yet visible, came the horde from the motorway.

I fired, again, and again, and again. I kept firing, as quick as I could, venting my anger and frustration and despair. Minutes passed. I don't know how many, I just know that when I searched my pockets for ammunition, more and more of them were empty.

"Kim!" Bill called again. I looked down. His shoulders were stooped as if suddenly he was carrying too great a weight. He was bleeding. I couldn't see from where, but his hands were slick with blood. He was hurt, he was tiring, and we were running out of time.

"Bill? Bill!" I cried, and then it sunk in. We were trapped, doomed unless we could escape. "The boathouse. I'll see if there's another boat."

"Where there's one…" he muttered.

I jumped off the back of the truck, and ran along the waterfront. The door was barricaded from the inside. I ran over to the window, smashed the glass, cleared off the fragments then pulled myself up and through. The doors by the river had been pulled back, allowing sunlight to dance eerily on the collection of boats hanging from the rafters. Canoe's, punts, rowing boats, it looked like Barrett and the others had taken the only motor launch. I didn't have time to be picky. There was a punt close to the water's edge, the sort you would hire for picnicking along the river on a summer's day, or at least it was the kind they used in the movies. It wasn't the kind of craft you'd take when you were chasing a motorboat, but it was the closest, and time was pressing.

I spent a long few seconds trying to work out how to release the buckles and levers hanging it from the ceiling before I gave up, and just sliced through the canvas straps. The punt fell to the concrete floor with a loud bang. Splinters of wood flew off in every direction, but I didn't think it had cracked or broken. I grabbed a couple of oars, threw them, the rifle, and the axe in. I shoved and pushed and then dragged it, until I was wading hip deep in the water. Then I climbed in.

Kneeling on the punt, I pulled myself around the boathouse, trying to grip the slick corrugated steel, scrabbling for hand holds, desperate not to let go, knowing that if I got caught by the current, then Bill was dead.

"Bill." I wasn't calling to him, it was more like a mantra I repeated to myself. "Bill. Bill. Bill." Over and over, as I inched around the building. "Bill. Bill. Bi…" I rounded the corner and saw him sagging, leaning on his pike as another zombie approached. Bent double he glanced towards me, and I saw a face masked with blood. He straightened. I think he tried to grin. I couldn't tell.

I pulled on the building, tugging the boat closer as he swept the pike up. There was little force to the blow, the zombie staggered backwards, but only half a step. Bill tried to lift the pike, but he couldn't. His hand went into his pocket and came out with the pistol. He fired. The bullet hit the zombie in the chest. He fired again. And again. And again. And he missed. And I couldn't help him.

"Run!" I screamed, I know I screamed. He didn't run. He fired again and the zombie collapsed. Now I'm sure he was grinning as he turned and, pike cradled in one arm, pistol in hand, he half limped, half fell down the slipway and into the water.

I grabbed a paddle, thrusting it deep into the water, pushing the boat along as much by will as by strength. Ten metres away and the first zombie was through the gap by the truck. Eight metres and Bill was standing chest deep on the slipway, holding himself up with the pike. The gun in his left hand waved back and forth as he fired again and again. Six metres and he fired and two more zombies were through the gap, a dozen more behind them. Four metres and he fired again. Three metres and something thumped against the bottom of the boat.

I looked down. I could see the concrete edge of the slipway, about a pace away from Bill, but nothing else. Bill fired again. There was another thump against the flat hull and the boat rocked. I couldn't look down, not directly down, not whilst paddling. The current was strong and the front of the boat was turning and Bill was so close. He pulled the trigger once more but there was no explosion of gunfire. The magazine was empty.

The boat rocked again, and this time I knew what it was.

"Don't jump!" I screamed. "Pull me closer. With the pike. With the blade. Pull me closer. Don't try and swim!" I screamed it over and over, as I paddled furiously, but now my effort was focused on keeping the boat from being caught by the current and dragged away.

Bill looked and he saw, and he understood and he grinned, and this time I saw that smile properly. He slipped the gun back into his pocket, and swung the pike up and over and down in a huge one-handed arc, his other arm flying out behind him for balance. The blade bit deep into the wooden slatted seat, the wooden shaft landing on the boat's edge with enough force to throw up a cloud of dust and splinters. The boat rocked violently as filthy water sloshed over the sides. Bill pulled. The jetty drifted closer. His eyes were on mine, his smile creeping upwards in relief at his approaching salvation, when a zombie snapped its jaws down on the hand outstretched behind him. He screamed. He slipped. He fell, half into the water, half into the boat. I grabbed the strap on his backpack and hauled him up into the punt, smashed the paddle into the zombie's face, then pushed against the jetty, propelling us into the middle of the river, where the only thing rocking the boat was the gentle motion of the tide.

Bill was barely conscious. He'd lost a lot of blood and one and a half fingers. His arm and legs were covered in cuts and bites. The tide that had seemed so strong when I was trying to reach the shore now seemed glacially slow as I tried to stem the bleeding. Every few minutes I would have to leave Bill and paddle for half a dozen strokes just to keep us moving faster than the zombies pacing us on the bank.

We drifted for about ten miles, and that took the best part of a day. Either the fall onto the concrete floor of the boathouse, or the blow from the pike, or half a year's storage in a damp shed, or all of those things combined had caused the boat to leak. That day became a repetition of bailing, paddling, fending off from the shore and tending to Bill. There was no sign of the motorboat. Of course there wasn't. We'd no chance of catching it.

We came ashore at the golf course simply because I couldn't go any further. I dragged Bill up here, and did what I could for his wounds. I had to cauterise the stumps where his fingers had been using a paperweight heated over a fire of old trophies and broken barstools. I don't think I'll ever forget that smell. He's been delirious since then.

It's four days since we left the Abbey. Sometimes he talks, but I prefer it when he's quiet. I don't want any more of his secrets.

I can't leave him. At first I worried about that, about what I would do if I found a boat with fuel, and whether I could risk taking him with me to follow after the boat to find Annette and Daisy. But I found no fuel. Now all I can do is wait for him to recover.

Did they think Liz was infected? It's hard to say. I've re-read what I just wrote, and I think that is how it all happened. My memories of that day, or what can really have been only a few minutes, seem like photographs, individual snapshots with no emotion or sound or depth to them. They probably knew Liz had been injured but there was no way for them to know she was infected. Maybe she called something out. It's possible.

Let's say that they did know that she had been infected, though personally I'm convinced she was immune, they were in no danger. There was no way that she could have climbed up onto the deck without help. It was clear when they didn't turn the boat towards the shore that they had no intention of letting anyone else aboard. No, killing her was unnecessary. There is no way, no story I can concoct, no excuses I can give, that can justify it as revenge or self-defence or anything other than cold-blooded murder.

To me that is nothing compared to taking the children. Barrett must have planned it. Her and Stewart, and maybe Daphne and Liz. From the moment they decided on heading to the river, they planned on getting rid of Bill and me. Why?

Did they judge themselves better than us? Well, obviously, but that's not it. Was it because we were a threat, some type of insidious danger to Annette and Daisy? No, those are the answers they would give, the justifications they will tell themselves at night, but it's not why. I think it was because we didn't fit into their vision for a new world, because their idea of a new world looks remarkably similar to the world that is now for ever gone.

They took the children. I don't think the girls are in danger, at least not in any greater danger than any of us face these days, but how can I truly know? There was that strange moment at the Abbey, when they started talking about that old farmer and his granddaughter. They were hiding something there, but what? Why should I care so much? Maternal instinct? No, that's the easy answer and it's not that. It's because someone has to, and we are all that's left. If we can't be the best people we can, right here, right now, then really, what is the point?

Bill won't wake, not properly. It's all I can do to get a mouthful of soup down his throat. I can't leave him, but I need to rescue Annette and Daisy.

July 11ᵗʰ – 7 p.m.

I think his fever has gone down a little. His mutterings are slightly less intelligible, if that means anything.

I never wanted to go into nursing. My mother tried to convince me, on many occasions, that nursing was a good choice of career. Not medicine, nursing. There was never any ambition I should be a doctor, not even when I was applying for university. Nursing was the career for me, and it was that old-fashioned thinking that put me off it. Stupid really, since I ended up working in a coffee shop instead. Maybe my mother was right. Maybe that was the point. I never had the grades for medical school. Maybe I would have been a good nurse. Probably not. Anyway, it's not like it would have made much difference in the end. The outbreak would still have happened.

I do my best to keep Bill hydrated, and to keep his wounds clean. For the rest of the time I work on getting us out of here. I found a motorboat, outside a house down by the shore. It looks sound, though by the look of the flowerpots and curtains, it wasn't used as a boat but as someone's home. Some relative who'd fallen on hard times maybe, but who didn't quite rate one of the dozen bedrooms in the house.

And I found fuel. Not much, but enough to check that the engine worked. It took an age to find it, though. Most of the cars are so smashed together that the tanks have been punctured and any petrol in them has evaporated. I found enough to check the boat's engine worked, but there's no more fuel anywhere within walking distance. I've looked.

There aren't many zombies left around here either. At least, there aren't many which can still walk, but not a day goes by that I don't have to kill at least one. When I turned the engine on, the noise was loud enough to call six of the undead. It took four more bullets to kill three. I used the axe on the others. The ammunition all fits into one pocket now. Twenty rounds for the rifle, eleven for the pistol. It's not much. I suppose I shouldn't waste the rest of it on the undead.

Around the truck and the boathouse I was driven by adrenaline. At the Manor, and at the Abbey, I'd been safe behind the walls. Out there on my own, it was completely different. I've never felt so alone, not even during that time back at the Manor when I was locked up in that room, with nothing to do but wait.

So now I just need to find fuel. I can carry Bill down to the boat easily enough, I mean, I carried him up here, but what's the point of moving him until we can actually leave?

Sometimes life is like a river, pulling you along a long defined path. All you can do is hold on and try and stay afloat. Sometimes you come to rapids, and all you can do is hold your breath and hope you resurface. I read that somewhere, in one of those supremely mistitled self-help books. I always wondered, when you hit rapids, why you didn't have a third metaphorical choice, why you couldn't twist the boat or raft or whatever, get it lodged in the rocks and try and jump across from stone to stone until you reached the shore. Apparently, I was told when I asked,

171

metaphors don't work that way. But why shouldn't they?

Where do you find fuel? How would I get it back here? I'd drive, I suppose. If I took Bill down to the boat first, would he be safe there if I went off for a day or two? Sometimes he screams in his sleep. Do I have a choice? I could find another car showroom, find more fuel, and drive back here. But how long would it take? Maybe I could leave him for a day, but no longer. There has to be something I've missed.

There are the fuel cans we left in the truck and the car. Could I make it back there? There's no way I could paddle up stream, but we went by a couple of bridges as we drifted down the river. They hadn't been demolished, but were crammed with makeshift barricades. The undead couldn't get through, but I could easily get over them. Then what? What of the zombies from the motorway? How many hundreds of thousands of living dead are now surrounding that bank of the river? No. That's not going to work. What though? What have I missed?

July 12th – 11 a.m.

I shaved my head. It seemed sensible. Easier to manage. I started by cutting it short, but then the mirror slipped and broke on the floor. That's when I cut it all off.

It's meant to mean something, isn't it, when a woman is shorn of her hair. Well it doesn't. Without being able to see what I was doing, it was easier just to get rid of it all. Besides, the only thing to wash with here is the industrial strength detergent they had for cleaning the toilets. No hair is better than pouring that stuff on my head. A broken mirror, that's bad luck isn't it? Well, luck doesn't exist and hair grows back.

I suppose mirrors don't. I mean, glass and silver industries will need to be created first, but so what? How many mirrors are there in every house? A dozen, at least. How many houses per survivor in the world? How long before we run out, before we even need to bother thinking about how to make new ones. Centuries, probably. Which makes it someone else's problem. I've enough of my own.

Speaking of which, and the reason I took some time off this morning, I've solved how to get the fuel to the boat. I'm not going to write it down, that would add a level of confidence in the plan that I don't yet have. All I need to do now is work out where I can find some petrol.

As soon as it was daylight, I took a bike out and cycled about fifteen miles. The ground was so churned up I couldn't tell whether they had been fields or parks or football pitches. I'd found the address of a garage on the broken rear window of a car, located the address on the map and thought it was worth trying. No such luck. The roof had collapsed, crushing everything beneath it. So where to look next? That's the puzzle.

July 12ᵗʰ – 1 p.m.

I was sorting through Bill's pack, seeing if there was anything we could leave, anything we could get by without, and I found that hard drive he's been carting around. It's still wrapped in plastic from the Manor. Call it curiosity, call it a distraction, but I'm going looking for a laptop.

July 13ᵗʰ – 2 a.m.

I found a laptop. Actually I found three. It wasn't that hard. I don't think Bill was really trying. I don't think he wanted to know what he was carrying around, not really. There are 71,394 files taking up two and a half terabytes on the hard drive. It's a whole mixture of formats, some I recognised, others I didn't, but the computer did. I didn't know whether I should start with the videos or the photos or the documents or the weirder ones with bizarre extensions I couldn't even guess at. I thought the largest might be the most important. I don't know if it is, I haven't got to it yet. My eyes were caught by the smallest, a text file titled 'BILL READ THIS NOW':

Hey Bill,

If you're reading this then I've had to leave. This is an automated dump of everything I've managed to discover on Operation Prometheus. I don't know how much you've learned, or how much you've guessed. You must have worked out some of it, and I'm sure Jen will have told you most of the rest.

Prometheus was the US and the UK's post-Armageddon strategy for unilateral pre-emptive degradation. It all started with the vaccine, but you know about that. At some point someone realised that there was no way for us not to lose World War Three, so they took M.A.D. to a whole new level. Come the end of the world, and that seems to be what we're facing right now, they want to ensure that the only people building anything more technologically complex than a fire on the ashes of the old, is us. Not the Russians, not the Chinese, no one. I've included all the target data I could gather, but I couldn't get access to it all. There should be enough to work out what the rest would be.

The above is not the point of this message. I'm almost certain Jen Masterton knows about Prometheus. Quigley certainly does. You've got to tell them that so does every other nation on the planet. Or the ones that count do, and they've got their own versions of the same plan. I've included that target data too. I've no idea how much is missing, but there's enough there to get the picture. With hundreds of impact sites all over the world, we'll be lucky if we end up back in the Stone Age.

If you can, you've got to tell Quigley and Masterton, and anyone else who'll listen, to stop Prometheus, but whatever you do, don't trust them. I don't know if Jen or her father told you about me, or what they told you if they did, but don't believe it.

I'm sorry for everything. I did try, and you have to believe that everything I tried was ultimately for you. If I can, if it's not too late, I'm going to head your way. Until then, stay safe.

Good Luck.

Sholto.

After reading that, I sorted the files by date. I found the satellite images easy enough. It took a while to work out what I was seeing, then I found the one of the Hoover Dam. After that, I had a better idea what to look for. There's one of a canal, which could be Suez or Panama, I can't tell. There are dozens that I first took to be tiny odd shaped islands, until I realised they were offshore oil platforms. Some of the images look like ports, some like cities, others like mines, or factories in the middle of the desert, others seem to be clusters of ships out at sea. Exactly where these images are of, for the most part I couldn't begin to guess.

I went out and found a map, a good one, and was able to work out where some of the targets in Britain were. There's an image of the Isle of Wight, another of the power station at Dungeness. There's another I think is Birmingham, and one I'm certain is Glasgow. There are others too, but conscious of the computer's battery life, I turned it off at that point.

It's a lot to take in. More than that, it's a lot to try and understand. There are, I think, some pictures of London. I'm not certain. It might be that I expect there to be and so I'm seeing familiar shapes and patterns which aren't there. Bill was in London when Barrett saw the explosions over what must have been the Isle of Wight and Dungeness. If London was a target, then for some reason it was spared. By whom and why, I've no idea. And if London was spared, then where else is still standing?

As for who Sholto is and what he was apologising for, that's another puzzle, one that I'm not going to expand my theories on here. You see, really, I don't think it matters. I can see that it is important, but it doesn't change what I need to do next. There is only one file in there that will help me rescue Annette and Daisy.

July 13ᵗʰ – 3 p.m.

Bill regained consciousness. Sort of. I think regaining consciousness probably has some kind of technical definition. Some doctor would probably describe his condition as stable with periods of lucidity or something equally vague.

I don't know if the fever's broken. I think his temperature has gone down but I don't have a thermometer to check. Even if I had one, I don't know what's normal. He woke for a bit this morning and croaked out for water. He's fallen asleep again, but that has to be a good sign.

I know where I can find fuel. It's not far, and I spent most of the day getting ready. The boat is good to go. There's not enough water, but we'll just have to hope for rain. There's no way I'm drinking that stuff in the river. Maybe I'll find water stored with the petrol.

I've added spare clothes, an old torch I found next to the fuse box in the beer cellar, blankets, a couple of new bags, and the food. I'm going to give Bill another twenty-four hours and then he has to decide. He can come with me, or continue his search for answers to questions no one cares about. Either way, I've lingered here too long.

Day 124, Riverside Links Golf Club Oxfordshire

06:00, 14th July

I'm awake. I'm alive. I thought I was dead, but I was dreaming. It was a terrible dream, made worse by waking up and finding that reality is little more than a nightmare.

Kim has gone out. Water. We… I… My hand. You have ten fingers, how many do you really need?

I can stand. Just, and not for long. It's…

15:00, 14th July

I slept. I ate. I slept a bit more. I am feeling better. I think I must have been unconscious through most of the pain. I'm just weak now. Kim found water. She says she has checked everywhere nearby. We've only six pints left. She's found a boat and knows where there is fuel. She won't say where. I checked the journal. She's been writing in it. She didn't say where in there either. Tomorrow she's going. She won't tell me where.

July 14th – 7 p.m.

Bill is sleeping again. I said I'd record the conversation we had this evening.

"It's a simple choice," I told him bluntly. "I'm going after Annette and Daisy. You can come with me or you can stay, recover, and go find your answers. It's your choice, you've got to make it."

"It's not as simple as that," he croaked back.

"It is. I'm making it that simple. The past or the future."

"No," he tried to shout. "We need to destroy all trace of it. What if someone finds it? What if I'm carrying the infection, what if everyone who seems to be immune is—"

"What of it?" I snapped. "You really think that changes anything?" I picked up the map. "I found Lenham Hill. It's not far. Less than ten miles. In a few days' time you'll be fit enough to walk there."

"I—" he began. I didn't give him a chance.

"What do you make of the note? You've read it enough times. What's Sholto apologising for?"

"I don't know. Really."

"Do you want to know?"

"You mean you do?" he asked

"No," I said. "I mean, is it important to you? I don't know you, Bartholomew Wright. You saved my life. I saved yours. That doesn't give us some kind of deep spiritual connection. I don't know what you want, but when I leave here, I'm going to find the girls and then I'm going to find somewhere safe for them. Somewhere safe for me too, but that isn't as important, and don't ask me why. I can't explain it. It's just how it is. So what is it you want?"

"You don't get it."

"No. You don't. Let's say you find that those thousands of vials are still there. And let's say that you find out who's responsible. Whether it was an accident or it was on purpose, so what? Who are you going to tell? Me? Annette? Daisy, when she grows up? Do you really think that matters to us, to our lives? You think that knowing any of these things has anything to do with living long enough to have a life?"

"How can we do that," Bill said, "when all the time we're just struggling to survive?"

"That's the problem," I said, standing up. "We're not survivors, you and I, we're not looking for rescue." I held up a hand. "I've been thinking about this. I've had the time, a lot of time, whilst you've been unconscious, and we're not survivors. That's just another word for victim, and whilst we may have been victims of circumstances and whilst we both may have been victims once, we're not anymore. You know what those satellite images are?" I pointed at the hard drive. "You know what they represent?"

"Yes, of course," he said bitterly. "That I could have stopped it. That I wasn't just responsible for the evacuation, for the murder of millions of Britons, but of millions others besides. Billions, all over the world."

"NO!" I shouted. "If it means anything it's the complete opposite. It's proof that you were a cog in all the manipulative machinations of some master Machiavellian. You weren't any more important to the grand scheme of things than I was, and that doesn't matter anymore. We're not captives to that old world order. We're not survivors, we *survived*. That part of our lives is over. It's the next part, what we do with it, that's what's important now." I subsided a little. "Sanders, Liz, Chris, even Cannock, they were survivors. They got so far, and that was it. Their worlds became nothing more than getting by day to day. Just dragging existence out for a few more years, one day at a time. That's no more a life than what I had in that cell. Look at us," I said, hefting the rifle. "Look at this, what we are now, *who* we are. We're the barbarians inside the gates, all right. If you go out and find the who and why and how of it all, that's not going to turn back the clock. The undead aren't going away. You can look for your answers, you can spend your whole life doing it, and maybe you can even find them, but the world is going to keep on turning, indifferent to you and all that you find."

He was silent for a while.

"We'll have to go far away, somewhere no one recognises me," he said, finally.

"So you're coming with me?"

He didn't say anything for a long while.

"The way Barrett and the others looked at me—"

"You should have said who you were to start with. Or, yes, made up some lie about what happened, or better yet, burned that journal. But it's too late for any of that now. You want to come with me, or not?"

"The future or the past, that's the choice, is it?" He closed his eyes for a moment, sighed, and then asked, "Where are we getting the fuel?"

"You need to say it. I need you to say it, and I need to know you mean it. I'm serious. There's no turning back. If we stumble across some of those answers on the way, then that's fine with me, but we're not looking for them. We've one job. Find the girls and get them somewhere safe. Yes?"

"Yes," he said. "We'll find them. We'll take them somewhere safe." He paused for a moment, and then smiled. "Manipulative machinations of some master Machiavellian? How long did you spend working on that one?" Then I smiled too.

"So, where are we getting the fuel?" he asked.

"Easy," I said. "Lenham Hill. That's why I needed you to say it out loud."

Day 125, Riverside Links Golf Club Oxfordshire

06:45, 15th July

"I make it a bit less than ten miles to Lenham, according to that map," Kim said, this morning.

"Let me see?" I asked. "Well there's no direct route. I make it about

179

fifteen, assuming that none of the roads are blocked."

"We're going in a straight line. Over the golf course, then down the train line. That brings us to within a kilometre. We'll see what the land is like there. Maybe we can drive up close. Or we walk."

"You're certain there's fuel there?"

"No. There was a whole load of manifests and supply documents. They got a lot of petrol delivered, diesel too, just before the outbreak. We're talking tankers of the stuff, and since it was an M.O.D. place, I can't see it being requisitioned."

"But what if it was? Or if there are people there, like you said, out of all the places in the world, this one is—"

"Then I've got the addresses of three car showrooms within a couple of miles of it," she cut in. "We'll find some fuel somewhere."

"It's a long shot," I said.

"It's better than just sitting around here." And that was it. The matter was settled.

My next question was more practical. "How are we going to drive there, without fuel?"

"A golf cart."

"Golf cart?"

"What else do you expect to find at a golf club? I reckon they were designed to go up and down at least ten miles of grass without being recharged, so two batteries should see us there and back. I've found us four. They're easy enough to change over, and when they run out, we dump them. Satisfied?"

I wasn't. I'm still not. I feel exposed sitting out here, waiting for her to finish loading up the rest of the supplies. At least a golf cart should be silent, and since I can't walk, what other choice do we have?

09:45, 15th July

The cart is quiet. It's no faster than walking, particularly on the uneven ground of the golf course. There's something farcical about all of this. I'm sitting by the train tracks, watching Kim push the cart up the embankment. Even the undead on the golf course, unable to move far with their crushed limbs, heard us coming, but They couldn't even crawl towards us. They could only let out a low moan as we went by. Yes, this is almost funny.

We're just going for the fuel. I had to agree to that again. If the place is abandoned, if it seems safe, and if there's time, then we might search for information on the virus and we may try and destroy the facility. But only if there's time. Kim's right. Annette and Daisy come first. The past can wait.

11:15, 15th July

We've stopped about a mile from Lenham Hill. Kim has gone on to scout ahead. We saw a strange sign, a 'road closed' sign, with the word 'zombies' scrawled over it. We've hardly seen any of the undead since we left the train line, though we had to deal with a couple when we went through a tunnel. Rather, Kim had to deal with Them whilst I just sat and watched.

There's something sinister about those signs. Kim has gone to check, just in case.

Day 125, Lenham Hill, Oxfordshire

20:00, 15th July

"Three zombies. Already dead," Kim said when she returned. "Shot. And there were another two signs, just like the first, each in the middle of a road."

"We can't go back," I said. We'd discussed it when the first battery died, a mile along the railway line. We'd discussed it again when the second ran out when we were in the middle of the tunnel. Now, only a mile away from Lenham Hill, we'd just swapped in the fourth and final battery.

"I think we can make about four miles," Kim said. "Whoever shot those zombies, whoever left those signs, if they're still around here, then four miles isn't going to get us far enough away."

"Then we need that fuel."

We left the cart in an otherwise anonymous terrace at the edge of a cricket club, and with Kim holding me up, walked the last thousand yards or so into a small copse, overlooking Lenham Hill.

"There's no hill," Kim said.

"No, well, that's the point," I said. "Second World War mentality. Misinformation dragged forward into the Cold War. It's just another old airfield, long ago sold off to a private company, at least as far as anyone else might suspect."

"It was an old radar station?"

"Sort of. During the war it was an airfield, then a staging post for commando raids then, after the war, it became the site of one of the post-nuclear communication centres. It was part of a string of bunkers across the country, linked by underground cables. A sort of pre-Internet post-apocalyptic communications system. You have to remember that Britain was broke after the war, so the sites they picked were chosen purely on where there was an existing underground facility. Then the bombs got bigger, these places became obsolete and were mothballed. Or that's what I thought."

She levelled the rifle and peered through the scope. "I can see a hanger, an old red-brick, and a couple of newer office type buildings. Where's the bunker?"

"At a guess? The concrete hut where the two landing strips intersect," I replied.

"It looks deserted. I don't like that."

"You'd rather you could see machine-gun nests and searchlights at every corner?" I asked.

"No, I mean, if someone's going out and shooting the undead, then there should be some kind of signs of life about this place."

"You're assuming that whoever shot those zombies came from here. They could be somewhere in the town, or in one of the villages around here, or it could have been someone passing through any time in the last few months," I said.

"I can't see anyone down there," she went on, ignoring me.

"The kind of people who'd be stationed there would be good at not being seen," I said. Suddenly, Kim leapt up and turned around.

"What is it?" I asked, startled, as I turned around whilst I scrabbled in my pocket for the pistol.

She smiled. "Sorry. It's just that if this was a film, that's the bit where some grizzled sergeant appears out of the darkness and points a gun at you."

I tried not to laugh. I failed. The absurdity of the situation was too much. "Time's against us. You want to risk going down there?"

"Try the hanger first. That's our best bet."

The hanger was empty, at least of fuel. Most of the space was given over to a partly dismantled prop-plane. Sections of engine had been taken apart and arrayed along a series of now dusty workbenches. If I hadn't known what was under our feet I would have taken it to be an entirely legitimate, if close to bankrupt, business.

We went round the other buildings, checking the walls for any sign of some underground fuel storage tank. We found nothing. Then, we turned towards the concrete hut in the middle of the airfield. Both of us wanting to get it over with, we headed towards the bunker.

We didn't see the scorch marks until we reached the doorway. A few fragments of burnt wood hung limply from a frame that was no longer hiding the steep steps leading down to a stout, reinforced, metal door.

"We're not going to find any fuel down there," I said.

"I know," Kim replied.

"We can go," I suggested. "Just get the cart as far as we can, search the cars, find fuel that way, or—"

"I think it might be too late for that. Look up," she said.

I did. Above us, over the doorway, was a camera. It swivelled one way, then the other. Then the door clicked open.

We could have left. Of course we could. We didn't. We just looked at one another and shrugged. Somehow, in that same strange way that I

183

knew I had to climb into that window at the Manor, that same luck that landed me with a broken leg during the outbreak, the same instinct that had kept me alive when billions had perished, it was all telling me that, despite every appearance to the contrary, it was going to be okay.

Nevertheless, I checked that the pistol was still in my pocket. I took out the torch, but then had to wait an infuriatingly embarrassing few seconds for Kim to twist the end so that the light would come on. It is so maddening the simple everyday things that require two working hands!

The torch illuminated a narrow staircase that descended a dozen steps before ending in a short landing.

"You think you can make it on your own?" Kim asked.

"I can try," I replied. She nodded, and raised the rifle in front of her.

We were half way down when we heard the door shut behind us.

"Figures," Kim said.

At the landing, we turned the corner and found another staircase. We kept going down, staircase to landing to staircase, about seventy feet in total, and I was exhausted when we finally reached the bottom. We were standing in front of a steel door that resembled an airlock from a submarine. It was hanging loosely by one hinge. Whether it was there to keep something in, or to keep it out, it had clearly failed.

"What if whatever's down there isn't human?" Kim asked.

"The door up there clicked open and closed," I said, still trying to catch my breath.

"That's not very reassuring," she muttered, pushing the door aside, and stepping through.

We walked into a reception area. There were no pot plants, no magazines, no chairs except one behind the solitary desk. Beneath the desk was a computer tower unit, shattered and ruined by an unmistakable bullet hole.

"This is getting…" Kim began, but didn't finish the sentence. Opposite the door we had come through was another pressure door, its hinges broken like the first. She pushed it open and we stepped into a long corridor.

I played the torch up and down and across its sides. "No light fittings," I muttered. "Nothing but nozzles. Probably part of a fire suppression system," I said. Then I remembered what it was we might find here, and I realised what kind of systems might be in place and what those nozzles might dispense.

"Sightseeing later," Kim said, and we hurried on, through another broken door and into a wider corridor. The torch wasn't powerful enough to make out anything more than shadows at the far end, about two hundred yards away. As I looked, I saw that the corridor had once been a large rectangular chamber, subdivided and partitioned into individual work spaces.

I glanced into the one closest to the door. There were computers, with similar matching bullet holes, screens, a light-desk and a cabinet, but my attention was taken by the bullet holes in the wall. Two, close together, at head height, surrounded by a horrible red smear.

"At last," a voice called out. "You made it."

I spun around, shining the light towards the far end of the corridor where I thought the voice was coming from. Kim moved away from me, edging to the opposite wall, her rifle raised.

"You took your time," the voice continued. It was male with a US accent, but that was all I could tell. I took a tentative step forward, trying to gauge how much danger we were in.

"You know," the man went on, "I was starting to think you wouldn't come at all."

I took a few steps towards him. I could just make out the man, standing in the doorway to a cubicle. Behind him, a workbench was dimly illuminated by half a dozen screens.

"Spotted you on my security system," he said, pointing to the screens. "It's amazing what you can do with some batteries, an improvised wi-fi network, a couple of webcams and a whole lot of time."

I stopped about twenty yards away from him, and played my torch up and down the cubicles to either side and opposite him. They were empty, unless you counted the bullet holes and bloodstains.

"It's a mess. I know," he said. "I tidied up as best I could, but there was so much to do. You saw my early warning system?"

"The camera on the door?" I asked, wanting to keep him talking. He was a large man, a few inches taller than I was, with the kind of athletic figure you can never get from a gym. I tried to see his face, but there were too many shadows to properly make out his features.

"No, no... well, yes. I mean, the cameras are there to tell me if I need to run and hide. Not that I've had to. No, I meant the signs. The road signs. You saw those?"

"With the word zombies scrawled across them?" Kim asked.

"That's them," he said turning to look at her. "Cell phone with a motion sensor. If the sign gets knocked over I get a call." He turned and walked back into the cubicle and was suddenly hidden from view. I had to take another couple of steps forward. The partition between the next cubicle, the one between myself and him, was transparent. He slapped his palm down on a desk covered in half dismantled phones, all connected by a spider web of wires.

"That was the first thing I did when I arrived," he said. "On my way up here, I got trapped in an old church for a week. You saw that? The horde? Must have been millions of zombies. Shame really. I was looking forward to finally seeing the British countryside, and They had to go and ruin it. I almost starved then. Would have died of thirst if it wasn't for the water in the font. That's why I rigged those signs up. Helps to keep people away, too. Which is never a bad thing. Have to keep going out to change the batteries, but it's better than sitting down here in ignorance."

"How long have you been here?" Kim asked. I glanced over at her, wondering if the question meant she had some kind of plan, but it was too dark to make out anything more than her silhouette.

"Oh, a week. Two. No, three. Maybe three, but who's counting? Oh, I'm sorry, where are my manners. Would you like some coffee? Or tea? Or water? That's all I can offer. I'll have to unplug this lot." He began to disconnect a series of plugs from a large metal box. "They blew the generator. Literally. Grenades, going by the burn pattern. Left me having to use this portable battery pack. It's meant to be rechargeable, but the hand crank broke, and it's not like I can call up the manufacturer to complain. Found two here. The other's doing duty by the front door. I thought they'd be coming back for them, since they left the vault intact."

"The vault?" I asked. "With the vials in it?"

"Right. 67,892 vials," he said. "I checked and double checked, and I think they're all accounted for. No," he added to himself, "no, I'm sure they are. That's why I put up the cameras. I figured they'd left the job only half done, and even if they didn't all come back, I thought the food, the fuel, the battery packs, that'd be enough for one or two of them to get an idea to loot the place. Hence the cameras, like I said."

"The fuel's still here?" Kim asked.

"Sure. Gas and diesel, still in the tanks. As far as I can tell, anyway." He plugged in a small travel kettle. "Makes you wonder, doesn't it. Makes you think that maybe they're not coming back after all. Of course that could be what they want you to think. Is there a game within a game? It's so hard to know. It's why you can never be too careful." He bent over the power unit. "And I suppose we can afford to spare a little light as well, eh?"

He flipped a switch. A few fluorescent lights, rigged up on the table and across the floor flickered and went on. The light was dim, but compared to the gloom before it was as bright as day. I put the torch down on a work counter, and lowered my hand to my pocket.

"From what I've gathered." The man waved his hand at a pile of partially disassembled computers on the table. "Someone stormed the place on March 15th. And they had someone on the inside. You see up there," he pointed at the door we'd come in through. I looked and saw a panel had been removed.

"Shaped charge. They all went off. Someone initiated the self-destruct system. The first part of which is to blow all the doors except the air lock at the front, and the door to the outside at the top. Then, this is meant to have sprayed out." He walked over to a small cylinder lying on the floor, and tapped it. "Highly flammable. Like, napalm mixed with Thermite. Then there's another explosion and the place should have burned down. Steel, concrete and everything in between. The only thing that's meant to be here is a crater. Except, it didn't go off." He waved his hands to take in the room. "The doors blew open, and then someone waltzed right in. The rest was grenades, bullets, and knife work. Not a good end, judging by the bodies."

"And where are they?" Kim asked.

"Downstairs. The vault. Wasn't space anywhere else. When I realised I was going to be here a while, I figured it was better down there than up here, you know? Stuck in a few of these too." He tapped the cylinder again. "Because, like I said, you can't be too careful."

I took a few steps closer, trying to get a better view of the man's face.

"What I can't work out is if they took anything with them," he went on peering down at the workbench. "Two bullets to the head. Each. I mean, was that it? Was that all they wanted to do? Just kill everyone here?"

The man turned towards me, and for the first time I saw him properly. He was at least a decade older than me, with traces of grey streaking through hair I'm sure would have been dyed six months ago. The eyes were tired, the beard was roughly trimmed, and the expression barely concealed an inner mania that, if anything, made him seem generations older than he was. I knew then, and I know now, that I had never seen him before in my life.

"Doesn't really matter," he went on expansively. "I only came here to blow the place up. Figured someone had to. Thought I might find an address for the doctor. I knew he'd come back to the UK, but I doubted he'd come here. Thought I'd kill two birds."

He walked over to another work table, this one covered in a pile of charred paper. "This is how I knew how many vials there should be. Not that they'd left a list, or anything. I had to work out how many they made. But why torch this lot and not burn the whole place down? Why destroy the hard drives, and in such a theatrical manner, rather than take them away? Why leave the vials here? Why? You know why?"

"Transport?" Kim suggested. I glanced at her. She'd raised her rifle and was peering at the man through the scope. He didn't seem to mind.

"Right," he said leaping up again, seemingly oblivious to the gun pointed at him. "Exactly. Transport. They didn't have any, or any space to spare in whatever vehicles they had. That's the only possible answer. So," he said turning to me, "do you think that would have been a problem for them?"

I didn't know what to say. Clearly this man thought he knew who we were. Since I had no idea who that was, I had no idea what the right type of response was to keep him talking and his hands away from that canister. I slipped my hand into my pocket and gripped the pistol.

"Sorry," he went on, as I was still working out what to say, "you don't know, I didn't show you. Hang on, look at this." He went over to the other desk. "Got it finished a couple of days ago. Not great, sure, had to combine pieces from different angles. Sort of a photo-fit picture." He tapped at a few keys on the laptop "Here" he said swivelling the screen around to face us.

I recognised the image on the screen instantly.

"Quigley."

"Got it in one," he said. "Sir Michael Quigley. The Foreign Secretary. Or Prime Minister, or Tyrant in Chief or whatever he was calling himself by then. He came here in person. Puts a bit of a spin on it, doesn't it? Everyone who was here worked for him, so why did he need someone on the inside? The game within the game, that's what I'm trying to work out. I know, after that demonstration in New York went wrong, after the outbreak, he came back to the UK. I also know he left the doctor over there in the US. Then, a few days later, Quigley comes here, tells the inside man to disarm the system, and then he makes sure everyone inside is killed. Was he covering up his involvement? Or was he as surprised as the rest of us?"

He stared expectantly at me.

"I... don't know," I said, and I didn't. I searched around for some innocuous comment, something that would just keep him talking. "Wouldn't he have been on the Isle of Wight?" I asked.

"Check the date stamp on that image. No, he missed the nukes. I reckon if he survived New York, and survived Prometheus, then he's got to be out there somewhere. The question is where. I found some addresses. That's about all I've got to show for my time here. Before the outbreak they'd have led somewhere, but now? Who knows?"

I looked over at Kim. She was now flicking the rifle back and forth between me and the man, her eye glued to the scope. I thought she was trying to signal something, but couldn't work out what. I gripped the pistol tightly, lifting it slightly, to check it hadn't snagged on any errant strands of cloth. I edged sideways, away from the cubicle wall, to where I thought I would have a better shot. I just needed a few more seconds.

"So there's nothing else to find out here?" I asked.

"Not really. No. I suppose I would have left soon, but I couldn't decide where to go next. I didn't want to go, you see. I mean, I knew if I was going to find you anywhere it'd be here. I tried the house of course, but you'd already left. So where else on this entire planet could I look? Some part of me knew you'd come, and I was right. Here you are." He grinned.

I glanced over at Kim. She had lowered the rifle. The kettle began to boil. I stepped out from the partition. I had a clear shot. I raised the gun.

"Who are you?" I asked.

"What?" he asked, surprise in his voice. "Jen didn't tell you?"

"What? Who are you?" I asked again, the gun trembling in my hand.

"I thought she'd have told you—"

"Who are you?" I shouted.

"But you must know. Don't you... I... I'm Sholto," he said. "I'm your brother."

Epilogue:
Sholto

16th July

Day 126, River Thames

"Tell me again," I asked for what must have been the fourth time.

"Really?" Kim asked. I glared at her. She'd taken it in her stride, and I was somewhat resentful of that. "Personally," she went on, "I want to know what your real name is. I mean, it's not really Sholto, is it?"

"N'ah," Sholto said. "Though it's as real as any other name I've had these last thirty years or so. You can call me Thaddeus if you want. That's the name on my birth certificate. Thaddeus and Bartholomew. Two brothers. There's a Sherlock Holmes story with two brothers, Thaddeus and Bartholomew Sholto. They were twins, which kind of messes up the comparison, but I figured it was enough of a clue to get Bill here digging. Turns out I was wrong. When Jen Masterton gave him that Sherlock Holmes anthology, I was certain he'd get it—"

"No, I worked that part out," Kim said.

"Wait. What? You did?" I asked.

"Sure," she replied. "Whilst you were unconscious. It was in your journal, and it's not exactly hard to find a copy of Conan Doyle in this country. Was it you," she asked turning back to Sholto, "who put the bookmark into that copy in his flat?"

"The Orwell one? Right again. Last time I was over here. Only the third time I came back since I left. I figured since Jen Masterton was dropping her oh-not-so-subtle hints by giving you that book, that I should do the same. So I stuck in a Big Brother bookmark. I really thought that you might get the hint, but no. I had to break into your flat to do it. Sorry about that. But I wanted to check it wasn't bugged."

"What. Wait. Jen knew too?"

"Right. I told her before I confronted Lord Masterton. I figured that maybe she had some sway over her father. No such luck. She's just a chip off the old block, like father like daughter. She used what I told her to blackmail her way up the ladder. Giving you that book, well, maybe that was her way of giving you a hint. She should have told you. I thought she would of at the end."

"Was his place bugged?" Kim asked.

"Wait," I said. "Go back to the bit about Lord Masterton. You confronted him? You didn't mention that earlier."

"Was that to do with Prometheus?" Kim asked.

"Hang on. One at a time," Sholto said, adding, "This thing keeps dragging to the left. I think there's something stuck on the rudder."

After Sholto had explained who he was, twice, the initial surprise gave way to remembering why we had gone to Lenham Hill in the first place. The fuel tanks, installed long after the bunker itself, were accessed above ground via a nozzle disguised as a water valve. Sholto had stashed an electric car in a garage in the village. We loaded it with fuel cans, but before we left there was one last thing we had to do. Standing by the car, about a thousand yards from the edge of the aerodrome, he turned to Kim.

"You want the honours? Ladies first and all that?" he asked, holding out a smart phone. This time, I could see her roll her eyes. "No? Suit yourself. Here," he handed me the phone. On the screen was a comically large red button. "I was bored," he said.

I pressed the button. A dialogue came up, "Execute programme. Yes. No." I looked at him

"I was bored, but I did have other things to do," he said. "Press yes."

I did. There was a muffled bang. The earth shook, the car rocked. A gout of flame speared skywards from the entrance to the bunker. Then there was a roar of sound, as the ground above the facility shook. Earth flew up and outwards. Then there was a secondary explosion as the fuel tanks, buried only a few metres below the surface, erupted, sending a towering column of flame into the sky. The concrete of the airstrip buckled and suddenly collapsed inwards, the hole getting larger as the ground nearby starting caving in. And then it stopped, leaving a crater of bubbling burning earth, beneath an oily black cloud of smoke.

"Probably should have closed those airlock doors," Sholto said.

Then we drove back along the train line to the river.

"Yeah. I can't see what it is," Sholto said, bending over the side of the boat. "Something's tangled with it or bent it out of shape. I can't tell from here. Anyone fancy going into the water and having a look? I was kidding," he added with a grin.

"It's not going to be a problem is it?" Kim asked.

"Couldn't tell you. Up until a few months ago the most I knew about boats was that the pointy end is the front. I'd not taken mine out more than a mile from shore. So, your guess is as good as mine. Wouldn't want to take this out to sea. But I think we'll be fine along the river."

"Can we go back to what you were saying about Lord Masterton," I said. "You hadn't mentioned that before. You said you'd confronted him?"

"Right," he said, walking back to the wheel. "I'll start again from the beginning. Our Dad worked for the government. Essentially he was a hit-man, though since it wasn't official, it didn't get called that. As far as anyone else was concerned he drove a truck. Deliveries across Europe was his cover, the official reason why he spent so much time away from home, his son, me, and his wife. A wife who, whilst he was away for three months, gave birth to a second son. You. That last mission before he died, no, not a mission, that sounds far too glamorous. The last job, something went wrong. When he came back, either not all of him did, or maybe he brought back something with him. PTSD, flashbacks, whatever you want to call it, he started re-living whatever he'd been through. He killed our mother. Then he came back to reality and he killed himself, but not before making a phone call to his handler."

"And that was Lord Masterton?" I asked.

"No. That was Quigley. Though I didn't find that out for years. I saw it all. I'd snuck out. I often did, and I was trying to sneak back in through the garden. The murder, the suicide, I saw that, and then I saw the car pull up a few minutes later. I saw a man get out. I saw him go into the house, and bring you out. Then I watched him start the fire." He rolled up his sleeve to show a white scar on his arm.

"That's what brought me out of it. When the flames got close enough to set my jacket alight. I ran. I don't remember much of what happened next, not until the next morning. I was walking along a street somewhere. I couldn't tell you where, I didn't recognise it. Don't remember anything about it, except for the newsagents putting out the boards with the morning headlines. It made the front page. House fire. Four dead. Mother, Father, teenager and their infant son.

"After that, life got tough. It hadn't been great to begin with, what with Dad away a lot, with Mum's world suddenly just being about this new baby. Even before you were born, well, the euphemism is that I'd gone off the rails a bit. With literally nowhere left to go, thinking I was being hunted, I fell in with the only people I knew. It was a gang, basically. Not your off-cut thugs, but a real organised crime outfit. They were the middle men for guns, drugs, people, you name it. Four years, I spent with them. I'd dress up as a public school boy, carrying a duffel bag with heroin or whatever inside, and a cricket bat poking out the top, muling stuff across London and beyond.

"Officially I was dead, you see, and I thought you were too. Well, I was just a kid, and I thought that some mysterious man had shown up and killed the baby brother I'd resented. Let's just say I was pretty messed up. I didn't care about anything or anyone.

"Then, one day, four and a bit years after that fire, a bag of cash in one hand and a bag filled with passports in the other, I walk into a room and find the people I'm meant to be handing this stuff to are all dead. So I'm standing there, looking at these bodies, and I think to myself that maybe it was time to think about the future. I figure that of all those passports there's got to be at least one that looks vaguely like me. So I run, and this time I didn't stop running until I got to the other side of the Atlantic.

"I bought myself a new identity and then I found that I had a bit of a talent for making money. I got rich, but I couldn't stop thinking about that man, the one who'd taken my brother away from that house and, I assumed, murdered him. I started plotting my revenge, and that took a long time.

"All I had to go on was what that man looked like. It isn't much to go on now, and was even less back then. I bribed and blackmailed, and worse, I'll admit it. I got access to databases and records, or at least to the people who had access. But it was slow going. It took years. I was getting nowhere, until I saw him on the news. There he was, a new Member of Parliament, part of some trade delegation. After that, things sped up. I figured out a dozen ways of getting revenge, but by then I'd realised he had to work for someone, and I wanted to get them all. So I continued digging and bribing and blackmailing until I found out that it was Lord Masterton who'd signed off on those missions. It was him that had sent Dad overseas.

"So that's when I finally came back. I was going to kill them both. Except then I found out you were alive. More than that, Masterton had paid for your schooling, you'd grown up with his daughter, and you'd grown up with the same name our parents gave you. I figured... well, I figured maybe I'd give him a second chance. I got back on the plane and went home again.

"I kept an eye on you, as much as I could, tried to figure out what to do next. You seemed happy enough, even if you were squandering your life on politics. But if that was what you wanted to do, then you should get your chance. I didn't want Masterton or Quigley or anyone else using your past as a hold over you, so I made contact with Masterton's daughter, Jen. Told her who I was, told her I wanted a meeting with her father. Told her I wanted to try and smooth it all out. I met with him, told him what the deal was. That you got to live your life and that you were to be left alone. That was my big mistake. He engineered for you to stay in the UK. It was why he had that fictitious uncle of yours die, leaving you with that debt-ridden house and no option but to keep working for his daughter."

"Why didn't you just say something?" I asked.

"Because by then, I'd started to uncover something worse. Something bigger. Prometheus and the vaccine and everything else. I didn't know what a lot of it meant, but I could see it was bigger than some family reunion."

"And then the world came to an end?" Kim asked.

"Sort of. For me, it started falling down a bit before last February. If anything the outbreak saved my life. Even when you're as good at it as I was, there are certain questions you can't go asking without someone taking notice. I was about twelve hours ahead of them when those patients in New York reanimated. So, all in all, I'd say I'm pretty grateful for the apocalypse. I got out of the US, managed to get over here, and went to your flat. You were gone, of course, but by the way there was a dead goon outside your house, the way your computer was gone and you'd eaten nearly everything except the wallpaper paste, well, I knew you'd escaped." He grinned.

"I recognised him, you know," Sholto went on. "The dead guy outside your house. He was one of our Dad's successors. Probably sent by Quigley. Or Masterton. It's much the same thing. Since you had the computer, and the files I sent you, I reckoned if I was going to bump into you anywhere on this benighted island, it'd be at Lenham Hill."

I do believe him. I don't know why. That same instinct that told me to trust Kim tells me he isn't lying. He is Sholto and he is my brother, whatever that means. I went to Lenham Hill and I found answers, but they were to questions I didn't know to ask.

We're about five miles downstream of the golf course now, heading slowly, but quietly, back towards London. We'll find Annette and Daisy and rescue them, if we still can. Then I'll find somewhere safe for them and Kim, but not for me.

I still don't know if I am carrying the infection within me. Of the few scraps of paper Sholto had managed to piece together none shed any light on the virus itself. He thinks the doctor is out there somewhere and means to track him down. Perhaps we'll find him. Perhaps.

To be continued...

Printed in Poland
by Amazon Fulfillment
Poland Sp. z o.o., Wrocław